Praise for
MURDER AT THE GOD'S GATE

By Lynda S. Robinson
Published by Ballantine Books:

MURDER IN THE PLACE OF ANUBIS
MURDER AT THE GOD'S GATE

MURDER
AT THE
GOD'S GATE

Lynda S. Robinson

BALLANTINE BOOKS • NEW YORK

This book contains an excerpt from the hardcover edition of *Murder at the Feast of Rejoicing* by Lynda S. Robinson. This excerpt has been set for this edition only and may not reflect the final content of the hardcover edition.

Copyright © 1995 by Lynda S. Robinson
Excerpt from *Murder at the Feast of Rejoicing* copyright © 1996 by Lynda S. Robinson

All rights reserved under International and Pan-American Copyright Conventions. Published in the United States by Ballantine Books, a division of Random House, Inc., New York, and distributed in Canada by Random House of Canada Limited, Toronto.

Library of Congress Catalog Card Number: 95-94964

ISBN 0-345-39531-X

This edition published by arrangement with Walker and Company

Manufactured in the United States of America

First Ballantine Books Edition: March 1996

10   9   8   7   6   5   4   3   2   1

Cherry Weiner, my agent, is someone who will tell me the truth—even when I don't want to hear it—who will encourage me, fight for me, and believe in my wildest ideas. She has been behind the concept of a mystery series set in ancient Egypt from the start, and has supported and inspired me as a writer. This book is dedicated to her in friendship with my unending thanks.

1

▽

Year Five of the Reign of the Pharaoh Tutankhamun

Unas, pure one and servant of the god, was late. The last golden light of the sun god's rays inflamed the gold-and-silver inlay on the face of the massive outer pylon gate as the priest skittered inside the temple of Amun. Feeling even more insignificant than usual, he listened to the slap of his sandals on the flagstones. His footsteps echoed off the walls. He glanced up, but the ceiling of the temple was so high that it vanished into darkness.

The evening ritual was finished. Those not in residence within the temple grounds had been filing out of the god's gate for some time. Was he the only one left? He hated being alone in the temple after dark, but he had to put his list of royal artisans where he could find it quickly tomorrow.

Like an ant scurrying between the legs of an elephant, Unas hurried deeper into the temple darkness, past electrum-shrouded obelisks and pylons. He turned right before reaching the sanctuary, threading his way through groves of statues dedicated by kings and high priests. Now he couldn't even hear the fading voices of his fellow priests as they left the temple on their way home.

He passed a lamp stand, its light burning low, and casting uncertain light on the brilliant painted scenes of men and gods in endless registers on the walls. He entered a side room where the linens and oils of the god were kept. His list would be safe here, and he could retrieve it without going all the way to the treasury in the morning.

The room was lined with wooden shelves burdened with the rare oils, unguents, and linens used in the rituals of Amun. Unas wiped perspiration from his shaved head. He rubbed a palm on his kilt and transferred the papyrus roll to his dry hand.

Squinting in the gloom, he retrieved the lamp and set it on a shelf next to bottles of perfume. He reached up and shoved the roll between the necks of two bottles at the back of the shelf. He stepped back and frowned. A pile of linens had been carelessly placed on the floor. Stooping, he reached out for the white folds, then turned his head.

A sibilant hissing made him hold his breath. The shades of dead kings visited the god at night. He was sure of it.

He could hear something right now, beyond the safety of the lamp's glow, somewhere deeper in the temple. What if demons had wandered into the sanctuary? Unas flattened himself against the wall by the door.

The hissing had turned to a murmur, low, guttural, with a background hum. He shivered as the chill of the stone he was pressed against penetrated his skin. Where were those cursed temple guards? Lazy, that's what they were. They lounged around the outer pylons and traded stories and insults with the students on their way to the evening meal.

There was a stab of fear in his gut. He clasped his amulet necklace to ward off evil and took a step out of the storeroom. He couldn't stay here forever. He would slip into the hall and run for the pylons. Unas eased his toes over the threshold and froze.

"Don't be witless. They're camped beyond the border forts where the army won't look for them. Now are you going to help me or not?"

Unas let out his breath and smiled to himself. He'd been a fool again. Everyone said he was too skittish about shades and demons. He recognized that voice, although he hadn't heard it in the temple in a while. And the other, he knew it as well.

Walking down the hall toward the speakers in the room where copies of sacred texts were housed, Unas nearly stumbled as he began to perceive the significance of the conversation. His steps faltered, then halted. His body grew cold, as if his ka, his soul, had flown to the netherworld, taking with it all warmth.

What he was hearing couldn't be real. He rubbed sweat from his upper lip. How could he sweat when he was so cold? The voices buzzed and hissed. They poured dangerous knowledge into his heart until he grew so frightened that he began to back down the hall. His arm hit the lamp stand. He whimpered and caught it before it fell.

Unas stumbled into the storeroom again and closed the door. He gawked at the portal in horror and careened into one of the shelves that lined the walls. The impact disturbed a bottle of oil and he lunged for it. Catching the ceramic vessel before it fell, he replaced it, only to find his foot lodged in that pile of linens on the floor.

He kicked it aside and heard a tear. He went still and listened. If the two in the small library heard him, they would kill him. No one saying such words would hesitate to murder to keep them hidden.

No one came running to kill him, so Unas withdrew his foot. Dropping to his knees, he picked up the linens, but the stack wouldn't move. The lowest piece of cloth was caught under a loose flagstone. He slipped his fingers beneath the stone and extracted the cloth. Something went *clink*. Something below the flagstone.

Unas pried the flat stone up and slid it sideways to reveal a hole. Bowls. Who had put bowls under the floor?

He picked up the top vessel in a stack of five and held it near the light. Unremarkable. A modest ceramic dish, shallow and painted in a common design, blue on a buff background. Unas's fingers traced the lotus pattern on the inside rim, then paused at a series of ink marks.

No, not marks—words. Words in the cursive script of a scribe. His lips moved as he read, then fell open as his heart refused to let them form the words at the end of the line. His stomach roiled, then cramped, and his hands shook. The bowl crashed to the floor and shattered.

Unas started, then cringed and waited for the two evil ones to come for him. His skin grew clammy, and he lost all sense of the passage of time while he prayed for deliverance. He waited and waited. Nothing happened as he cowered on the floor in the midst of shards.

Finally, when he'd decided that they must have gone, Unas gathered the broken pieces. With jerky movements and an occasional whimper, he straightened the flagstone, the linens, and his kilt. The broken bowl, he must hide it. But not here. If he took it away, perhaps whoever had concealed them wouldn't realize one was missing.

Glancing about the room, he spotted a small wicker box. He emptied it of unguent vials and stuffed the shards in it. After several moments of girding himself, Unas pressed the door open a crack and listened.

He heard nothing but the indefinable sound of the vastness of the temple. He would take the long way out, through the four pylon gates in the direction of the avenue that led to the quay and the Nile. This route would take him farther away from those he hoped he was leaving behind in the temple.

After poking his head into the corridor, Unas melded himself to the wall and trickled along it, then bolted to the innermost pylon. Poking, ducking, and sliding, he made his way to the court of gilded papyrus columns between the middle pylons. As he entered the court, he stopped to listen again. His ears almost hurt from the effort to perceive the tiniest sound.

No footsteps tapped in his wake. No fists clutching knives appeared at his back. The evil ones had indeed left before him. Unas clutched his box under his arm and rushed by four towering obelisks.

Unas hurried past a tall, striding statue of some dead king and darted to the doors in the outer pylon. He squared his shoulders as he spied two sentries standing inside the doors. They stared, but recognized him and opened the portals. The muscles in their arms bunched as they hauled at the weight of cedar studded with bronze and overlaid with gold. He sidled out into the open.

Two guards walked up, greeted him, and helped their fellows shove the doors closed with a hollow boom. They were in good humor. They always were as the time drew near for them to yield their post to the night porter and sentries.

Unas hesitated. It was dark now, but he could hear the familiar flapping of the banners atop the tall, electrum-tipped poles that stood in front of each side of the pylon gate. He peered among the countless votive statues, painted white, red, green, and blue, solid and replete with inscriptions, in the forecourt. They had multiplied over untold generations as Theban citizens in search of the god's favor placed them there.

His breathing shallow and quick, Unas walked between two flagpoles and crossed the god's avenue of sphinxes. He turned south, then sped away from the sacred precinct of Amun. When he was out of sight of the guards, he broke into a run.

He pattered past shrine after shrine, house after house, turning north onto a street of workshops and homes owned by metalworkers, amulet makers, and scribes. His own house's white facade and painted doorway had never seemed so welcoming. With one last glance over his shoulder, Unas ducked inside and slammed the door shut.

Immediately he began to shiver. With the back of his arm he wiped sweat from his brow and bare head. Something was pressing into his side. He glanced down to find his hand pushing the wicker box into his flesh. He lifted it and knew fear all over again.

What was he to do? He'd heard such evil, and he was only a pure one, not a lector priest or servant of the god. If he told someone, how could he be sure that the recipient of his confidence wasn't a part of the evil as well?

Unas gripped the box and crossed the reception room. On his way he caught his foot on Ipwet's loom. He yelped, stumbled, and rubbed his ankle with a free hand. Kicking a spindle whorl out of his way, he hurried to the common room behind the reception chamber. He paused to listen to the rhythmic grinding coming from the roof.

Ipwet was preparing dinner. The thought of food turned his stomach, and Unas dodged around the central column and through the doorway that led to their sleeping chamber. At last he could shove the box under his bed while he paced and thought.

He glanced at the household shrine to the god Bes. Not a powerful god when compared to Amun, the king of gods. No help there. He would be hunted like a wounded hyena. They would destroy him if they found out he knew.

Should he tell that charioteer? Not a fortnight ago the warrior and his master, the great Lord Meren, had come for some information about unguent. A strange request. And he'd been so frightened. Unas nearly ran into the wall opposite his bed as he remembered the visit of the Eyes and Ears of Pharaoh.

The only reason he'd agreed to provide information was for the rewards. He had to flourish to please his wife. Ipwet was a young woman, much younger than he, who deserved a prosperous husband and fine possessions. If he could provide well, he might keep her affection, for women valued a man of accomplishment much more than a man who possessed merely youth. He turned and sat on the bed. Resting his forearms on his thighs, he hung his head over his knees and groaned.

He didn't want trouble. All he'd ever wanted was to be able to do his work well so that he could have a fine home and provide for the children he and Ipwet desired. So many other priests born to higher station grew fat on their privileges without having done anything to deserve them, while he worked long hours and made few mistakes. Others before him had risen through ability, so he still had hopes of greatness. Only now it seemed incongruous that he'd been so excited when his superior, Qenamun, had elevated him to chief of the pure ones of the treasury only last week.

Now his promising future was threatened. Especially if he told the Eyes of Pharaoh anything. No more advances, no prospect of lucrative assignments that brought a share in the income from the god's estates. Yet how could he not say anything?

What he needed was to know the will of Amun. There was every possibility that Amun had guided his steps tonight so that he could foil the evil. Or a demon could have influenced him to seek out the hearing of the sinful words. Which?

He hated dilemmas. He liked clarity and simplicity, like figuring the number of men required to drag an obelisk of a certain weight. Unas sank his head in his hands and moaned. He was a sparrow among vultures in this matter. They would pounce on him and snap his neck. He must give much thought to the choice of whether or not to speak and to whom. Haste could cost him his life.

Taking a deep breath, Unas rose and walked toward the threshold. Then he remembered the inscribed bowl. Veering around, he glowered at the box under his bed. It seemed to shriek danger in a high, raptorlike scream. He should destroy it. Someone could find it and accuse him of unnameable atrocities.

Unas snatched up the box and headed for the kitchen at the back of the house. Ipwet had come downstairs from the roof and was pressing out bread dough beside the dome-shaped oven. Faint wisps of smoke floated up through the vent hole in the roof. She glanced up and gave him a quick smile.

Her dark brown hair was tied back to keep it out of her way, and she wore her old gown, the one she used when doing heavy chores like grinding grain. He liked to watch her use the quern and grinding stone. Her arm muscles bunched as she shoved the stone back and forth, and her breasts bounced in time with her strokes.

"Guess what?" Ipwet said. "Papa brought a duck this afternoon." She breathed in. "Smell that, Unas. Is there nothing finer than roast duck?"

"Mm-hmm."

Unas removed the box lid.

"What is it?" Ipwet asked. She shaped a round loaf with her hands. "I hope it's dates."

He fished inside for the shards. One stuck his finger, but he managed to gather most of the pieces in one hand. Lifting them from the box, he walked to the oven and cast them into the fire. For good measure, he emptied the box at the mouth of the oven and brushed the smaller pieces toward the flames. Ipwet slapped his hands.

"What are you doing? You'll ruin my fire!"

Unas backed away as she shoved him. "I—I was trying to make it hotter."

"With broken pottery?" Ipwet knelt in front of the oven and peered inside. "If you've ruined my fire, you can just make another if you want any dinner." She straightened and shrugged. "It seems fine. Whatever made you do such a stupid thing? Oh, never mind. Go away, Unas. I hate it when you hover over me."

He craned his neck to see over her shoulder, but the shards had disappeared into the flames. His palms felt damp. As he left the kitchen he rubbed them against his kilt.

In the common room he went to a tall, narrow-necked jar in a stand, picked up a strainer, and poured beer into a cup. Gulping until he'd finished the drink, he poured another. Relief sprinkled over his body like one of those rare winter rainfalls. The bowl was destroyed, and he had nothing to fear. He was safe and could take his time in pondering what to do. Haste was an abomination. It led to mistakes; this time it could cost him his life.

Night shrouded the forecourt at the temple of Amun. The threshold of the double doors, where a porter should have stood, was empty. An owl circled overhead, then swooped and landed on the head of a votive statue of some long-dead nobleman. The man must have been wealthy, for the figure had at one time been painted and gilded. After a century, however, the figure had been shoved aside to make way for the offerings of a new age. The sheet gold had been surreptitiously removed, and now the owl picked at chips of paint to reveal fine black diorite stone.

A blur of white movement made the bird screech and launch itself into the air. A whisper of cloth as it moved against skin. The hush of a sigh. The statue seemed to give birth to a man who stepped away from its looming bulk.

Transparent pleated folds caught the gleam of moonlight. A bronze bracelet reflected moonbeams, as did a gold ring with a flat bezel bearing hieroglyphs of the owner's name. The man turned and watched the owl fly over the roofs of the shrines and buildings of the temple complex. Another, shorter man joined the first and spoke in an almost inaudible whisper.

"So you're sure you know this eavesdropper."

The man who had dismissed the porter said, "Of course."

"You got a clear glimpse of him? There is no mistake?"

"I assure you, lord. I know this pure one."

The short man nodded. "Then I will leave the matter in your hands. You know what must be done to keep us safe."

"I'm going at once to send someone to watch him. I know him. He will ponder and quibble and hesitate for days, long enough for an accident to take place."

"Just don't wait too long. They gather at the palace, and my men in the desert have found a suitable place in which to begin the work."

"Haste is unwise. Such tasks must be done carefully, or they only create more difficulties than they solve."

"You can afford to be unruffled. You're not walking

the palace floor tiles with royal guards and suspicious and bloody-minded bastards like Meren."

"Calm yourself," the robed figure said. "I will accomplish the deed in the fullness of its time. After all, our enterprise is blessed by the Hidden One, the great god Amun, who silences storms and protects his disciples."

The short man grunted. "Just you remember that he aids those who know when to strike with the swiftness of a thunderbolt and the deadliness of a cobra. I'm going home."

The robed figure bowed, and a film of linen swirled about his ankles.

"Hail to thee, friend, and may Amun give you peace."

"By the god's balls, one would think you murdered men every day after morning ritual."

"Not that often, my friend, not nearly that often."

2

▽

Meren stood beside General Horemheb before the temple of Amun, enjoying the last of dawn's coolness. He bent his neck back to peer up at the head of the colossal statue that crept toward him. A rhythmic work chant filled the air, punctuated by the gasps and grunts of almost two hundred bondsmen manning the lines that dragged the statue's sledge. On the base of the statue stood an overseer who coordinated each tug of the lines with his chant and the clapping of his hands.

"The high priest will soil his pure white robes when he sees it," Horemheb whispered.

Meren suppressed a grin. "And you'll revel in every moment of his anguish."

Tons of red granite scraped across the oiled and graded path toward the north half of the pylon. Meren glanced over his shoulder into the shadows of the gate. No sign of the king, who had disappeared into the sanctuary for the morning ritual. The welfare of the Two Lands depended upon the king's intercession with the gods, especially Amun, and Tutankhamun performed the ceremony as had his ancestors throughout the centuries.

If the king were unable to attend, the high priest took his place. There was much urgent business, but the king hadn't wanted to miss today's ritual. If he had, he would have missed the arrival of his statue and its effect on the high priest, Parenefer.

Meren glanced at Horemheb with masked affection. They had been friends since they were youths training to be warriors, and had remained so when their duties separated them. Beneath his court wig, the general's hair had turned light brown from long days spent drilling in the sun.

Horemheb wore his hair cut short and brushed back from his face, but it was so lively it stood up and away from his head like the feathers of an angry hawk. He had a rectangular face with three horizontal lines on his forehead. Meren had watched these lines appear and grow deeper over the years. His nose sat slightly askew on his face, the result of an injury when he got in the way of a stampeding chariot.

Horemheb bore a habitual expression of intense determination, as if he sensed a horde of Asiatic nomads lurking just over the horizon. He walked aggressively, almost stomping, as though dogging the steps of some negligent army recruit. He had a noisy temper when dealing with soldiers, allies, or friends and the biddable demeanor of a sleeping crocodile when in the company of strangers or enemies. Meren had seen him switch from fist-pounding fury to poison-sweet courtliness in half a heartbeat. And on the battlefield he possessed the guile of a leopard and a skill Meren hoped never to encounter pitted against him.

However, what was most intriguing about Horemheb was that it never occurred to him to regret his humble origins. He was Horemheb, general of the king's army, royal scribe, councillor to pharaoh, a man of consequence. His common birth was unimportant.

At the moment, the general rocked back and forth on his heels and scowled at the temple quay. The barge upon which the statue had been shipped was docked there, and it had been the object of excitement for the crowd gathered to witness the king's arrival. But Meren knew Horemheb. His friend had forgotten the statue; the general's heart dwelt on the Hittite threat.

"Patience, old friend," Meren said. "We've the rest of the day to argue about brigands, war, and troops."

They both understood that the colossus served as important a function in its way as did the forays of the army, for this statue—so monumental that it almost rivaled the mighty pylons of the king of the gods—this image of the king was to stand before the temple. And in its magnificence and scale, it would tell the people of Egypt that pharaoh was more powerful than any priest who might dwell within the temple it guarded.

Thus, earlier, the statue's arrival had caused the high priest of Amun to contort his face as if he'd swallowed an asp. His chagrin was echoed in the faces of the gathered priests. They huddled in clumps, like sullen pigeons, and scuttled back as the teams of laborers hauled the statue down the avenue.

As the complicated maneuvers that would slide the colossus into its correct position began, Meren saw a pair of royal guards emerge from the gate. A wave of movement started as spear-carrying men in bronze-and-gold armor gestured at the crowd. Courtiers turned, the statue forgotten. Heads lowered. Meren nudged Horemheb, and they both knelt.

Horemheb turned his head toward Meren and grinned. "I've been waiting for this ever since the king conceived the idea."

"Just be careful Parenefer doesn't see how much you enjoy his aggravation."

The sudden silence of this moment always impressed Meren. It was as if the kingdom ceased to breathe. Then he heard the *ching, ching, ching* of sistrums, the beat of drums. Louder and louder the noise grew, until it seemed to beat inside his body. At last it stopped, and he heard a cheer. Concealing a grin, he rose and found Horemheb already on his feet. He only had to follow the glint of gold to find the king.

Tutankhamun stood before the gateway between the high priest of Amun and the vizier Ay and gave off a sunlike radiance. The cobra on his brow, the thick bracelets and ankle bands, the scepters he held in one hand, were all of gold. Even his sandals gleamed with the stuff. Gold symbolized the majesty and divinity of pharaoh, but Meren knew how useless such trappings could be. The king's youth, his strength, his commanding soul, allowed him to wear the raiment of a living god without being dominated by it. Beside the king, Parenefer looked like what he was, a cracked and dried-up old coffin filled to overflowing with resentment and hate.

Meren watched the high priest as the king spoke to the crowd, telling them how the statue was intended for the greater glory of Amun, his father. Parenefer's skull always shone due to the scented oils rubbed on it after shaving. The skin stretched tight across the bones as if to make up for the loose flesh at his jowls and neck. Age spots dotted his face, his arms, and the backs of his hands. Wrinkles furrowed his mouth, running from his nose down the flesh above his upper lip and into the mouth itself like wadis etched in a desert landscape.

Shortsighted, Parenefer jutted his head forward from his slumped shoulders and squinted at the world like a suspicious and wary vulture. His life and character had been marred by the dissolution of the temple of Amun by the pharaoh Akhenaten. Declared anathema, hounded and hunted as a criminal, Parenefer had survived in hiding, plotting and fomenting defiance of pharaoh, until Akhenaten died.

Although he and his god had been restored to their

former prominence, the high priest's ka had been warped. He couldn't forget the deaths of his friends and his humiliation at the hands of Akhenaten, nor could he forgive Tutankhamun for being the brother of the heretic. Meren and Horemheb trusted the Hittite ambassador more than they trusted Parenefer.

Horemheb spoke, barely moving his lips. "See. I told you it was worth the wait."

The high priest craned back his head and studied the face of the colossus, noted the straight, small nose and flared nostrils, the full, sensual lips and slightly rounded cheeks of youth. Parenefer's lips pressed together in a tight seam. He turned vermilion, and his cheeks puffed out so that he resembled an elderly, indignant frog. He turned away.

"Well worth it," Meren said softly.

Hearing the commander of the royal guard snap an order, he hurried to take his place behind the king as Horemheb went to the quay where the royal barge was moored. Meren fell in step with Maya, chief of the treasury. As they paused to allow the king to speak to several commoners, Meren glanced over his shoulder at the swarm of workmen around the colossus.

He found himself meeting the direct stare of a priest. His gaze traveled over hollow shoulders, wide hips, noted the way the man's oversize ears stood out from his head like slices of dried melon. Narrowing his eyes, he felt a stab of familiarity. There was something about the man. Perhaps it was the way his shaved skull came to a point; perhaps it was only the fear in his eyes.

Meren was used to seeing fear in those who met his eyes. Then the priest opened his mouth and took a step. He stopped abruptly, looked to the side, and started. Without looking at Meren again, he plunged into the midst of the gang of workmen, artisans, and architects at the base of the statue.

Meren searched in the direction the priest had looked, but found only more priests and a few courtiers. Whatever or whoever had startled the man was unremarkable in appearance.

Maya put a hand on his arm. "Meren, the king."

The king's chamberlain was beckoning to him. He crossed the ramp to the royal barge and knelt before Tutankhamun.

"You may rise before my majesty."

Meren stood and met the barely suppressed amusement of a king who, after all, was barely fourteen. He frowned as openly as he dared in response, and the amusement slid from the boy's face. A mask of dignity and graciousness descended upon the king's features, and he turned to accept the farewells of the high priest and chief prophets of the god. Meren allowed himself a silent sigh. Tutankhamun had already challenged the power of the priests once today. It wouldn't do to arouse them any further.

As the barge moved away from the quay, Meren stood beside the king, his head bent to catch the low pitch of Tutankhamun's voice.

"Did you see him?" the king asked. "Did you see how red he turned when he realized how great was the size of my image?"

Meren risked a sidelong glance at the king. Tutankhamun was maintaining a regal demeanor. He stared straight ahead at the west bank, away from the eastern city and its countless temples.

"Aye, majesty. Thy image is indeed that of a living god."

Tutankhamun lifted a brow and met Meren's bland gaze.

"It was your idea too," the king said. "So don't pretend you don't enjoy his discomfort."

"But our joy must be a silent one, majesty."

The king sighed and turned to take a last look at the monumental image of himself. Meren looked at it as well, then squinted. A priest had climbed onto the base of the statue and was facing them, staring at the royal barge as it retreated from the sacred precinct. Meren closed his eyes as the glare of the rising sun assaulted them, then opened them again.

The priest was still there, unmoving, and Meren could have sworn he was the same man whose fear had so impressed him only a few moments ago. There was something unsettling about that solitary figure. No doubt it was the contrast between the priest and that mountain of a statue; he did look rather like a beetle next to an elephant.

The king spoke to Meren, and he forgot the priest. When next he looked, the little figure had disappeared from the statue base, and he thought no more about him.

Back at the palace the king vanished into the royal chambers to divest himself of his crowns. Meren and several councillors remained in one of the smaller audience chambers. Light filtered through the high rectangular windows and illuminated the fluid scenes of the king hunting in the marshes that bordered the Nile. The deep blue of the river was re-created by the glazed floor tiles. Meren preferred this room to the great audience chamber with its vastness, its loftier columns, and its air of chilly sanctity.

He took a goblet of wine from a servant as Maya joined him. The treasurer was a favorite with Meren, for he was more interested in the efficiency of those who served under him than in his own advancement. From a family of ancient nobility, Maya felt he had little to gain in scrambling after more power. He had enough, and devoted his attention to meddling in the personal lives of those about him—for their own benefit, of course.

Having little patience with those who viewed life as a series of battles, Maya preferred enjoyments. He liked fastidious workers who saved him trouble. He liked music and feasting, acrobats and good stories. Meren felt he gave a much-needed lightness of spirit to pharaoh, who was surrounded by men of gravity and bore overwhelming responsibility of which he was too well aware.

Now Maya was nodding in the direction of Ay, who was engaged in a quiet quarrel with Horemheb.

"What's happened, Falcon?" Maya whispered. He'd given the name to Meren years ago, observing that his friend's intelligence was as quick as the falcon's flight. "This sudden audience was your idea, wasn't it?"

It was, but Meren wasn't going to admit it. He'd had too many disturbing reports of unrest in the fallen kingdom of Mitanni on the northern Euphrates and among the vassal states and allies of the empire that stood between Syria and the borders of Egypt. Everyone knew the Hittites were behind the turmoil.

When Meren didn't answer, Maya nodded at Horemheb. "He wants to campaign in Palestine and Syria after the next harvest."

Meren took a sip of his wine. "That's not what they disagree about."

"Oh? What is it, then? Because we have to do something about the Hittites."

"Indeed, but Ay doesn't think the king should go on the campaign."

"Too young yet?"

Meren inclined his head.

Maya, whose easy temperament and skills at organization had endeared him to the king and the vizier, turned toward Meren and frowned. "And what do you say? You've trained him."

"No boy of his age, however godlike, can master a warrior's skills in so short a time. Perhaps in another year. Until then . . ."

"And our beleaguered Horemheb says the empire can't wait that long."

"He could be right."

"Then one of the other princes can provide a royal presence."

Meren shook his head. "You know it's not the same for the troops."

He took another sip of wine and surveyed the audience chamber. Huy, who served as one of the viceroys of Nubia—those lands to the south over which Egypt maintained dominance—stood talking with the Nubian prince Khai, who also helped govern the south. Nakhtmin, general and royal scribe, had joined in the discussion with Ay and Horemheb.

He was surprised to see Ahiram, a foreign prince, in attendance. Ahiram was the son of Rib-Addi, the king of Byblos, one of the ally princes whom Akhenaten had failed to support against insurrection. Rib-Addi had succumbed to the depredations of rebels incited by the Hittite king Suppiluliumas. Poor Ahiram had been sent to the Egyptian court to be educated, only to find himself fatherless and without a city or a throne to which he could return. Perhaps Ay had requested Ahiram's presence, since the foreign prince was familiar with the country around Byblos and Tyre.

Everyone suddenly snapped to attention when the royal guards burst into the room, spears tapping on the floor tiles. Tutankhamun entered, marching smartly as only youth can, and clapped his hands.

"Yes, yes, get up, everyone. My majesty consents to dismiss ceremony. We'll deal with Nubia first. Huy, what happened to that expedition to the gold mines?" The king dropped into a chair covered in embossed sheet gold.

Before Huy could answer, the overseer of the audience hall swung open the double doors and poked his head into the chamber. Meren came to alert immediately, for the old man's eyes gleamed as he sought the gaze of pharaoh. Tutankhamun nodded, and the overseer stepped aside to allow Kysen into the room. Upon seeing his son, Meren knew something had happened.

He'd left Ky in charge of the daily ordering of the affairs of his office—reading summaries of disturbances throughout the kingdom and receiving reports from their various intelligencers—while he attended this audience. Now Kysen hurried forward to cast himself at the king's feet. He lifted his face from the floor, and Meren's unease vanished. Kysen grinned at the king.

"O living god, divine and golden one."

Tutankhamun swiped his hand to the side. "Please, Ky."

"Majesty." Kysen was grinning broadly. "They're home!"

Tutankhamun thrust himself out of his chair and clapped his hands again. "Where are they?"

Kysen turned and nodded at the doors. Through them burst a noisy group of young men followed by musicians playing music to which several foreign women danced. These were followed by servants bearing inlaid treasure boxes.

The king burst out laughing and shouted, "Tanefer!"

The call was repeated by everyone in the hall. Meren ducked aside as a woman whirled her body at him. He smiled as he watched the young men stride toward the king. Disheveled, stained, and dusty, their leader nevertheless walked into the king's presence easily, as if he frequented the houses of kings every day, which he did.

Prince Tanefer knelt before the king, who raised him. To Meren, the resemblance between Tanefer, who was older by fourteen years, and the king was apparent, especially in the large, rounded eyes and full lips. They had gotten them from their father, the pharaoh Amunhotep, but Tanefer inherited the darker skin and softly curling black hair of his foreign mother.

The king and Tanefer exchanged a rough hug. Then Tanefer shouted an order, and the music rose. Drums beat out a sensual rhythm as Tanefer whispered something to the king. Then he began to clap his hands and sway.

Meren recognized the traditional warrior's dance of the royal charioteers. He folded his arms and smiled as Tanefer snatched a goblet of wine, raised it to the king, and kept on dancing. Tutankhamun laughed and answered by swinging into line with Tanefer. The king grabbed Kysen, who obliged by falling into step and dragging another new arrival, Rahotep, with him.

Around the room they swirled, stamping and leaping, until Tanefer ran into Meren, who ducked under a flailing arm and swung into line beside him. He whirled quickly in a circle, then kicked out with one leg. Tanefer jumped over it, but Meren snagged his ankle and yanked. Tanefer dropped to the floor, yelped, and rolled as the line of men ran into him.

Tutankhamun offered his arm as he passed, and Tanefer grabbed it. Leaping to his feet, he bent over, planted his hands on his thighs, and puffed to catch his breath. The line broke up as everyone guffawed at Tanefer and sucked in air.

The king pounded Meren on the back. "That will teach him to parade before us like a Babylonian king."

Tanefer raised his head and grinned at Tutankhamun. "But, majesty, in reality I should be a king, king of Mitanni after my deposed uncle. I would be if I didn't find the Two Lands the chosen place of the gods. And besides, the divine one needs mirth and pleasure. It's my task to provide them as a solace in his days of care for the empire."

This last comment attracted Meren's attention, as it was meant to. He stared at Tanefer, who was bowing to the king. As he straightened, Tanefer glanced at Meren, who read his meaning and faded out of the group. He circled around to Ay and whispered to the old man. Ay nodded. Leaning on his staff, he penetrated the crowd of young men and spoke to the king.

"Perhaps thy majesty desires to speak privately with his envoy to Palestine and Syria?"

Tutankhamun paused a moment, glanced at Meren, and said, "Yes, my majesty desires it at once. Huy, Khai, Maya, go away for a while. We will summon you again."

In a short time only a few confidants were left—the vizier, Horemheb, Prince Tanefer, and his companions, Prince Rahotep and Prince Djoserkarenseneb, called Djoser. Prince Hunefer stalled beside the king.

"Why must I go?" he whined.

Meren raised his eyes to the ceiling. Hunefer possessed the wits of a beer vat, but suffered from the fantasy that he deserved rewards and honors though he'd done nothing to earn them.

Tutankhamun gritted his teeth and scowled at Hunefer while he tapped his sandaled foot. "You have to go, half brother, because I told you to."

Meren slipped to Hunefer's side and smiled at him. Hunefer started at his sudden appearance, refused to meet Meren's gaze, and sidled out of the room. Meren made sure the overseer of the audience hall had closed the doors and that the royal sentries were in place beside them. When he returned, Tutankhamun had taken his chair again. Tanefer, Rahotep, and Djoser stood in front of him with the others gathered behind, all except Ay. The vizier's age and revered status allowed him to sit on a stool near the king when in private. Meren joined the group as Tanefer began.

"Majesty, Karkashar has fallen to the Hittites."

Tutankhamun gripped the arms of his chair and cursed. "You're sure?"

"Aye, divine one," said Rahotep. "We scouted the ruins ourselves. They burned and razed the city and carried off the women and children."

Rahotep's glance slid away from the king. His opinion was unspoken but known to every man there. He could have prevented the disaster had he been pharaoh instead of Tutankhamun. But then, as far as Meren knew, Rahotep felt he could do anything better than anyone else.

Djoser shuddered. "Not one man was left alive, majesty. You should have seen the battlefield. At first I thought I saw some of the bodies moving, and then I realized it was the . . . the flies and maggots."

Meren eyed Djoser, who was pale under his layers of dust. Djoser, like Tutankhamun, Tanefer, and Rahotep, was the son of Amunhotep the Magnificent. But he was a half prince, the son of an Egyptian noblewoman rather than a princess. A scholarly man in his early twenties, he had gone on this expedition in a misguided attempt to become a warrior. He had returned with a limp and an air of one haunted by netherworld monsters. Meren didn't think he would attempt battle again, no matter how much he envied the king and Tanefer their warrior's skills and allure.

"Then we are left with the cities of Palestine between us and the Hittites," the king said.

"Not for long, majesty," said Tanefer.

"Yes," Horemheb said, "not for long. I can begin

preparations for the army and navy at once. By next harvest we'll—"

Ay raised his hand. "There's no need for haste. After all, pharaoh doesn't need the allegiance of vassals whose only desire in life is to wheedle gold from his coffers and murder each other. These northern peoples know nothing of peace and harmony. Let them devour each other while we play one against the other."

Meren stepped aside as Tanefer abruptly bowed himself out of the group of men who burst into argument. He followed the prince, who ducked behind a column, and found him standing with fists balled, arms rigid, and eyes closed. Hearing the deliberately controlled deep breaths, he waited a moment before speaking.

"He doesn't mean to offend you."

Tanefer opened his eyes and gave Meren a mock smile. "Meren, my love, my old friend. Think you he's forgotten that my mother was a princess of Mitanni?"

"Perhaps." Meren leaned against the column. "You look too much the Egyptian, my friend, and more like your royal father than the king does."

They stood together in silence while the king and his councillors argued. Meren had always felt sympathy for the princes and half princes of the kingdom. Only the sons of the great royal wife had a right to the throne, so these men were cast aside, regardless of their talent. Some, like Tanefer, preferred a warrior's life of freedom to the responsibilities of kingship. Some such as Djoser were temperamentally unsuited from birth to govern, while Rahotep and Hunefer lived lives of resentment and envy because their concubine mothers' blood cost them a throne.

In contrast, Tanefer's great passion was surrounding himself with objects of beauty. His attitude toward statues and luxurious furniture and jewelry was odd; he wanted to look at them rather than use them.

To Meren and everyone else a statue had a purpose: a gift to the gods, a repository of one's spirit, an image that enlivened one's soul for eternity. Jewelry was for adornment and for magic. Furniture was for convenience. Luxurious materials symbolized a man's status.

Tanefer wanted to look at these things as one looked at a beautiful woman. In the same way, he reveled in the artistry of the cavalry and was one of pharaoh's most accomplished charioteers. At twenty-eight, six years younger than Meren, he was rising fast in the military and had a reputation as a brilliant strategist. Meren thanked the gods for such as Tanefer, for the heretic pharaoh, Tutankhamun's dead brother Akhenaten, had left the empire weakened.

"Tanefer," Meren said, "it was not Ay who refused to come to the aid of Mitanni."

"I know, brother of my heart, but Tutankhamun can't let the destruction continue. The Hittites will eat away at the edges of the empire until we find them at our very borders."

Tanefer turned to face him, and Meren saw the uneasiness he'd concealed from the king. "Listen to me, Meren. The Hittites fight differently than we do. They use a three-man chariot that's heavier than ours. It carries two warriors instead of one and a driver. They're slower and less maneuverable, but they can destroy a line with a massed charge. With three men they can devastate us at close quarters. Meren, the Hittites might be able to—"

"Take Egypt." Meren nodded. Tanefer had confirmed what he'd been hearing from other sources. "You may be right, old friend, but they won't do it today, or tomorrow, or even next year. Akhenaten allowed the army

and navy to fall to pieces. Horemheb and Nakhtmin
need time to rebuild."

"But—"

Meren pushed away from the column and squeezed
Tanefer's arm. "Be at ease. I've heard you, and I believe you."

"There isn't much time. Right now they're fat with
victory, and complacent. If we attacked now, we might
even push them out of Mitanni."

"And put you in place of the Hittite minion who rules
there now?" Meren grinned at the astonishment in
Tanefer's face. "Oh, don't look so worried. I but jest
with you. For a man who lives on merriment and lightness, you fail to recognize another man's joke too often."

Tanefer shook his head and pointed at the king, who
was listening to Ay. "I can see it already. Ay will con-
vince him to delay. Delay and negligence lost my uncle
his kingdom and cost him his life."

Meren stood beside Tanefer and gazed at the king.
"And haste, dear Tanefer, could cost pharaoh his."

3

▽

Unas scurried through the black streets of western
Thebes, his ka lighter than it had been in two days, for
he was no longer afraid. He was unsuspected; he could
continue at the temple without risk. Yesterday he'd seen
Lord Meren among the attendants of pharaoh and had
almost spoken to him. Luckily he'd lost his courage; the
man he feared gave no sign of disturbance.

In the darkness of the hour before dawn he could
barely make out the shapes of the sphinxes that lined
the avenue before the temple. He walked between two
of them and down the street toward the first pylon, the
gate of the god. It was still early, and there was no one
about.

Unas approached the colossus. It stood surrounded by
scaffolding, ready to be finished. Most of it had been
carved at the quarry far to the south near Aswan, but it
still had to be polished. Soon master stoneworkers and
their apprentices would arrive with their rubbing stones
and buckets of crushed quartzite to smooth and polish
what surfaces weren't to be painted and adorned with
gold.

Nearing the ladder that scaled the statue to the platform surrounding its head, Unas paused as he heard a
loud snore. He poked his head around the base of the
sculpture. The noise was coming from the gate between
the pylons. That lazy porter was asleep again. Sniffing,

Unas patted the list of tools and supplies he'd folded and stuck in the waistband of his kilt. The sentries must be pacing their route on the far side of the temple. Not that they would disturb the porter, who could sleep through the howling of fiends.

Unas, on the other hand, always woke early, a habit that benefited him this morning. Last night the master sculptor had sent a boy with a message asking that they meet early to go over the day's work plan. He grasped the ladder and began climbing.

Halfway up, he paused and glanced around. He could see lights in houses now, and far off a donkey brayed. He continued up the ladder, smiling. Being the first to arrive and the last to leave afforded him much pleasure, for his industrious habits had attracted the attention of the prophets of the god. In their hands lay all opportunities for advancement.

His head reached the floor of the top scaffolding. He grasped the ends of the ladder and put a foot on the floor. Pharaoh's granite eyes, as large as Unas's head, stared at him.

As he hoisted himself onto the scaffolding, he heard the creak of wood. Something white dashed at him as he straightened up with his feet planted on the edge of the platform. Unas's mouth fell open, but the man who leaped from behind the giant head of the colossus was too fast for him.

Unas screamed, flailed his arms, and plummeted. He felt one last jolt of pain, and then nothing.

The man on the scaffolding peered over the edge at the body below. Then he surveyed the area around the statue, keeping his head cocked in the direction of the god's gate and the porter. A loud sucking noise floated toward him, signaling continued slumber, and he quickly climbed down. He stood over the body for a moment before turning and melting into the darkness beneath the high wall that surrounded the temple. What was left of Unas lay undisturbed except for visits from flies.

As light appeared behind the eastern temples of the sacred precinct, several priests walked down the avenue to the pylon. They didn't glance at the base of the statue, and in any case the body lay on the far side, away from the gate. The priests roused the porter, scolded him, and went into the temple.

Not long afterward, a group of men arrived at the quay in a skiff. Disembarking, they shouldered baskets and sacks and headed for the pylon. As they approached, talking and laughing, they veered aside and directed their steps toward the colossus.

They passed granite feet larger than two men, rounded the corner of the base on which they stood, and came to an abrupt stop. Silence enveloped the group, broken by the buzzing of flies. Then they all chattered at once.

"It's that priest, Unas."

"What happened? Did he fall?"

"Look at his head. His meat has spattered all over the flagstones."

"He must have lost his footing."

The oldest man, whose skin was cracked, split, and scarred from years of working with stone in the sun, raised his voice for the first time. "Quiet, all of you!"

He walked over to the body and stared at it while the others kept their distance. In his years as master stone sculptor, Seneb had seen many wonders—the colossi of Amunhotep the Magnificent's funerary temple, the arrival of the Mitanni princess Gilukhepa and her hundreds of waiting women at the court of Thebes, even water turned to cold clouds of white snow in mountain-

tops far to the north. Never had he seen a dead priest at
the base of a statue.

He looked from the body, up the ladder to the platform that surrounded the neck of the statue. He rubbed
his chin, then dropped the basket he was carrying. Old
Unas had been a scribe, and scribes could stumble over
their own toes.

"I'm going to see the priests. All of you stay here
and let no one touch the body."

"But, Seneb—"

"Stay here, I said."

Seneb broke into a trot. He went to the gate and confronted the porter, who was leaning against a stone wall,
rubbing his eyes and yawning. It took him several attempts to make the man understand, but eventually he
was allowed inside and encountered a servant sweeping
flagstones.

The servant conducted him to a pure one, who
handed him over to his chief, who listened to Seneb's
report without comment. Then he was left standing
under a papyrus column while the priest vanished into
the black inner temple. After a while the man reappeared, trailing behind a tall priest in a luxurious wig
and gold headband.

He moved with slim, almost fragile grace. His bones
were thin, giving him a deerlike aspect. The gauntness
of his face and its length reminded Seneb of the old
heretic Akhenaten. The sheer quality of the linen he
wore along with the gold scarab pectoral at his breast
put Seneb at ease. Here was a priest of rank. This man
wouldn't pass off responsibility, and he'd know what
to do.

"I am Qenamun, chief overseer of the god's treasury
and lector priest of Amun. You've found one of our
pure ones?"

"Aye, master. It's the priest who was working with us

on the statue of the living god. Unas was his name. He's fallen from the scaffolding."

"Fallen? Are you sure? Amun protect us. Conduct me to him at once."

Seneb discovered that "at once," to a lector priest, meant a stately progress out of the temple, with care taken not to get dust on his priestly overrobe and fine sandals.

The group of artisans around the body parted so that he and Qenamun could see. As moments passed, more and more laborers, priests, and visitors to the temple clustered nearby, muttering among themselves. Seneb watched the lector priest survey the body.

It was obvious to him that Qenamun was one of those whose priestly station was inherited through a noble family. His bearing and his dress spoke of privilege. His elaborate wig, worn over a shaved head, had its braids bound by hundreds of bronze rings. His parched-looking skin had been oiled. No doubt it soaked up moisture like the desert floor.

Seneb was about to explain how they'd found the dead man when Qenamun stooped over the body and began to make magical signs. The artisans backed farther away as a group. Seneb, conscious of his station as their leader, only retreated half the distance of the others.

Qenamun turned away from the body and addressed him. "This is a most unfortunate accident. You said he must have slipped and fallen from the top of the ladder?"

"Yes, lector priest."

"Very well. You and your men will remain here on guard. He's one of those under my command. I'll send servants to remove him to his house."

"Yes, lector priest. And then I must report to the office of the treasurer, Prince Maya."

He cringed inwardly when, without warning, the priest rained white coals of fury on him.

"By the gods, you will not!" Qenamun's voice hissed and spat venom. "Insolent lowling, this is a matter for the servants of Amun, not a breaker of stones. You'll do as I command and nothing more, or I'll see you condemned to the stone quarries in the eastern desert."

Qenamun turned on his heel and left Seneb standing in an empty space between the body and his fellow artisans. His gut squeezed and did a few somersaults before he regained his composure. He glanced over his shoulder to find everyone staring at him. He glared at them.

"What are you looking at, dung-eaters?"

He ordered them to form a cordon around the body and took his place with them, facing away from the dead man. Several curious boys on their way to the school in the temple tried to shove between their legs, thus offering him an opportunity to swear and shout at someone. As minutes passed and no one came to take the body away, Seneb had time to think.

He was a royal artisan, answerable to his overseer in the royal workshops, who was answerable to another superior, who eventually was answerable to Prince Maya, chief of the treasury and Friend of the King. To whom did he owe allegiance, Maya or that scorpion of a priest Qenamun?

He turned to his son, who was also his apprentice, and spoke quietly. "Djefi, you will go back to the royal workshops at once and report this matter to the overseer of stonemasons. Say to him that I've done this in spite of being forbidden by the lector priest. See to it that he understands none of us are to blame, but that we must report anything that happens regarding the image of the living god, may he have life, health, and strength. Can you remember to say that?"

"Yes, Father."

"Then go now, before the priests come back. Hurry!"

He followed his son's progress until he disappeared into the crowd. Curse all priests. Why did this one have to die on Seneb's statue and call down upon his head the notice of great ones? He knew from experience that their attention was as the attention of hornets, and much more dangerous.

Meren rose from his stool and began to stretch his arms and legs as he listened to the treasurer's objections to the king leading an army into Syria himself. Since they'd first discussed the prospect, Maya had become more and more worried that pharaoh would get himself killed in battle. He wanted no part in urging the king to take such a risk.

The councillors had broken from their meeting after more than four hours of debate. The king had led them outside to the reflection pool. Whenever he could, Tutankhamun sought the outdoors. Having three daughters and an adopted son, Meren understood the king's restlessness. No youth forced to spend hours dealing with matters of finance, law, and diplomacy could be blamed for longing for physical release.

He moved closer to a servant who plied an ostrich feather fan in his and Maya's direction. Thrusting out his arm, he pressed it across his body with the opposite hand in a stretch while he gazed across the pool over blue and pink lotus flowers. Under a baldachin that shaded him from the sun, the king was listening to Ay. Even from this distance Meren could tell that Tutankhamun was growing angrier.

In the council meeting a division had emerged between the king's advisers. General Horemheb and Prince Tanefer favored a military campaign against the rebellious vassals of Syria and Palestine. Everyone agreed one was necessary. But the king wanted to lead the army himself, and Horemheb and Tanefer concurred. After years of neglect on the part of the heretic Akhenaten, the army needed training, and it needed a warrior pharaoh at its head. Ay and Maya understood this, but both kept repeating one refrain—the king was too young.

Meren bent over and touched the ground with his fingertips. He straightened when he heard the king's voice carried over the water.

"I'm not too young, old man. And whatever my years, I'm still pharaoh, and I'll do as my majesty pleases!"

Tutankhamun burst out of his gilt chair. It flew to the side and hit a table that bore an electrum flagon and goblets, sending everything crashing to the tiles that bordered the pool. Ay dodged a rolling goblet as the king stormed away from him. The vizier watched his charge stalk back into the palace, then glanced at Meren.

Shaking his head, Meren walked around the pool to join the vizier as a guard escorted a treasury official out to meet Maya. He was still shaking his head as he met the vizier under the baldachin.

"Ay, Ay, Ay."

He'd known Ay all his life. The brother of the king's mother, the great Queen Tiye, wife of Amunhotep the Magnificent, the vizier was famed throughout the Two Lands for his skill in government. He was even more renowned for surviving the reigns of Amunhotep the Magnificent, Akhenaten, Smenkhare, and now Tutankhamun. His eyebrows slanted upward along with his eyes, giving him a startled appearance.

In Meren's opinion he hadn't been surprised since the

age of the pyramids. The knuckles on his hands were swollen and ached, and his back curved like a scythe. The vizier's body moved slowly, except for his eyes, which never rested. His gaze skittered across Meren now, then darted back to the place where his royal nephew had vanished.

Ay's aged voice grated out his words. "He's too young, and the little cock knows it." Ay stopped talking and lowered his skeletal frame into a chair as servants righted that of the king. When they'd gone, he continued. "And sometimes I wish he was still young enough to require a regent."

"The quarrel would be the same," Meren said as he leaned against one of the support poles of the baldachin. "When you and Horemheb were vice regents, you always favored caution, like the oryx on the plain, while Horemheb favored action, like the lion who hunts the oryx."

"But at least he listened to me, young one."

"The divine one still listens, but he's growing into a man. If you don't let him test himself, he'll cast aside all your counsel and do something even more dangerous than usual."

Ay scowled at him. "Then you don't think he's too young for battle?"

"Of course he's too young."

"By the womb of Isis, then why do you chastise me for telling him so?"

"Ay, where is your fabled diplomacy? The king is an untried youth in need of experience and all too aware of a kingdom watching his performance. His mistakes and embarrassments are discussed from the delta to Nubia, over every morning cup of beer, in every tavern, stable and cattle pen. Offer him something else besides opinions about his lack of prowess."

Ay sighed and lowered his chin to the palm of his

hand. "I'm too old. I forget what it was like to be so young. That's why I'm glad you're here. He needs you young ones about him."

"Like Tanefer?"

"Tanefer? That wild colt? Half the responsibility for this quarrel lies upon his shoulders."

"We have to do something, Ay."

"I know. I know. Now go away and let me think, young one."

Meren returned to a chair at his shaded place on the opposite side of the pool, only to find Maya in a fit of irritation. His hollow jaws worked, and his mouth slanted down even more than usual while he ranted at his aide.

"Why must you disturb me about so inconsequential a matter when I'm in counsel with his majesty? Handle the matter yourself."

"But the overseer of stonemasons is upset," the aide said. "And you always told me that master craftsmen can create much havoc if they're disturbed. And after all, the priest did fall off his majesty's image right in front of the temple of Amun."

Meren had been downing a cup of water when he heard this. He wiped his mouth. "What's this?"

Maya threw up his hands and said, "Some priest has fallen to his death from the scaffolding around the colossus of the king in front of the temple of Amun. An accident about which I don't wish to know and don't care."

"What priest?" Meren asked before gulping down more water.

The aide consulted a scrap of papyrus. "A pure one, my lord. The pure one in charge of the supplies of precious stones and metals to be used on the statue. His name was, hmmm, his name was Unas."

"I don't care what his name was," Maya said. He sat

down, crossed his legs at the ankles, and glared at the aide. "Go away."

The aide turned, but Meren held up his hand so that the man paused.

"Maya, I think I understand why the matter was brought to your attention. If you will recall the delight the king takes in this brilliant image of himself, its monumental size—and its strategic position in front of the temple?"

Maya groaned and rubbed his temples. "His majesty will be furious. By the staff of Ptah, he's already angry, and now . . . I don't want to add to his frustration."

"You're right," Meren said lightly. He glanced at Maya out of the corner of his eye and went on in as negligent a tone as he could produce. "However, if he knew the matter was already being taken in hand?"

"Ah!" Maya's pained look vanished, and he sat up. "You'll investigate? I know it's an insignificant matter, one you'd hardly touch yourself if it weren't for the king. Could you?"

"If you like."

"Excellent." Maya waved his aide away and beamed at Meren. "My thanks, Falcon."

As Maya chattered on, Meren nodded and smiled while he thought furiously. He'd recognized that name. Unas. Unas was the name of the informer paid by his aide, Abu. Only a few weeks ago he'd seen him in the temple of Amun when investigating the murder in the place of Anubis. His informer among the priests of Amun was dead. Now he remembered. Yesterday he'd seen the little man with the pointed skull staring at him from the base of the statue, and now he'd fallen off it.

Meren didn't like the conjunction of events. He didn't believe in accidents, not ones that happened to his informers. And yet it could be a simple accident. He'd been too long among courtiers who would murder their own husbands and wives to gain power. After all, Unas was one of thousands of pure ones in the service of Amun. Still, he had to be sure the death was an accident. Which was why he'd maneuvered to take charge of the investigation, an easy task, considering how much Maya disliked upsetting the king.

Maya was almost as protective as Ay. Tanefer was right when he accused them of holding the king back, of nursing him like a sick calf. One had to be careful and suspicious if one wanted the king to live to reach manhood. Pharaoh lived with too many enemies—even his own wife. No, it was better to be suspicious than foolishly trusting. He would inform the king of the priest's death, but he wouldn't be able to investigate himself. His presence might arouse the hostility of the high priest. He'd send Kysen.

Having decided his course of action, Meren closed his eyes and listened to Maya's analysis of the risks to the king in warfare. He was nodding his agreement for the third time when a familiar voice spoke from somewhere above his head.

"Wake up, cousin."

Meren's eyes flew open, and he stared into the face of Ebana, so like his own except for the scar that arced across it. His cousin stood over him, an elegant and regal figure in gold, lapis lazuli, and transparent robes. Wide of shoulder, as fit as any charioteer, and as deadly, Ebana raked him with a black, black gaze.

Meren clamped his hands on the arms of his chair, every sense awake, his body thrumming with the beat of alarm. Ebana, who hated him, who served the powerful high priest of Amun.

Ebana gave Meren a cobra's smile. "Prepare yourself, cousin. Your spy in the temple is dead."

4

▽

Meren shook his head, leaned back, and loosened his grip on the arms of his chair as he smiled. "Ah, cousin, we've just heard of this accident at the temple. My spy?" He gave Maya a glance that held both amusement and resignation. "Why is it that everyone at court believes that I have spies in their households and in every temple in the kingdom?"

"Because you do," Maya said calmly.

Meren would have liked to cuff the treasurer on the ear, but Ebana interrupted.

"I saw your man speaking to him only a few weeks ago. It's not like you to expose your minions so carelessly, but I had him watched after that." His eyes glittered and fixed on Meren's face. "And now he's fallen to his death from the top of the king's statue. No doubt the good god avenged himself upon his traitorous servant."

Sighing, Meren said, "Unas wasn't my spy."

"You know his name."

"Gods, Ebana," Maya said. "We just learned it together a few moments ago."

Meren had been watching his cousin through his lashes. If something weren't done, Ebana would create a scandal that could eventually involve the king. He sighed again and gave Maya an apologetic look.

"Would you mind, old friend, if I spoke to my cousin alone? Family quarrels and rivalries, you understand."

Maya registered no surprise, nor did he object at being edged out of a matter that involved his underlings. With a smooth acquiescence, he left them alone. Meren knew he would be inundated with queries later, which was why Maya could keep his curiosity under rein now. When he was gone, Meren rose so that Ebana could no longer look down on him.

He turned away and, beckoning a slave, whispered that Kysen be summoned. Then he dismissed the servants with their fans and walked away from the chairs. He stopped when he reached one of the sycamores that surrounded the reflection pool in orderly rows.

He glanced back at his cousin. Wide of shoulder, with a flat belly and long legs, Ebana had a body that closely adhered to the canon of proportions painters used to depict gods and kings. People said the cousins looked alike. Meren had never paid much attention to their resemblance. He did remember how Ebana used to laugh at him for being embarrassed when girls would linger in doorways and drape themselves on rooftops as they drove their chariots through the city.

That had been when they were like brothers. Leaning his shoulder against the tree, he waited for Ebana to join him.

"I haven't come for a loving family talk," Ebana said. He confronted Meren with arms folded across his chest. "I've come to report to his majesty."

"You know well that I was only pursuing a murderer when I talked to that priest. I talk to priests of Amun all the time, Ebana. Do you suspect each of them? And if you do, perhaps I should suspect you of killing this one."

Ebana flushed. "I'm no murderer, and don't try to distract me."

A breeze caught and tossed the leaves of the syca-more. Meren breathed in cool air, closed his eyes, and raised his face to sunlight dappled by leafy branches. "Follow your own reasoning. Of all the priests of Amun, you're the one I talk to the most. Therefore, you're the one most likely to be my spy. Does Parenefer suspect you?"

When Ebana didn't answer, Meren opened his eyes. Had he not shared a childhood with the man, he couldn't have read anything in his expression. Ebana's eyes weren't simply the dark brown of Egypt. They were true black, like the Nile at night. Only Meren could catch a glint as if the full moon had dropped into them, and the skin around them seemed pale from ten-sion.

"I didn't know," Meren said softly.

"You know nothing. I have orders to report to the king. I could tell him what I know of your spy."

"Don't," Meren said as he began to rub the scar on his inner wrist. "You'll only annoy him and create fur-ther strain between the temple and the court."

"Amun has no fear of—"

"Ebana, sometimes you're wearisome beyond endur-ance. I've had a letter from my sister. She's at home with Bener and Isis and says they're both learning the running of an estate quite well. I have to admit that I didn't think Isis would do well. You have daughters. You should understand how the youngest always man-ages to slip away from responsibilities."

"The way you slipped away from yours to me?"

Ebana touched his temple where his scar began. It crossed his left cheek and slanted down his neck, where it disappeared under a gold-and-carnelian broad collar.

Meren shoved away from the tree trunk and planted his feet apart. "Damn you. I tried to warn you, but I found out too late."

"I'll never believe that you didn't know Akhenaten had condemned me. You knew how unpredictable were his humors."

"Why won't you understand? He almost killed me as well. I'd only been released a few days when I found out he'd sent men after you. I could barely stand, yet when I heard he'd taken it into his head that you sympathized with Amun, I tried to come to you. I could trust no one with a message, so I tried to warn you myself."

Ebana wasn't looking at him. His gaze had gone distant. His mouth contorted as he sank into the memory.

"You found them, didn't you? My wife. My son. The guards dragged me away from their bodies. I never saw them again."

Slowly, Meren reached out. He touched his cousin's arm, but Ebana shook him off.

"You know I took care of them. Did I not conceal them and have them taken to Thebes? The old king never found their bodies, did he? I tried, Ebana."

"Did you?"

Meren met his cousin's gaze. For a moment he glimpsed the old Ebana, his friend and companion, the one who had studied with him, hunted with him, sailed with him. Then the pit of distrust and old hurts opened between them again. Meren subdued the pain of loss he always felt during one of these confrontations. Ebana chose to live in a netherworld of timeless grief and hatred. He couldn't make his cousin whole again.

"Leave it," Meren said softly. "Leave it before it destroys you." Ebana said nothing, and Meren veered away from the matter, glancing over his cousin's shoulder in the direction of the palace. "Difficult as it is to believe, I've other tasks of greater importance than this accident. However, as a favor to Maya, I'm sending Kysen to inquire into the happenings at the god's gate."

Ebana looked over his shoulder to watch Kysen's approach. "Ah, your peasant son. Have you no seed left in your loins, that you have to adopt the spawn of a commoner?"

Meren stepped close to Ebana. "Shut your teeth, cousin, or I'll reach down your throat, pull your spine out, and make you eat it."

Moving back, he smiled sweetly at Ebana before welcoming Kysen. He heard Ebana curse him, but by the time Kysen greeted him, his usual mask of unconcern had settled over his features. With Ebana lurking beside him, he couldn't warn Kysen of the significance of this death. He could only hope that Ky had learned enough to recognize danger without help.

Kysen approached the statue of the king before the gate of Amun, his head throbbing from a night spent drinking beer and losing wagers at games of senet to Tanefer, Ahiram, and several other friends. He should have looked at a calendar this morning, for surely today was a day of misfortune for him. He knew his eyes were red-rimmed. His head felt like it had been filled to bursting with swamp water. And now he had to spend the day with his father's serpent of a cousin.

The noise of the temple aggravated his pain, for the house of Amun was more a city within a city, its great walls enclosing not only the home of the god but lesser shrines, the House of Life, workshops, a treasury, libraries, the high priest's residence, and service buildings. In addition there was a sacred lake, and every building contained its own staff of busy priests, servants, slaves, and sometimes priestesses.

Blinking against the sun's glare, he shaded his eyes and tried not to kick up dust as he walked. Something was wrong. Ordinarily the death of a lowly pure one wouldn't concern the great Servant of the God, Ebana.

Neither would it have attracted his father's attention. Yet both men had been reserved as they gave him the task of investigating the accident.

Meren rarely spoke of Ebana. His silence hadn't kept Kysen from recognizing the violence of whatever secret lay between the two men. Nor had it disguised the place Ebana still held in Meren's affection. Few had such a claim on his father. Kysen had learned long ago that Meren guarded his ka against deep attachments outside the family. He suspected the reasons lay in too many losses—father, mother, a beloved wife and infant son, comrades in warfare.

The sun was rising high above the walls of the temple now, glinting off the gold-and-silver inlay of the god's gate. The light sent jabs of pain spiking behind Kysen's eyes. He squinted and stepped into the shadow cast by the statue of pharaoh. Workmen crawled over the great stone figure, climbing the scaffolding, carrying baskets of tools and waste flakes.

Kysen stopped beside the base and studied the ground. "You let them move the body? Where is it, and where was it found? Gods, they've tramped all around here."

Ebana rounded on him.

"Don't address me as if I were a fruit seller, boy. Surely Meren has beaten some civilized behavior into you by now."

A white-hot poker drilled its way through Kysen's skull, and he felt his cheeks burn. Ebana always managed to make him feel like fish dung, but he'd learned a little from watching his father.

He inclined his head at Ebana and said, "I was abrupt. However, I doubt anyone could rid me of my plain blood, adopted cousin." He paused to lift his head and stare dagger-straight at Ebana. "It sometimes makes me—unpredictable—to those whose raising was softer."

"By Amun's crown, your blood may be plain, but you've acquired the clever tongue and slippery wit of your second father."

Ebana turned to point at a dusty spot near the base of a ladder that scaled the statue. "He fell from the top of the scaffolding. There."

Kysen knelt and brushed dust and flakes of stone away to reveal dried blood, a few dark hairs embedded in it. Standing, he looked across the flagstones, then up the ladder, then back at the blood. All at once, he looked around, scooped up a heavy mallet from a basket of tools, and began scaling the ladder.

"What are you doing?"

He ignored the impatience in Ebana's voice. Reaching the top of the ladder, he mounted the platform. All work on the statue stopped. Two artisans on the scaffold stared at him as he turned to look down at Ebana. More stoneworkers, apprentices, and laborers stared up at him from the ground.

"You'd better stand back, O Servant of the God."

He didn't wait. Stretching out, he dropped the mallet. The tool plummeted to land almost directly below the ladder.

Kysen stared at it, then muttered. "A man's weight. He trips, falls, tries to grab the ladder and misses. Perhaps he hit the rungs going down. Still . . ."

Turning, he found the artisans still staring at him. The most senior of the two was eyeing him keenly.

"You found the priest?" Kysen asked.

"Aye, lord. I'm Seneb. We found him on his back. His head was split."

"Did you see any marks on him?" Kysen asked. "Any bruises, cuts?"

"Lord, if you mean had he been attacked, no. There were no marks of violence."

"And when did you arrive?"

"Just at dawn, lord."

As they spoke, Kysen sensed the suppressed excitement of the stonemason and his assistant. They hadn't known Unas long, for he'd only recently been assigned to the task of supervising the statue. There were so many priests of Amun, and the royal craftsmen had been at the quarry with the statue until it came to Thebes. As the questioning continued, Seneb became less reserved.

"We saw no one around the body, so I went to get a priest. I'll make a wager that the porter was asleep. We talked to the night sentries before they went home. They came to look at the body, you see. They said they must have been walking the circuit on the far side of the temple, or they would have seen Unas arrive."

Kysen nodded. He went back to the top of the ladder and stood gazing over the edge of the scaffolding. The stonemason joined him.

"Seneb," Kysen said. "No doubt you've seen a lot of rock fall in your time."

"Aye, lord."

"If a stone weighing about as much as a man were to fall from this scaffold, where would it land?"

"Almost directly below, lord. There."

Seneb pointed a cracked and dusty thumb at a spot near the foot of the ladder. Kysen glanced from the spot to the patch of blood.

"Not where the priest landed?"

"Too far away, lord, but a man is not a rock."

"But if he tried to grab the ladder?"

"Such a movement might keep him at the foot of the ladder, or thrust him away, to the place where the blood is."

"Ah."

Kysen tried to estimate the distance between the blood and the ladder—several arm-lengths at least.

"Um, lord."

"Yes."

"I've seen men fall from scaffolding. Their wits sometimes riot and they kick out, hit the ladder, and thrust themselves out even farther than this one did."

"My thanks, Seneb."

He lapsed into silence as a priest emerged from the crowds swelling in and out of the temple. This one, like Ebana, wore a wig over his shaven head and therefore must not be on sacred duty at the moment. He was dressed in cloud-white linen and gold.

"That's the one who came when we found the body."

Seneb was standing at his shoulder. They exchanged glances, and Kysen knew the man was waiting for encouragement.

"What did he say?"

"He didn't want me to report to the treasury. Said it was the concern of the temple, but this is the statue of the living god. I'm a royal craftsman. Pharaoh—may he have life, health, and strength—pharaoh has been generous to his stoneworkers. We couldn't allow such an evil to go by without reporting to our chief."

Now he understood. "Fear not. Your chief is pleased, as is his superior, and those at the palace who interest themselves in this matter. All will go well with you and your men, Seneb. You can work in peace without fear of the temple."

"Thank you, lord. May Ptah, god of artisans, protect you."

"And you," Kysen said as he climbed down the ladder, leaving a much-relieved stonemason atop the platform.

He joined Ebana and the new priest and was introduced. He'd already formed an impression of Qenamun from observing him from above. The man walked as if his joints were hot oil, smoothly, with a glide that surely would make no sound. Close up he seemed as slender as a walking staff. He had long, thin bones, almond-shaped eyes, and thin nostrils that quivered, thus completing his resemblance to a gazelle. Beside Ebana's dense muscularity, he appeared almost fragile.

"So the body was sent to his house," Qenamun was saying. "No doubt by now it has gone to the embalmers across the river. And of course we've given the sad news to his wife."

"Of course," said Kysen. "How quick and attentive of you."

Qenamun gave Kysen a chilly smile and bowed slightly. "All diligence is needful in the service of the good god. Have you any other questions?"

"What of the porter? Where is he?"

"The man was asleep at his post. He's been punished and has been set to hauling refuse. Laziness and negligence are an abomination to the god."

"I would like to question him myself."

"What foolishness," Ebana said. "The man knows nothing, and he's not here."

"I'll go to him."

"You will not!"

Kysen only lifted a brow, a gesture he'd acquired from his father.

Ebana scowled at him. "You're not dragging us down to the refuse pits. Qenamun will send him to your house around midday to await you."

Murmuring his assent, Qenamun executed a sinuous bow and left them. The sun had moved, causing the shadow of the statue to shift. Kysen moved with it and wiped sweat from his brow with the back of his hand.

"An imposing personage, Qenamun," he said.

Ebana said nothing.

"Are you going to tell me about him, adopted cousin, or shall I bribe servants and humble pure ones?"

Shrugging, Ebana said, "Qenamun is a lector priest."

"You don't like him." When this comment was met with further silence, Kysen sighed. "Ah, well. I was hoping to go home to a midday meal, but it seems I must enter the temple and ask questions until nightfall simply because you won't be agreeable."

"You're an insolent pup."

"Who can bribe or coerce what I need to know out of any servant in that temple."

Ebana studied him, allowing his hostility to show in his gaze, but he finally spoke.

"Qenamun is one of our most talented lector priests. He's learned in magic, a man of power whose spells have aided many in need of help. For a price."

"You *don't* like him, do you, Ebana."

"The man is a scorpion," Ebana snapped. "I detest him because he creates discord, lovingly, as a spider spins a web. One of my underlings befriended him a few years ago when we were repairing the damage done to the temple by the heretic. They worked together. Then one day I was talking to Qenamun and he mentioned that my underling was repeating heated words about me to others. I was furious and exiled the man to a temple estate in Nubia. Later I found out from a friend that Qenamun had repeated the same story about one of his underlings."

"But why?"

"To eliminate rivals, those who could stand in his way. The usual reasons."

Kysen felt the throbbing in his head increase, and heat rose up at him from the flagstones. "Gods, I hate aristocrats."

He swore silently at himself as Ebana turned to smile at him.

"Go home, Ky," he said. "There is nothing here but dried blood and the death of a careless fool. You're not going to blunder into the temple and dare to question those of high station and noble blood. Remember, the high priest of Amun comes from the same lineage as pharaoh; his Servants of the God are princes and nobles as well. You don't belong in there. Go home."

"Unas didn't work among princes and nobles. Oh, don't get a heated belly, I'm going."

Kysen turned on his heel and stalked away from his father's cousin. Shouldering his way through the crowds streaming in and out of the temple, he looked back only once. Ebana was still standing where Kysen had left him, but he was looking down, his features set and still as he examined the dark patch of blood at the foot of the image of the living god.

5

▽

Ebana watched Kysen vanish into the throng before the gate of the god. Had he succeeded? He didn't know.

Nothing had gone as he'd anticipated in his dealings with Meren today. Knowing Unas's death certainly would attract Meren's attention, he had tried to distract and confuse by launching an attack that would put his cousin in the wrong. He'd never expected Meren to set the boy Kysen the task of inquiring into the death of the pure one. Turning, he made his way back into the temple, through the great pillared halls and to the House of Life.

As he went, Ebana cursed Meren's ability to twist words against himself into condemnation of his accuser. The stratagem had been to throw Meren off guard; it may have failed.

And then there was that peasant's spawn, Kysen. The boy had grown from a cowering, awkward whelp into an aristocratic warrior. With his wide jaw, rounded chin, and half-moon eyes, he didn't look like his adopted father, except in the straight, severe line of his mouth. In that feature father and son resembled statues of the great king Khafre.

He'd lost count of the time spent wondering why Meren refused to take another wife and get himself a son. Many women died during childbirth. Sit-Hathor had died in labor, and so had her infant son.

That had been many years ago, long after the girl had finally fallen in love with her husband. He remembered how he'd thought her a fool not to admire Meren when she first married him. That was long ago, before the heretic brought chaos and death to their family.

The memory of his own wife, her face streaming with blood, gnawed at him. Pressing his lips together, he forced his thoughts away from the past and stepped over the threshold of the House of Life. He hadn't realized how great the heat of the sun already was until he entered the semidarkness of the building. Glancing around, he took a moment to drink in the peace offered by this place of knowledge, history, and learning.

Alabaster lamps gave off cool yellow light in pools where scholar priests studied ancient records. Row after row of columns stood like a forest before him, and beneath them stood chests filled with papyri. Near the door sat a carved basin with a spout at its base through which flowed a trickle of water. Notches in the wall of the basin allowed the telling of time as the water level dropped. He remembered how bloated with pride he'd felt as a boy upon learning how to interpret the markings.

He nodded at several priests as he made his way past a row of columns, through an open door, and down a corridor to another portal. Two priests flanked the threshold. They'd stirred to alertness upon seeing him, but as he drew nearer, they relaxed their tense stance. He entered the room without speaking to them. The door shut.

There were many such rooms in the House of Life. It was a small, windowless chamber lined from floor to ceiling with cupboards. In those cupboards lay bundles of papyri stored in leather cases. Ebana loved this room, for it contained some of the oldest chronicles in the kingdom, dating from the time of the great ones who built the pyramids.

As he entered, he heard a sibilant whispering, as of wind stirring sand grains across the floor of a rock desert. Only one man could hiss like that—Qenamun.

The lector priest bent gracefully to address an old man in a pleated robe spangled with gold roundels. He glanced up as Ebana came forward, and closed his mouth. Kneeling, Ebana felt Parenefer's hand on his shoulder. The high priest squinted at him, shoving his head forward in a movement that so resembled that of a vulture.

"Rise, my friend," said Parenefer. "Qenamun was just telling me how ably you fended off the Eyes and Ears of Pharaoh."

Ebana cast a sidelong glance at Qenamun as he rose from the floor. "Was he?"

Parenefer's mobile features settled into a scowl. He was one of those men whose appearance benefitted from the ritual requirement of shaving. His skull was well-shaped, with no deforming bulges or dents, and his pronounced bones lent strong definition to his face.

Ebana knew the man to be much older than himself, and yet age seemed only to give him strength. Perhaps it was the splendor and power of his office, or of his lineage: Parenefer's family had held priestly office since before the time of Thutmose the Conqueror.

Or it could be, like himself, Parenefer defied time through the remembrance of old wrongs. The old high priest had been cast out of his sacred office by Akhenaten and had almost died in exile, of grief, fury, and lack of food.

There were times, when recounting the tale of his humiliation, that Parenefer seemed to lose himself in the past. Once, late at night, he'd listened to the story from Parenefer's wine-slick lips seven times. Each telling grew more malignant than the last. Aye, one could live long on the fatted meat of such rancor.

"You don't agree with Qenamun."

"Unfortunately," Ebana said, "Meren twisted the whole matter around on its head. He said that he talked to many priests, which is true. And that all of them couldn't be spies, which is also true. He's harder to surprise than a Syrian bandit. I told you he'd be suspicious no matter how we handled the matter."

"So long as his suspicions continue to sail on the wrong course, I'm content. Qenamun has warned our friends at court. They've taken heed."

Ebana went to a cupboard and touched the strap on a document case. "You don't know Meren as well as I do, holy one. It's enough that this accident has directed his attention to the temple. Now we must advance with perfect craft. One misstep, the wrong intonation in my voice, an unguarded look from Qenamun, and we're destroyed."

"That's why you're handling this cursed pure one's death," Parenefer said as he rose from his chair. "We need someone to act as intermediary between the temple and the court. What ill luck that this fool had to stumble off the king's statue at this of all times. I hope the Devourer eats his soul in the netherworld. Tripping in the dark like that. Who told him to be so diligent and arrive early?"

Qenamun floated over to stand at Parenefer's elbow and murmured, "Unas was anxious in his labors for the good god, far too anxious. His agitation made him clumsy at times."

"I care not," said Parenefer as he approached the door. He held up his hand to forestall Ebana from opening it. "Take care of this matter, both of you, for if you don't, all of us could end up drinking the poison cup of the condemned. All of us."

* * *

Kysen reached the end of the high wall that surrounded the temple of Amun, turned a corner, and glanced over his shoulder to make sure he hadn't been followed. He didn't want Ebana interfering when he inquired at the house of the pure one, Unas. Several priests seemed headed in his general direction, but they passed him, footsteps quick in the pursuit of temple business.

Unlike Akhenaten's planned heretical city, eastern Thebes was a hodgepodge of temples, hovels, noble residences, and workmen's houses huddling next to each other in noisy confusion. He passed the walled residence of a prince, turned a corner, and met a row of much more modest houses. The upper stories were dotted with narrow window slits, and he could see women on the roofs. Before him stretched a line of irregular housefronts broken by thresholds, most with their doors thrown open to allow air to circulate.

He knew only the street where Unas lived; his house would be the one with mourners and a crowd of relatives. Near the end of the street he saw several people enter a doorway and heard a woman wailing inside the house. There were no professional mourners. Possibly the family hadn't arranged for them yet, or could not afford them, or would not.

He had pressed close to the wall of a house as he surveyed the street, keeping out of the way of people, cattle, and donkeys. Now he took a step back into the traffic, only to have a hand come down on his shoulder and pull him to the side again. Kysen whirled, his hand going to the dagger at his side.

"Abu, damn you, you should have spoken."

His father's aide dropped his hand. Like most charioteers, he was tall. People gave way to him in the streets; no one thwarted the progress of a man wearing leather-and-bronze chest armor with a scimitar and dagger at his side. Especially not a charioteer, who was usually well-born and experienced in battle.

Abu was almost as giant as Karoya, Tut's Nubian bodyguard. His build was heavy and his muscles seemed to live a life of rippling activity beneath his skin. A few years younger than Meren, Abu rarely smiled, and when not on duty went on sprees of wine drinking that rivaled any indulged in by warriors half his age. Kysen had never dared inquire as to the cause of Abu's melancholy or his drinking lapses.

He scowled up at Abu, who gazed down from his advantage of four fingers'-width of height. "He sent you."

"Ky, know you who this Unas was?"

"I'm not an apprentice at this," Kysen said. The throbbing in his head was making him irritable. "Father wouldn't have sent for me if this pure one hadn't been important. An informer? One of yours, I assume."

Abu was wearing a warrior's short wig. He wiped perspiration from beneath it as he nodded.

"The lord sent me to assist you."

"There's no sense lying. Ebana has baited him again, and Father is seeing plots and threats in every word and movement."

"The lord has great perception, and he's usually right in his suspicions."

"Yes, but this death appears to have been an accident, Abu. Qenamun said that the priest was an excitable man, anxious to succeed, and clumsy when agitated."

Abu lowered his lashes. "True, and he hadn't sent word of any danger to me, nor have I heard that he knew anything of import that could have gotten him killed. Nevertheless, Lord Ebana accused your father of having suborned Unas and would have stirred up trouble with the king had he not been prevented."

"Why?" Kysen held up his hand to forestall an answer. "Either to bring embarrassment upon Father, or . . . No sense concocting imaginary tales when I don't know the whole of it. Come, and don't pretend you haven't been sent to guard my back, Abu."

They went to the house. Abu banged on the closed door, stepped back, and crossed his arms over his chest. Kysen rolled his eyes, for he knew the charioteer did this to make his arm muscles swell. He was flexing the sinews of his thighs as well. Whoever opened the door was going to be startled by aggressive flesh and gleaming bronze.

The door creaked, and a bent, leathery figure appeared. Another wail boomed out at them. Kysen beheld a fragile old man with wisps of silver hair and a kilt that sagged on his bony frame. Watery eyes blinked at Abu. Dry fingers gripped the door.

"The agent of the Eyes and Ears of Pharaoh, the noble lord, Kysen, son of Meren, inquires of the family of the Osiris Unas," said Abu.

At this formal announcement, with its customary reference to the dead, the old man stepped back, allowing them to enter. He made obeisance to Kysen, bending and lifting his hands.

"I'm the father of Ipwet, wife of Unas, lord."

Kysen nodded but was distracted by the body, which took up most of the space in the small reception room. Beside it squatted a woman who rocked back and forth on her heels and sobbed into her gray hair, which was strewn with ashes.

"My wife," the old man said. "Word came only a short while ago from our daughter. Unas was my wife's cousin, lord."

Kysen glanced over his shoulder at Abu, who maneuvered both husband and wife away from the body. Kysen knelt beside it. Unas had been placed on his back on a litter for transport, and no one seemed to have touched the body yet, for it still bore a film of dust.

Unas had been a hollow-shouldered man, light of frame, like most Egyptians.

What distinguished him was his shaved skull, which came to a rounded point at the back. The left side, at the back, had been cracked, leaving a hole that exposed the meat of his head. Kysen could see blood-smeared pulp. The flesh surrounding the wound was ravaged and flecked with pebbles and dust.

Though wrinkled, the priest's kilt was hardly soiled except where he'd landed on it. His hands were empty and bore no traces that would signal a struggle. The man appeared to have sailed off the scaffolding so suddenly that he hadn't even had time to grab for support.

Kysen brushed flies aside as he noted the pallor of Unas's skin. It was waxy, and blood had collected in the portions of the body closest to the ground. His eyes had already flattened, and he was stiff. Kysen's gaze swept over the figure. His nose twitched as he caught the smell of loss of bowel control. His bile rose in his throat, and he swallowed, blood pounding in his temples. He stood up before the smell made him spew his stomach contents over the body. Cursing Tanefer for urging him to drink the better part of a flagon of wine, he stood and signaled to Abu.

"I see no signs of violence."

"The embalmers have been sent for," Abu said. "They will come at any moment."

Kysen hesitated. He would like to have the assurance of his father's physician that Unas had indeed died from a sudden fall, but interfering with Unas's embalming would draw the attention of Qenamun and Ebana and incite another confrontation between the temple and his father, and for little cause that he could see. He would have to trust to his training; provoked, the priests would throw up blockades to further inquiries.

"Allow them to take him," Kysen said. "Where is the rest of the family?"

"There's only the wife, Ipwet. She and Unas hadn't been married long, a little over a year. The parents arranged the marriage in order to see Ipwet settled before they died. She's their youngest. I believe she has seventeen years."

Kysen looked down at Unas. The priest must have had two score years at least. Not unusual, considering how long it took a man to acquire the means to set up his own house. Many years were spent by most men in this quest, so that they could earn the privilege of taking a wife and begetting a family.

"Look about the house," Kysen whispered to Abu, "but be discreet. We can't justify acting as if this death were other than an accident."

Abu barely nodded his head. "The wife is in the bedchamber." The charioteer pointed toward the back of the house.

Kysen found the chamber empty except for two low wooden beds and a few furnishings. A portable lavatory sat in one corner. Against a wall sat a chest filled with clothing. Another, smaller box contained cosmetics. The floor was covered with woven rush mats. Beneath one of the beds, partially concealed by a cover that hung over the side, sat a wicker box.

Stooping, he retrieved the box and opened it. Empty except for a few buff-colored flecks of pottery. He closed the box and replaced it under the bed. Where was the wife?

He left the chamber, glanced at the common room, and then headed for the kitchen. As he approached, he heard a sob. A woman's voice floated out to him.

"Poor Unas. Poor, poor Unas."

Unas's wife was in her kitchen, but she wasn't alone. Kysen paused just to the side of the doorway to watch a young man drop to his knees beside the woman called Ipwet. Gathering the sobbing woman into his arms, he muttered soft words into her hair. Kysen remained still and quiet.

The young man couldn't be much older than himself. Where Unas had been hollow of shoulder, with a splayed belly and pronounced knees, this man could have been a royal archer. Nor would he lack for admirers among women. The clean lines of his body and his obvious vitality must have intimidated a skittish and aging man like poor Unas. Poor Unas indeed. Kysen entered the kitchen.

At his appearance, the young man looked up. His eyes, under straight brows, widened, taking in Kysen's rich garb. Ipwet stirred, then gasped as she beheld him. For a moment Kysen felt a twinge of guilt. Once, he had been one of those who started with fear at the appearance of a great one. He knew what it was to dread the wrath of those whose mere birth had placed them in control of his very life.

"I am Kysen, agent of the Eyes and Ears of Pharaoh. I've come to inquire into the circumstances of the death of the pure one called Unas. I offer condolences to the wife of Unas." He glanced suddenly at the man. "Who are you?"

Blinking rapidly, the young man hesitated before answering. "I am Nebera. I—I am, was, a friend of Unas. I live next door."

"What are you?" Kysen asked quickly. "And how did you spend this morning?"

Nebera opened his mouth, but Ipwet spoke for the first time.

"Nebera is a worker of metals and jewelry, an apprentice to a master in the royal workshops. He heard of Unas's death when word was brought by the stonemasons there, and he came to offer comfort."

"I must return to work soon," Nebera added.

What was it about these two? It wasn't just that they clung to each other with the intimacy of lovers. It was their habit of speech. Their conversation was like a tune sung by professional singers. First one sang, and then the other, in easy exchange, as if each knew his part and that of the other as well. These two reminded him of his oldest sister and her husband—twin souls in harmony. Ipwet spoke for Nebera, and Nebera for Ipwet.

Kysen murmured his assent, and Nebera turned to Ipwet.

"I'll return as soon as the day's work has ended."

Ipwet nodded, shaking the gleaming curtain of dark brown that was her hair. She lowered her gaze to the floor as Nebera left. Her hand toyed with the deep blue beads of her faience necklace. In the dim light of the one oil lamp, Kysen could barely perceive the slight flush on her cheeks. The kohl on her eyes had run when she wept, and her hair was mussed.

In spite of her disheveled appearance, Kysen could see why Nebera was so anxious to return to her. Ipwet had great doe's eyes, plump lips, and lean arms and legs that spoke of limber strength and invited a man to imagine to what interesting uses she could put them. She also had an Egyptian woman's frank way of meeting a man's gaze with a look that spoke of fearlessness and pride. Kysen would have wagered that no husband of this woman would dare stray or mistreat her. If she was this formidable so young, what would she be like as a grandmother?

"Lord, why have you come? My poor Unas fell from the scaffolding of the statue of the living god, may he forever have life, health, and strength."

"Formidable indeed," Kysen muttered.

"Lord?"

"It's naught. The Eyes and Ears of Pharaoh often inquire into sudden deaths that involve persons connected with the affairs of the living god, no matter how slight the association may be. How was your husband this morning?"

"The same as usual, lord. Agitated over his new responsibilities in the treasury of the god, perhaps. But Unas often grew excited about his work. He dreamed of rising in the service of Amun until one day—ah, but such dreams are of no consequence."

"And you have noticed nothing odd about his manner in the last few days?"

"No, lord. He was the same. Diligent, remaining at his duties long after everyone else. The other day I scolded him for being out after dark. I was already cooking the evening meal by the time he came home." Ipwet smiled, but tears quickly welled up in her eyes. "I scolded him for nearly ruining my fire."

She turned and wiped her eyes. Her fingers came away black with kohl. Stooping, she picked up a rag beside the oven and wiped her face.

"Was he worried about some matter at the temple, that he would ruin your fire?" Kysen asked.

"I know not," Ipwet said. "I was busy making bread, and he came in. To watch, I thought, but instead he threw broken pottery into my fire. Unas could be so irritating, always trying to please, so anxious, always hovering."

Kysen furrowed his brow. "He threw shards into the fire? Why?"

"He said he was just discarding them. He was only trying to capture my attention, I think."

Kysen said nothing. Meren had always taught him to look out for practices that were out of the ordinary, signs of inconsistency or lack of logic. Although Unas seemed to have been an excitable, jittery man, even one in fear of losing a much younger wife wouldn't throw shards into a fire for no reason.

Or would he? Ipwet might have quarreled with him. If a vessel had been broken during the quarrel, some of the remains might have been tossed into the oven. It could be that Ipwet shrank from revealing the quarrel to a stranger. Then Kysen remembered the flakes of pottery he'd found in the box in Unas's bedchamber. The priest might have kept these shards in it. Such elaborate preservation of such humble objects—extraordinary indeed.

Kneeling before the oven, Kysen took a pair of wooden tongs and stirred the ashes. At first all he found were coals. Then, with Ipwet holding the lamp close, he scraped out several small, blackened shards. He was about to give up when his gaze caught a spot of buff and blue at the edge of the oven floor, away from the ashes. He fished it out.

It appeared to be a piece from the rim of a bowl, and it bore portions of a hieroglyphic inscription. Kysen lifted the fragment closer to the lamp flame. Two lines curved side by side like twin throwing sticks. Beneath the one on the left was a tick mark shaped like the tip of an arrow. Beneath the right one was another curved line like the one above it, only more rounded.

A common piece, this buff pottery. There were thousands upon thousands of such clay vessels in Egypt. Nevertheless, Kysen dropped the fragment onto Ipwet's rag along with the blackened shards and folded the cloth, tucking it into his belt.

"Can you tell me why your husband went to the temple so early?"

"A boy came with word from the master sculptor asking to meet early at the statue."

"Did you know this boy?"

"No, lord. I thought he came from the sculptor."

"And such a message," Kysen said, "it was unsurprising?"

Ipwet was beginning to look at him with curiosity.

"The request was unexpected, but not unusual. Is aught wrong, lord?"

Kysen shook his head. Seneb hadn't mentioned sending for Unas, and he was convinced that the sculptor would have done so if he'd been the one to request an early meeting. He would have to question the man again.

"There is nothing wrong. May the good god Amun comfort you in your grief, mistress."

At his words Ipwet's lips trembled, and fresh tears gathered in the corners of her eyes.

"I thank you, lord. My husband was not a great man, nor was he—comely—but his soul was gentle, and he took humble pleasure in doing good work."

Kysen watched her large eyes narrow in a wince. In that moment he understood that Unas's wife was suffering, but she was suffering much more from guilt than from grief. He withdrew from the kitchen, found Abu, and left.

"Send for the master sculptor Seneb," he said as they walked away from Unas's house. "Unas received a message given by a boy that is supposed to have come from Seneb requesting an early meeting."

"You think the message was false?"

"Seneb said nothing of the message to me when I talked with him, but he could have been avoiding trouble. I know what it's like not to want the attention of the great. If the message is false, this death may be more than an accident."

"Which means . . ." Abu paused while he avoided a group of women balancing tall water jars on their heads. "Which means we begin to look for someone who knew Unas's habits, who knew that the porter neglected his watch for sleep, who knew the route of the temple sentries and when the artisans would arrive for work."

"A priest," Abu said. "Or the wife of a priest, or a friend. Unfortunately, there are countless possibilities when dealing with a murder that has occurred at so well-traveled a place as the god's gate."

6

∇

The king had retreated from the blast of the afternoon sun to an audience chamber. For this Meren was thankful, but he would rather have remained by the reflection pool than endure this bickering among pharaoh's advisors. Tutankhamun had summoned support for his side of the argument, so now several of the younger men were gesticulating in front of a weary Ay. Meren's gaze traveled from the short and wiry Ahiram of Byblos to Tanefer, Djoser, and Rahotep.

His concern mingled with that for Kysen. Something was wrong at the temple of Amun, something that had so disturbed Ebana that he'd brought the matter to court. Now Kysen was in the midst of inquiries that would pit him against Ebana and possibly Parenefer.

Far more powerful men than Ky had lost their lives in such struggles. There had been sudden deaths by poisoning, purported accidents that cut a life short, unexpected scandals that ruined reputations. The reach of the temple of Amun was high and deadly.

Djoser rose abruptly from his kneeling position beside the king, distracting Meren from his worries. The king's brow furrowed as he directed his stare at Djoser. Meren could see that he was confused by Djoser's lack of zeal for battle. Raised in the tradition of warrior pharaohs, Tutankhamun hadn't the experience to understand a man who preferred tranquility and the rhythmic cycles of the farmer to the glory of court and battle.

Meren sighed and rubbed the sun-disk scar on his inner wrist. He caught himself and shoved a thick warrior's bracelet down over the wound. He bore much of the blame for the king's headstrong desire for conquest. Knowing how great was the Hittite threat, how easily barbarians could invade Egypt and prevail over a people so used to peace and good living, he had taken care to train the king for battle.

The king's father, Amunhotep the Magnificent, had built great temples and ruled by divisive manipulation of allies and enemies alike. Thanks to his neglect and that of Tutankhamun's older brother, however, such tactics would no longer suffice. The time for war was coming.

So now he was faced with a young stallion kicking at the stable door, who threatened to injure himself in his efforts to gain freedom. Meren rubbed his chin and stared down at the plastered floor. He stood in the middle of a painting of a reflection pool. A yellow-and-blue fish goggled at him from between reeds of deep green.

His attention snapped back to the group surrounding the king. Ahiram of Byblos and Prince Rahotep were arguing—again. No matter the issue, they were never on the same side. Ahiram had made a point for the war side, which Rahotep immediately rebutted.

Ahiram balanced on the balls of his feet. He was a small man, but powerful of build. He wore his curly hair longer than Egyptians did and cultivated a pointed beard that grew at the tip of his chin. Meren had always thought it gave him a goatish appearance, but had spared Ahiram his opinion.

Not so Rahotep, who criticized anyone except pharaoh with the brutal honesty of a child of four. No matter who was offended, Rahotep would offer his views.

Perhaps Rahotep disliked Ahiram because of their similarities. Both felt the sting of imagined insignificance, Rahotep because of his peasant mother, Ahiram because of his foreign birth and lost throne. With natures based on such weak foundations, neither man seemed capable of reaching peace of the ka.

A warning trumpet blew in Meren's head when Rahotep suddenly jumped to his feet. Ahiram stuck his thumbs in the belt of his kilt. His bearded chin jutted forward so that the tip pointed at his adversary.

"Such maidenly aversions cost my father his life, and me a throne."

Rahotep narrowed his eyes and sneered at Ahiram's beard, the essence of civilized Egyptian disdain. "Watch your tongue, barbarian. My ancestors were exacting tribute from your kind while your family was still raising goats in the wastelands of Syria." He made a point of staring at the beard as he said *goat*.

Meren edged closer to the group as an abrupt silence fell. Even the king stiffened and dropped his hand to a ceremonial blade in his belt. The air crackled with the threat of bloodshed.

"You well know Byblos is an ally. Speak not of tribute when you mean trade, fool."

Meren darted a glance at the king's chief Nubian bodyguard, but Karoya was already moving to Tutankhamun's side. At the appearance of the towering warrior, Ahiram broke off glaring at Rahotep. Danger ebbed from the moment, and Meren glided between the two men.

"All of us are weary from a long morning of duties, and the divine one still must receive merchant emissaries from the Mycenaeans and the Libyans."

"As always, Meren plays the arbiter," Prince Tanefer said as he smoothly drew Ahiram away from Rahotep.

"It's possible we won't have any peace until we drive

the Hittites back into their forsaken mountains and take their children as hostages the way Ahiram was taken," Rahotep said, almost earning a kick from Meren.

"My father sent me to Egypt willingly for training. I was never a hostage!"

Ahiram lurched out of Tanefer's grip. His hands fastened around Rahotep's neck. Meren shouldered Djoser aside, grabbed one of Ahiram's fingers, and bent it backward. Ahiram yelped, his hold broken, and Meren changed his grip so that he could bend the man's arm backward and pinch flesh and tendons against bones. The whole movement lasted less than a heart's beat, and then Meren stepped back and smiled lazily at Ahiram.

"Govern yourself in the presence of the golden one," he said. "You know better, my friend. It's not like you to chance rousing Karoya." Meren jerked his head in the direction of the royal bodyguard.

Ahiram's head swiveled around in the same direction. Karoya had drawn a knife. He'd cocked his arm back, the blade gripped in his fingers, aiming at Ahiram. The foreign prince flushed and raised his empty arms away from his body in a gesture of compliance.

His dark face expressionless, as if killing Ahiram meant no more to him than stepping on a beetle, Karoya glanced at Tutankhamun. The king's hand made a slight, sideways movement. Karoya sheathed the knife.

"Divine one," Ay said. "Lord Meren is right. Duties await thee."

"Very well," Tutankhamun said, and waved his councillors permission to retire.

Meren spoke under his breath to Tanefer. "Bring everyone to me. We all need a good meal and relief from this heat."

Tanefer nodded as he left.

"Lord Meren will attend my majesty."

He was surprised to find the king studying him intently. Ay passed him on his way out and gave him a look of sympathy. Karoya had retreated to his station behind the dais upon which the king sat. Approaching the king's gold and ebony chair, he dropped to his knees and bent his head.

"Oh, be done with that," the king snapped. "What use is it for you to kneel to me when you know well that I am the one who must obey, who must perform and follow tradition and orders?"

Meren straightened, but didn't get to his feet. He raised a brow. "What is thy will, divine one?"

"You've been quiet all day. When Ay argued for caution and pointed out how young I was for a campaign, you said nothing. When Horemheb and Tanefer scoffed and spoke of the ravages of the Hittites, you remained silent." Tutankhamun rose from his chair and threw up his hands. "Curse it, Meren. It's not like you to straddle a boundary stone. What do you think?"

Meren sank back on his heels and stared up at the king, who was pacing back and forth like one of his pet lions. At last he shook his head and spoke.

"It is my misfortune to think two things at once, golden one."

The king halted and stared at him. Meren rose.

"If we allow the Hittite menace to go unchallenged, we invite a powerful enemy to camp at our very borders. Our armies and allies have been neglected. Their faith fails them, for they have seen their pleas for aid ignored and have needlessly shed blood because of it. They need a warrior king to lead them."

"I knew it," the king said. "I knew you understood."

"And if you plunge into battle with them before your time and are killed, no victory, no amount of land or tribute, will make up for the evil that will befall Egypt."

"But you've said my skills are great."

"They are, as is your heart and courage," Meren said.

"But have I not also said that the span of a warrior's training is as the length of the Nile? Consider, majesty. How long is the reach of your arm compared to mine? Try to touch me."

The king reached out, and Meren darted forward, arm outstretched as if gripping a short sword. His hand tapped against the gold and lapis beads of the king's broad collar. He drew back in silence as Tutankhamun's gaze darted from his chest to Meren's arm. A flush crept over the king's cheeks.

"Damnation to you," Tutankhamun muttered.

"Had I been a Hittite, I could have sliced your heart in half."

"Get out!"

Meren bowed and backed away.

"Wait."

Tutankhamun gripped the back of his golden chair. Meren cocked his head to the side as the king pressed his lips together.

"I didn't mean to shout at you."

He had difficulty in concealing his admiration and his surprise. It was as close to a request for forgiveness as he'd ever heard from a living god.

"Thy majesty is much beset."

Tutankhamun came to stand before him. "My majesty wishes you to reconsider your advice." He touched Meren's arm briefly. "You of all of them should have faith in me."

"I do, majesty."

"Then consider well, for I'm not done with this matter, and neither are Horemheb and Tanefer."

"As thy majesty commands."

"Don't affect obedience in private, Meren. I know you're going to do just as you wish."

"I give you my promise, majesty. I will ponder long and well."

"And before you leave, tell me what mischief your cousin has been spreading. Ah, you didn't think I knew about his visit."

"Thy majesty is all-knowing," Meren said. He told the king of the death at the foot of the statue. "Such an affront to thy majesty's image must not go without inquiry."

"There's more," Tutankhamun said. He walked over to Meren. "Tell me the whole of it."

"It seems that Ebana imagines that this pure one was in my pay."

"And was he?"

"Only indirectly, majesty."

"Do you think they killed him for it?"

Meren shook his head. "I don't know. If Parenefer had the pure one killed, why bring the matter to my attention and risk my conducting an inquiry?"

"But you will anyway," the king said. "So perhaps they're attacking before you do, to distract."

"Aye, majesty. I'll know more after Kysen makes his examinations."

"Very well. I can see you wish to go, but don't forget my words. I want to lead my armies, Meren."

He left the king then, relieved to escape without having pushed the boy into fury with his defiance. As he went, he realized that this matter of the king's campaign was no longer a councillors' squabble. Now it was a matter of state—an affair of life and death.

Almost an hour after leaving the king, Meren stepped through the gate in the wall surrounding his town house in the palace district of western Thebes. The charioteers behind him took the path to the left around a reflection pool, through another gate in a wall, and past the house to the offices and barracks that lay to the rear. The porter closed the gate, leaving Meren standing alone in the shade of the first of a double row of acacia trees that lined the walk surrounding the pond in front of the house.

As he had left the king, he'd come face to face with the high priest of Amun in the throng outside. After the confrontation with pharaoh, he'd been in no mood to tolerate Parenefer. He could still hear the old man's high voice grating like a bronze saw against granite.

"Ah, the lord Meren, in secret conversation with the son of the god as usual. How great is the fortune of the Two Lands that its young lord should so depend upon the council of a servant."

He grew cold all over again in remembering the sudden quiet that had settled over the courtiers and government officials. The stares, most of them sly or calculating, none of them revealing the rankling envy and fear Parenefer had taken care to feed. Meren pinched the bridge of his nose and squeezed his eyes shut.

Even Horemheb had looked at him strangely. But the damage was done. He had to remember that scorpions like Parenefer were always lurking, and they had yet to sting him fatally.

Opening his eyes, he shaded them and glanced at the small family chapel, shining white in the sun of the front courtyard, before walking down the path to the house. In the distance he heard the whinny of his favorite thoroughbred from the stables. Kysen might be back from the temple of Amun by now.

The morning's confrontation with Ebana still worried him. It wasn't like his cousin to make open accusations that led nowhere. He speculated that Parenefer had instigated the trouble, perhaps as revenge for the placing of that statue in front of his temple, perhaps for some other evil and obscure reason he had yet to discover. Parenefer would have known that Unas's death would attract his attention. It could be that the high priest had decided that an attack was better than waiting to be accused of eliminating a suspected spy.

In the house, Meren gave orders for the preparation of a large meal, then retreated to his apartments. He'd bathed, changed, and gone to his office behind the house by the time Kysen sought him out. He retrieved his juggling balls and was tossing the three leather spheres. His hands made soft padding sounds as the balls hit them.

It wasn't long before his son came into the room, carrying a pitcher of beer and two goblets. Setting these aside, Kysen picked up a fourth ball and tossed it at him. Meren grabbed for it and missed. Another ball hit his arm while the others fell and bounced at his feet.

"You still haven't managed that fourth one," Kysen said as he poured beer.

Meren stooped and picked up the balls, storing them in a cedar box. "Not when it's thrown at me."

"Did the juggling settle your temper?"

"What temper?"

"Come, Father, I saw your expression this morning. And Ebana always manages to stir you to hornet madness."

Meren shut the lid of the cedar box and picked up his goblet of beer. "The inquiries at the temple, what of the death of the priest?"

"Some day you must tell me about him."

Meren took a long sip of beer before speaking. "The priest."

"I'm not sure whether he died accidentally or not. Ebana might have been trying to goad you," Kysen said. "Unas appears to have been an excitable little moth of a man, over-diligent and clumsy as well. Most likely, he missed his step and fell through his own carelessness. There are no marks to betoken a struggle."

"However?"

"However, if someone did discover his connection with you, well, this could be Parenefer's way of warning you to keep away. And there is a difficulty."

"What difficulty?"

"Unas's wife said that he went to the statue early because of a message given by a boy from the master sculptor asking for the meeting. Yet the sculptor says he sent no message. I believe him, for he's the one who brought the accident to our attention, and he has a reputation for straight dealing and honor."

"Have you found this boy messenger?"

"No. He's vanished."

Meren set his cup aside. "It could be that the wife is lying, or she may have been mistaken about who sent the message."

"I've sent Abu to see her again. He's good at scaring the truth out of people."

"If Unas didn't fall by accident, the murderer would have to be someone who knew the arrangements for work at the temple, those of the guards, the porters, the priests, and the royal artisans as well."

"In other words, someone from the temple, or his wife or her lover."

"Lover?" Meren asked.

"Yes, a man much younger than Unas, who no doubt attracts the attention of many women."

"I see," Meren said. "Yet another example of the delights of marriage." He went to his chair and slumped into it. "God, I'm sick of questioning everyone's motives, of suspecting even the slave who pours water over me in the bathing stall."

He looked up at Kysen, who was regarding him with surprise. "Even I can grow weary of stratagems and machinations, Ky."

"Is that why you took me for your son? To have

someone so beholden to you that you could trust him completely?"

"No."

They held each other's gaze, and Kysen finally lowered his.

"Forgive me, Father."

"You shouldn't listen to Ebana. His ka is poisoned."

"I won't listen to him if you won't," Kysen said with a grin.

"Insolent colt."

"About the priest. The wife, Ipwet, is but a girl, one of spirit and pleasing. And the lover seems to have been on his way to the royal workshops when the priest died. If Unas was murdered, we may never know whether it was because of his family or because of his service to you."

Meren was listening to Kysen's view of the situation when Abu appeared, leading in the porter of the temple of Amun, Huni. The man fell to his knees and touched his forehead to the floor in front of Meren, who backed away as a pungent odor reached him. The man's hair was greasy and stuck to his scalp. His skin bore a layer of dust matted with grime. Beneath the smell of refuse Meren detected a whiff of cheap beer.

"Look at me," Meren said.

Huni raised his head. The whites of his eyes were discolored with a network of red veins, and he blinked at Meren slowly, as if he'd just swilled a few buckets of beer.

"Did you see the pure one Unas fall from the statue of the king?"

"No, lor'. Didn't see nothin'." Huni's fingers plucked at his kilt and his hair as if he were trying to repair his disheveled appearance.

"Because you were asleep," Kysen said as he walked around to stand beside Meren.

The porter sat back on his heels and placed his hands on his thighs. Huni's glance slid away from them as he fell to studying his broken and dirty fingernails.

"I never," he muttered, "sleep on duty."

"I have reports that it's your most skilled accomplishment," Kysen said. "I hear that if there were tournaments for sleepers, you would win the gold necklace."

"False reports," Huni whined.

Meren raised his glance to Abu, who instantly approached the porter, gripped his neck, and pulled him erect. He lifted the man by his throat until he balanced on his toes, gurgling and choking.

"I have no patience with mewling lingerers," Meren said. "Admit that you were asleep or tell me what you saw. Raise your right hand if you slept through the whole thing, porter. Ah, you slept. Then you will tell me who allowed you to serve as porter. Release him, Abu."

Huni dropped to his knees again and crouched there gasping. Finally he was able to speak.

"Wasn' a porter no more 'til a few days ago. The chief of porters took me back an' put me on night duty."

"Why?" Kysen snapped.

"Don' know, lor'. But now I'm banished forever to the refuse gangs. It's a terrible punishment. Terrible."

A fresh whiff of the man's odor sent both Meren and Kysen back several steps. Meren put his hand over his nose and gestured to Abu. "Get him out of here, and leave the door open."

When the two had gone, Meren looked around the office for a fan, but found none.

"Damnation," he said. "I'll have to have the whole chamber freshened."

"I think he was telling the truth," Kysen said.

"With Abu choking me, I would. By the gods,

Mutemwia has been straightening in this room again. No wonder I can find nothing." Meren left off his search for a fan. "I must order circumspect inquiries about the posting of Huni to the god's gate at night."

"Ebana isn't being forthcoming."

"I should speak to him again," Meren said.

Kysen agreed, but neither held much hope of prying anything from Ebana. Had Unas's death been an obvious murder, Meren would have requested from pharaoh the power to order his cousin's compliance. Without such power he could only request it, and Ebana's cooperation was doubtful where Meren was concerned.

If Meren pushed his cousin too hard, he could incite a quarrel that would embroil the entire court. His position would be precarious in such a battle. And perhaps that was what Ebana had wanted all along.

Meren and Kysen continued to discuss Unas's death and how to handle the priests of Amun throughout the afternoon. When a servant announced the arrival of Ahiram, Meren put aside the matter of Unas's death, for the moment.

"Come," he said to Kysen. "You should be thankful you weren't in the audience hall when Ahiram tried to strangle Rahotep."

They met the first of their guests in the pillared main hall, where servants had set out chairs, cushioned stools, and low tables laden with baskets of fruit and bread. A maid was pouring wine from a tall jar into a goblet for their guest. Ahiram barely glanced at them and uttered no polite greeting. Meren could tell he was still angry: when disturbed, he had a distinctive habit of speech.

"I'm in no mood for revelry, me."

Meren laughed. "Then I won't send for my harpists and singers."

"Ahiram, you jackal, how is it that you tried to choke Rahotep?" Kysen asked as he offered their guest a chair.

Meren shoved a basket of fruit into his son's hands and said, "Not now, Ky. We've just spent most of the day quarreling. This meal is for the respite of my friends."

"Respite!"

They all looked up to find Tanefer parading to the threshold, a cup of wine in one hand, a flagon in another. He moved loosely, with abandon and ease. As was his habit, he wore his dagger in a scabbard on his upper arm.

"Respite indeed," Tanefer repeated as he came in and looked back over his shoulder. "They're in here, Djoser."

Soon they were all seated and being served roast goose accompanied by new-baked bread. Rahotep joined them last of all, taking a seat well away from Ahiram. Servants passed among them, refilling goblets with wine or beer from jars whose necks had been decorated with garlands of lotus flowers. Meren kept Ahiram distracted while Tanefer entertained Rahotep and Kysen. As usual, Djoser listened quietly to everyone and said little himself.

As dusk approached, a wine-heavy somnolence came over the group. Kysen engaged Rahotep in a game of senet.

"I'll beat you," Rahotep said. "I beat everyone. I'm the best senet player in the Two Lands."

Meren saw Kysen press his lips together to prevent a retort. He'd warned Ky long ago about Rahotep's bragging. Rahotep considered himself the best at everything from swordplay to breathing, and saw to it that the entire kingdom knew it. Meren felt that his bragging covered an utter lack of faith in his own merit. And somehow he couldn't become annoyed with Rahotep for long. His rudeness and clumsiness were so childlike that when he offended someone, he was often bewildered at how he'd managed to offer insult.

Djoser, too, seemed indisposed to listen to Rahotep's blustering. He requested that musicians be summoned. When they arrived, he settled on cushions with a basket of pomegranates and grapes and listened to the harp, flute, and sistrum.

Tanefer left him to join Meren and Ahiram. The conversation drifted from the hunt to speculation about a newly widowed noblewoman, Lady Bentanta, who had taken an interest in Meren. Meren endured Tanefer's gentle teasing while his own thoughts pursued a different course. He didn't like the conjunction of the controversy among the king's advisers and this sudden death of a priest, and the currents of dissatisfaction at court seemed more disturbing than usual. This was one reason he'd invited Tanefer and the others to his home. Due to their station and birth, these men had great influence on those of lesser rank.

In addition, Ahiram commanded the Bows of Ra, an elite regiment of two hundred royal archers, and Tanefer's regiment of charioteers, the Golden Leopards, was second only to the king's own war band. Djoser nominally headed a squadron of infantry. No one expected him to remain its commander for long. Rahotep, however, had just persuaded the king to allow him a regiment of charioteers and supporting infantry. For these he was recruiting native and foreign soldiers, especially Mitanni, of whom he seemed to have acquired a good opinion while in Syria.

All of these men reported to General Horemheb. Any one of them, except possibly Djoser, possessed the knowledge, wealth, and skill to menace pharaoh should he choose. Meren's task was to know the character of each. Only in this way could he guard the safety of the king.

"Am I right, Meren?"

"What?"

"Don't fall asleep," said Tanefer. "Brother of my heart, I've just wagered this gold ankle band that you've refused to favor the Lady Bentanta."

Meren held out his hand, and a maid placed a silver dish laden with his favorite figs in it. He rose and went to a couch. Lowering himself to a half-reclining position on its cushions, he bit into a fruit.

Unfortunately, Tanefer and Ahiram followed him. Tanefer dropped on a leather cushion near his elbow, plucked a fig from Meren's bowl, and took a bite.

"He won't answer, Ahiram. What say you? Has he let her into his bed?"

"I would, me," said Ahiram between gulps of wine. "A widow—gods, think of her experience, and she's still young enough to—"

"Ahiram," Meren said softly. "You really should learn not to flap your tongue about women."

"Then settle our wager," Ahiram said.

Meren lay back on the couch and stared up at the plastered ceiling and green-and-white frieze of papyrus fronds that bordered it. "I regret that you've been reminded of the loss of your father by this whole question of a new campaign next harvest."

He glanced at Ahiram, but the Syrian was staring at Tanefer as if the younger man held the secrets of the underworld. Tanefer studied his fig, then took another bite.

Meren had expected to provoke a string of complaints, Ahiram's forte. His laments at his ill fortune were well known at court, and he could spend an entire evening listing injustices done to him, reasons why his plans for achievements hadn't succeeded (always someone else's fault), slights received. Meren often learned interesting things from these tirades.

"I know the old king abandoned your father to those rebels and bandits," Meren said.

"Dung-eaters in the pay of the Hittite king."

Meren tried again. "How it must sting to have been raised as an Egyptian, to be trained to take your father's place and continue in friendship with the empire—and then have those who promised so much fulfill nothing."

Ahiram looked away and shrugged. "That was long ago."

"Not so long," Tanefer said. He was staring into the pool of wine in his goblet.

Meren watched the way the corners of his mouth drooped, and for once regretted the necessity of probing old hurts. Tanefer's mother had been a princess, daughter of the king of Mitanni, who came all the way from the banks of the northern Euphrates to wed pharaoh's father and vanish into his palace as one of several lesser wives.

He remembered Gilukhepa. A woman, like many in the household of pharaoh, dissatisfied with her allotted place in the shadow of the great Queen Tiye. Over the years, her dissatisfaction had putrefied. She had tried to bathe Tanefer in that putrefaction, but her son possessed a merry and magical ka that could no more live upon misery than a crocodile could walk like a man.

He surrounded himself with beauty, having built one of the most gracious and largest houses in Thebes. He kept entire workshops of artisans who decorated his houses, created his jewelry, armor, and weapons, designed his tomb. Tanefer had a gift for beauty. Most of the young men around pharaoh envied him his easy yet regal manner, his brilliance in battle, his barbed wit.

"You could have been king," Meren said.

Tanefer set his goblet down on the floor and began

tossing a fig in one hand. "My uncle is dead, murdered by one of his cousins no doubt, and my relatives vie for what is left of Mitanni. Think you I wish to leave the font of civilization to lie in a bed of serpents?"

"Byblos is a magnificent city, and rich," Ahiram said. "I wouldn't refuse to rule it, me, should the empire find its testicles again."

"That kind of campaign would take years," Meren said. "Think of the cities that lie between Egypt and Byblos."

"We wouldn't have to fight if the old king hadn't—"

"Peace! We're here to enjoy Meren's food." Tanefer slapped Ahiram on the back and whispered a lurid jest.

Ahiram barked his laughter. Having won his game of senet, Kysen came over to join in their merriment. Meren was left free to approach Djoser and Rahotep, who were listening to the musicians. Words of the song floated up to him as he took a chair beside them. *My beloved rules my heart. Oh how long is the hour since I lay with her.*

The harp's music rippled through the air, and Meren could see that its tranquility was at odds with Djoser's thoughts. Evidently Rahotep was trying to amend his friend's poor spirits in his clumsy way and hadn't succeeded. Djoser's foul mood contrasted with his fine raiment. Of all of them, he was the one most attentive to dress. At the moment he was contemplating his sandal, a rich object of gilded leather. Djoser liked sandals. Meren once estimated he had a pair for each day of the year.

Rahotep was still trying to cheer his friend. He was generous; for once he'd found someone to whom he could compare himself easily and always rank himself the better.

"It isn't every man's fate to be a warrior," Rahotep said. "Many of the great of Egypt weren't. Remember the architects Amunhotep, son of Hapu, and Imhotep, who was also a sage and magician. Why, Imhotep designed the great step pyramid and is revered as a god."

Djoser downed half a goblet of beer, then wiped his mouth. Even this much drink couldn't seem to quell his agitation. His eyes darted from side to side, and he appeared to shrivel inside his skin as he spoke.

"You didn't puke on the battlefield. You didn't drop your own scimitar. You didn't lose governance of your horses and have to be rescued from your own chariot."

Djoser gulped down the rest of his beer and slurred his words. "I have to prove my worth. Everyone is laughing at me, but I'll kick their laughter back in their throats. No one should laugh at a prince . . ."

Meren exchanged glances with Rahotep.

"I'll see that he's taken home," Rahotep said.

Meren nodded. "Has your humor restored itself?"

Rahotep began to store the senet tokens in compartments inside their box. "Ahiram wouldn't have dared put his hands on me if I had full royal blood."

"His temper will be his downfall," Meren said. "I've seen him so maddened that I thought he'd touch pharaoh himself."

He could see that Rahotep didn't believe him. He'd known these men for most of his life, but Rahotep was the only one who bore common blood, and was the only one who constantly remembered it. His mother had been a peasant who caught the eye of pharaoh. And with every breath he drew, Rahotep regretted that she'd never been anything more than a concubine. He even hated his appearance, for he'd inherited his mother's wide, flat face and spreading nose, which he deemed to be peasant traits. Kysen had often remarked that Rahotep would appear far more princely if he weren't constantly digging his little finger in his ear.

Meren listened to Rahotep discounting the concerns

of Djoser, consigning them to insignificance beside his own burdens, and knew that he'd been right to invite his friends home. There was much fuel here to heat the cauldron of strife that was the court. To keep it from bubbling over, he needed to listen to howls of discontent, to keep his ear alert for the sounds of hounds metamorphosing into jackals and hyenas.

7

▽

North of Thebes, at the edge of the eastern city, the waters of the Nile had cut deep into the bank, causing eddies and slowing the current of the river. Here lay a small marsh, between the river and the beginning of cultivation. Ebana guided his chariot carefully along a road made of the back dirt produced by digging canals.

The going was slow, for it was late, and only the moon's light illuminated his way. Finally he pulled up and dismounted. He removed a spear from the case attached to the chariot and walked down a dike to the marsh, where a papyrus-stalk skiff awaited him.

Stepping into the boat, he shoved off, using the oar that lay within the vessel. Water rippled around him, obsidian-black and cool. His entry disturbed a hen-bird, who scrambled out of the water to the cries of her nestlings. Ebana glided between the tall papyrus fronds, taking care not to go too near the thick stands. The way his fortune had been going, he might disturb a crocodile or nudge a hippo.

The skiff slowed, then stopped. He sat quietly, listening to frogs and insects and the slap of water against the boat. He tightened his grip on his spear. If the need for secrecy hadn't been so great, he would never have risked crocodiles and drowning, not for the man he was to meet here.

A hazy dash of pink caught his eye—a rose lotus.

Moments went by, and as they did, it felt as if rats were doing a feast dance inside his gut. A curse wafted toward him over the water. Backstroking with his oar, he turned the skiff to meet another, sliding into the marsh from the river. The two craft drew alongside each other.

The newcomer spoke without preamble. "He knows!"

"Absurd," Ebana said. "Don't let him drive you like a frightened ox, or you'll betray yourself and us."

"I was with him today, and I tell you Meren knows something. Why is he so vigilant? He doesn't dabble in every accident and abrupt demise that comes to his notice."

"Because he can smell intrigue as a hound scents the oryx. It's his way, and I have prepared for it."

"He hasn't smelled me," the other said, his voice rising. "I swear it. The fault isn't mine."

"What are you speaking of?"

"Naught, naught. By the wrath of Set, I hate marshes. Too many creatures of the night."

Ebana studied the newcomer, whose head jerked from side to side as if he expected to be swallowed by a hippo at any moment. The fool was losing what mettle he possessed, and for so little reason—unless he had something to conceal.

"Hark you," Ebana said in a quiet, precise voice, "if your fear-blind haste has exposed us, I'll kill you myself."

That swiveling head twisted back to face him.

"No, no. No. Don't disturb yourself. I'll deal with the matter."

"Just keep yourself haltered, you fool. We were counting on the king and the others being distracted by this Hittite quandary, but with Meren sniffing the air, the high one thinks we should bide a while."

"Too late."

"Why?"

A hand came out to grip the side of Ebana's skiff.

"Too late. I got word early this morning. The work has begun."

"Curse it."

"Now do you see? By the time I could reach them, the acts will already have been committed. I expect shipments within a few weeks."

Ebana glanced down at the hand strangling the bundles of papyrus stalk that comprised the edge of the skiff. He could feel the tautness in the other's arm through the fabric of the boat. Infusing his voice with calm, he leaned over and unfastened the hand from his craft.

"Nothing has changed. Go about your affairs as is your habit. That's all you must do. And don't let my cousin's machinations make you flinch. He knows nothing. Nothing at all. Now go. We're in greater danger from the river than from Meren."

Ebana watched his ally disappear through a screen of reeds. Something was wrong. Something more than just the inconvenient death of a priest. Whatever it was, he was beginning to think that this particular ally must be dealt with—but not until after he'd accomplished the task to which he'd been set.

They had climbed out of the wide ribbon of green that was the Nile Valley, high onto the desert floor, and then into a valley formed by steep limestone cliffs. Meren climbed down from his chariot and handed the reins to Abu, who led the team away to be watered. Behind him came Kysen and Tanefer, Djoser, Rahotep, and several others.

The morning had been spent downing ibex, ostriches, and deer. Tanefer had found this deep valley where enough moisture gathered to favor the growth of vegetation around a minute pool. By the end of harvest, the water would evaporate. Tanefer's hunters had erected a net at one end of the valley, and the hounds had driven the game in from the other end.

Meren took refuge beneath a portable sunshade. A body servant came forward with a water bottle. He poured some over his face, which was covered with a layer of fine sand grains and dust, before drinking. He wiped his mouth and watched Kysen and Tanefer direct a hunter who was lashing a gazelle to a carrying pole.

Tanefer had organized this hunt, and Meren was grateful for the distraction; he'd managed to extract a period of grace from the king. A fortnight to decide whether to risk allowing pharaoh to fight the Hittites. Had it been so long since the day the priest had been discovered at the foot of the statue at the god's gate? Meren gulped down more water as Kysen left his host and joined him.

Tanefer was busy directing servants, hunters, and hounds. Kysen took a water bottle from a servant, dismissed him, and dropped down on a reed mat at Meren's feet. They swigged water and watched the preparations for the return to the city. Not far off, other men retreated to the shade of canopies, joking and laughing.

"Where is Ahiram?" Kysen asked.

"He discovered that Rahotep was supplying a brace of hounds and refused to attend," Meren said. He wiped gritty sweat from his forehead, then touched a cut on Kysen's inner forearm. "You're holding your bow too close."

Kysen grunted. "My right wheel hit a rock and I lost my balance."

Meren nodded, and they lapsed into silence as a breeze riffled down the length of the valley and cooled their skin.

"Has nothing come of your conversation with the lector priest yesterday?" Kysen asked.

"Naught. Qenamun's manner is as deft as his reputed skill with magic."

"Ebana dislikes him."

"So you said. However, being a schemer hardly distinguishes Qenamun from the rest of us." Meren waved his hand toward a group containing Djoser, Tanefer, and Rahotep. "Who among our friends does not indulge in stratagems and maneuvers? Rahotep is jealous of Tanefer—though he spouts accolades to his own perfection—and seeks advancement over everyone from pharaoh. Djoser's blood is turning to bile as his envy of us all increases."

"But they're outmatched in scheming by Parenefer and Ebana."

Meren gave his son a glance of sympathy. Kysen had spent the last few days attempting to inquire among Unas's fellow priests about his work, movements, and sympathies, only to have Ebana insist upon being present at each exchange. Thus he'd learned nothing of consequence.

Their only progress had been Abu's discussions with Ipwet and Nebera. At the time her husband died, Ipwet was in the company of several other young wives making barley bread. Inquiries at the royal workshops resulted in Abu concluding that Nebera had arrived there too early to have made a side trip to meet and kill Unas.

"It may be that I'm seeing evil and scheming where there is none," Meren said.

"Still, the porter Huni was readmitted to duty just in time to sleep through a fall to the death. I don't like the coincidence. But when I questioned the chief of porters, he said he'd decided to give Huni another chance to serve. Since Ebana was there when I saw him, I can't be sure if he was telling the truth."

Meren sighed and took another sip of water. "Suspicions plague me as well, but we can hardly fall to beating the man with such little cause. He's under the protection of the temple."

"I hate inquiries among the great," Kysen said as he rubbed his injured forearm. "And that cursed temple swarms with people, yet no one admits knowing anything."

"You haven't found the boy who brought the message to Unas, have you?"

Kysen shook his head. "And no one at the temple admits sending for him. Ipwet says she paid little attention when the boy spoke to Unas, so she can't be sure what he really said."

"Poor Unas," Meren said. "He doesn't seem to have been important to anyone."

"Hark you," Kysen said. "That porter will have some accident soon, or vanish to one of the temple estates on the Nubian border."

Meren sat forward on his stool, rested his arms on his knees, and shook his head. "And if he does, we'll reconsider our approach, but I've other matters to worry about as well."

"Ah, your fortnight is up, and the king is going to demand that you take a stance on this matter of the campaign."

"He's going to be furious, and I don't like disappointing him. His life is so full of cares and duties."

"He lives the life of a god."

Meren glanced up at Kysen's disbelieving tone, but he didn't argue. Kysen's childhood before adoption had been as filled with pain as Tutankhamun's. His father had sold him after having failed to beat him into a state of craven submission. It wasn't Kysen's fault that he sometimes couldn't imagine the life of a king to be an ordeal.

Meren rose, wincing at the ache in muscles that had taken many jolts as his chariot raced across the desert floor.

"Time to return home. The calendar marked this as a day of fortune, so I'm hoping I'll be spared another evening listening to Horemheb and Tanefer plan the provisioning of troops and the supplying of border forts. And if I'm blessed, the king won't remember my promise to take sides for a few days."

They left Tanefer and the other hunters gorging themselves on roast gazelle, and by the time the sun had reached its apex and begun its descent, they reached the house. In a short time Meren was standing in his bathing stall while a servant poured jar after jar of cool water over him. Reluctantly he signaled an end to the luxury and stretched out on the massage table nearby while his body servant rubbed oil into his skin.

While he was lying there, he perused several letters from his family. There was one from his sister, complaining that he neglected his daughters and should have visited them long ago. Was he neglectful?

Isis and Bener had to learn the skills of running a great estate and women's accomplishments that he couldn't teach them. Tefnut, his eldest, lived far away, in the delta with her husband. He missed them all, especially at night when he came home and caught himself listening for their bright laughter.

There was another letter, from his younger brother Nakht, whom he'd always called Ra. Meren unfolded the papyrus, skimmed the first few lines, and let it drop to the floor. More complaints about how Ra's judgment was always questioned by their steward.

Meren lowered his head to his crossed arms. He felt pressure build up at his temples, as if his head were being squeezed in a grape press. It was as if the members of his family grasped his arms and pulled in different directions; he felt that he was about to split down the middle. He whispered a request to his servant, who began to rub his head.

He was drifting off to sleep when the rubbing at his temples stopped. His eyes flew open, and he tensed and raised his head to see Abu entering the chamber, carrying a flat limestone flake, an ostracon, used to take notes to conserve papyrus. Meren sat up and wrapped a bathing sheet around his hips. His body servant vanished into his bedchamber.

"Forgive me, lord, but a report has arrived from the city police. The house of Unas has been robbed, or rather, it has been rifled. They don't think anything was taken."

"Have they caught anyone?"

"No, lord. The wife was visiting her parents, and the neighbor, Nebera, reported the crime."

Abu held out the ostracon. Meren took it and perused the report. Had it occurred at any other house, such a petty offense would have never been brought to his attention. He handed the report back to Abu as Kysen came in, freshly dressed, his hair damp.

"You've heard?" he asked. "I think Abu and I should visit the house tomorrow."

"I hope you discover more than the city police did," Meren said.

His thoughts racing, he stood and padded into his bedchamber. The others followed. He dropped his bathing sheet and allowed his body servant to wrap a clean kilt around him. Kysen tossed him a belt, and he waved his servant out of the room before wrapping it around his waist.

"I grow weary of sparring with intransigent priests," he said.

Kysen looked up from his perusal of the theft report. "But you said we couldn't provoke an open quarrel."

"That was before this new stroke." Meren rubbed the sun-disk brand on his wrist as he thought, then slipped a leather-and-bronze wrist band over it. "We must flush the birds from the marsh, Ky."

"The shards?"

"Aye, the shards. If they're significant, they may be just the goad we need to harry our prey into the open. But we can't tell the priests about them too directly. I suggest you let slip the tale of your discovery when we attend this evening's banquet at Prince Sahure's."

He smiled at Kysen. Many courtiers also served as priests in different temples. Word would spread to the priests of Amun like the blast of a desert storm.

"You think someone will come to rifle our house?" Kysen asked.

"No, but someone may make a mistake."

Later that evening Meren made polite conversation with Lady Bentanta at the banquet, all the while watching Kysen laughingly scatter the story of his discovery among the guests. He stood beside a column, a full wine cup in his hand, cursing his ill luck. Bentanta had run him to ground before he could vanish into another room.

"You're worried."

His attention swerved to the woman in front of him. She was lithe and tall, like a papyrus reed, and she teased him. No other woman had the temerity. She'd been widowed several years, had youth and wealth and several sons and daughters to keep her company. What was worse, she was as clever and perceptive as ever old Queen Tiye had been. He'd known her at a distance since childhood, but he had been betrothed young, at fifteen, and she was already married at thirteen. Meren regarded her with wariness. What had she noticed, and how?

"You imagine it, lady."

Bentanta made a disgusted sound, which irritated Meren even more.

"I've known you since you wore the sidelock of boyhood, Meren."

She drifted closer, and he smelled myrrh.

"Your eyes," she said in a whisper. "I've known you long enough to read your eyes when the rest of your face is a mask. Does the contention among pharaoh's councillors weigh upon you?"

He backed up until he hit the column. "You should know, since it's written in my eyes like the glyphs on a temple wall."

"Why, Meren, my warrior, prince, and Friend of the King, you're afraid of me."

He opened his mouth, scowling, but Bentanta chuckled softly. She left him then, allowing her arm to brush his as she floated away in a mist of sheer linen and perfume. He glared after her, but soon rearranged his features into a more pleasant guise and slipped deeper into the shadows beyond the reach of the lamps scattered about Sahure's great hall. Musicians struck up a tune, and a line of dancers snaked its way into the room.

Meren grabbed a spice cake from a pile on a table and tore it in half, wishing it were Bentanta's neck. The woman was too clever to be borne. She reminded him of Qenamun. Both had a way of discomfiting, of sliding between bones and tendons with words that should have been innocuous. Qenamun's motives, however, were even more unfathomable than Bentanta's.

He remembered his interview with the man the previous day. He'd sent for the priest because neither Kysen nor Abu had made progress in the matter of Unas's death. In retelling the story of the discovery of the body, Qenamun had been urbane, forthcoming, and open. He'd given no cause for complaint of a lack of cooperation, and aroused in Meren a deep suspicion of his motives. No priest of rank in the temple of Amun was so agreeable without good reason.

Qenamun had been born to his position; his father and his grandfather had been priests in a line stretching back almost to the time of the Hyksos invasions. A distinguished family, moderately wealthy, full of men who managed to survive wars, famines, political havoc. Of them all, Qenamun appeared the most successful. His detractors seemed prey to misfortune, his friends wary of thwarting him. Ebana said Parenefer was considering advancing him to the position of Servant of the God. This was Ebana's rank, and he wasn't pleased.

Qenamun had stood during the whole interview, hands folded in front of him, looking ingenuous in his fragile elegance, his luminous, dark eyes suffused with tranquility.

"I regret not speaking to you sooner," Meren said. "But matters of great weight interfered."

"The Lord Meren is gracious to concern himself with so small a matter."

"A death at the foot of the king's statue is more than a small matter."

Qenamun inclined his head. He resembled a gazelle bending down to take water.

"As you say, lord. But I have performed rites of purification all around the temple. Forgive me, but my experience has been that the evil aroused by sudden death can be expunged most effectively. There are several spells of great power for the purpose."

"Your reputation comes before you," Meren said. "I hear from many sources that your skill at magic and divination is a boon to the good god."

Actually, Qenamun had as great a reputation for instilling fear of his power as for doing good. His rise to prominence at the temple had a great deal to do with his skill at ruining the reputations of those in his way.

"My gift comes from Amun," Qenamun said, "and I have sought to use it in this matter that so concerns you, lord. For Amun is great of will, terrible and mighty of power. He guards his flock and casts into the lake of fire those that would oppose him."

Qenamun cocked his head to the side. His gaze melted over Meren like warm honey. Under that stare, Meren felt as if the distance between them somehow closed and the air he breathed grew hot. His lungs seemed to burn.

The priest was still speaking to him in a low voice. "Beware ye of Amun, king of the gods. His wrath is terrible against his enemies."

The closeness and heat alerted him to what Qenamun was doing. Anger spurted through his body like molten copper.

Tempted to find his whip and lash the priest for his effrontery, he lifted one brow and gave a soft chuckle. "As you say."

Qenanum lowered his lashes, breaking the lock of their eyes. Meren turned away from the priest to summon his aide.

"I thank Parenefer for allowing you to attend me. It appears that the pure one's death was indeed a simple accident."

"The lord is wise."

"You may go."

Qenamun bowed, lifted his hands. "May Amun-Ra, greatest of heaven, lord of truth, father of the gods, bless thee, my lord. And should the need occur, I would beg you to allow me to offer my skills for your service."

"I'll remember your offer."

A dancer twirled by him, tapping on a drum. The noise roused Meren from his reverie, and he looked down to find the spice cake still in his hand. The priest had disturbed him. Lector priests were scholars and magicians, but this one—this one was more. Seldom had Meren met one who could project power with his gaze in such a manner. The attempt to dominate had been subtle, wordless, and he detested the man for it.

Feeling guilt at abandoning Kysen didn't stop Meren from skulking out of the hall and returning home. He'd had enough of pleasantries, drinking, and the attentions of the amused Bentanta. Besides, the king was expected, and he didn't want to be questioned about his stance on the military campaign in the middle of a feast.

Near dawn the next morning he indulged himself by playing with Kysen's son, Remi, before he was due at court for an audience. He would rather have gone with Kysen to Unas's house or, better yet, avoided his duties and cavorted with the child. The boy spent his mornings playing in the courtyard by the reflection pool outside Meren's bedchamber. He was a top-heavy little devil of three, the scourge of his nurse and all the servants. At the moment he was hurling a leather ball into the pool despite Meren's scolding.

Meren scooped the boy up before he could jump into the water. Straightening, he settled Remi on one hip and found Abu coming toward him, leading a royal servant. The man stared past him at a point somewhere over Meren's shoulder.

"Lord Meren is commanded to the palace."

Meren sighed and stood Remi on his feet. "I'll come at once."

The man left, and Meren went to his chamber to finish dressing. As he donned elaborate court dress, Abu handed him a ceremonial dagger. Only he and Kysen knew that its edge was as sharp as a battle sword, or that the gold of its blade covered a functional bronze core.

"I suppose you'd better come too," he said to Abu. "It seems my respite is at an end, and I must throw myself into a crocodile pit this morning."

8

▽

Thebes was awake, and the sun beginning to set the top of the town wall aglow, as Kysen walked down an avenue that would take him to Unas's house. Since the priest's death, nothing had been uncovered that would lead them to the truth. What disturbed him most was the fact that they still hadn't found a reason for someone to kill Unas, if he'd been murdered. But the behavior of the priests of Amun . . .

Kysen felt that Meren had relegated the incident to a place of lesser importance while he struggled with far more weighty problems, especially that of the king's first military campaign. Of some concern were the bandit raids on small villages at the edge of the eastern desert half a day's sail from Thebes.

Then there were those letters from the family. One of the advantages of being adopted was that he could look upon the relationships between the members of the family without becoming embroiled in their complexity. In the last few years, he'd come to realize how great was Meren's burden as the oldest son.

Nakht, whom Meren called Ra, and one of Meren's stewards were fighting again. Although Meren had been persuaded to allow his younger brother to govern Baht, the family's great estate in the Thinite nome, Nakht's laziness assured the steward of the bulk of the responsibility. It had taken Kysen less than a day in Nakht's company to realize what governed his adopted uncle's life. He resented Meren.

As far as Kysen could see, Nakht wanted all of the privileges and prestige of Meren's position, but none of the responsibilities and hard work that came with it. And Meren indulged him because Nakht always managed to make his brother feel guilty for having inherited so much more than either him or their sister, as if he were responsible for having been born first.

Then there was poor Aunt Idut, who couldn't understand why Meren didn't advance her son to high office even though the boy was but fourteen and still in school. Idut cared more for pushing her son into great achievements before his time than for tending to her own affairs. Luckily Idut was busy training Kysen's sisters in the country at Baht.

He for one didn't envy either Bener or Isis. The complexities of beer brewing, the management of estate servants and farmers, the keeping of accounts, the mysteries of crops and weaving, all of these fell under their control.

It was from Idut that Kysen had learned of Meren's parents. The father, Amosis, had been a child of the god Set, evil-tempered, brilliant, a tyrant, who demanded that Meren excel at every skill, from those of a scribe to those of a warrior. He had punished Meren's slightest lapse, yet tolerated Nakht's indolence.

Idut he ignored except when he terrorized her along with her mother, Neith. Neith, a great beauty from whom Meren had inherited sculpted cheekbones and lithe height, never tried to curb her husband's rampaging temper. Instead she had devoted her life to forcing her children to accommodate it, cater to it, take the blame for it. As a result, Meren alternated between feeling responsible for the misbehavior and failings of his siblings and everyone else and furious resentment at his burdens.

With the embers of such old hurts and grudges perpetually smoldering in the family, Meren grew tense and distant with the arrival of letters from them. Once, Kysen had conceived of the idea of intercepting the letters and burning them, but he soon realized that if the letters weren't answered, the family would descend upon them, quacking and whining.

No wonder Meren avoided his brother and sister. The only family member who tended her own concerns was Meren's maternal grandmother, the ancient Wa'bet, whose guile and wisdom were as great as the green sea into which the Nile flowed. But Wa'bet lived to the north, near Memphis, and rarely traveled or tolerated visits from her family.

Kysen passed two laborers drawing a cart loaded with sun-dried mud bricks, a donkey laden with bags of wheat, and a group of boys on their way to school at one of the temples. Ahead of him, on the threshold of Unas's house, stood Ipwet's friend, Nebera. He'd sent word ahead for the metalworker to attend him, since he'd made the complaint to the police.

A purple bruise marred his left cheek, and his lower lip was swollen on the same side. Kysen glanced at the wounds, but said nothing. The report he'd read hadn't mentioned that Nebera had struggled with the thief.

Nebera, apparently unconcerned, escorted Kysen through the house. The front rooms seemed undisturbed, but the bedchamber looked as if a herd of goats had blundered through it. Chests sat with their contents strewn around them. Kysen stepped over shifts, loincloths, and kilts. His sandal hit a necklace of glazed ceramic beads. He sifted through the coverings of the bed, which had been ripped from it to reveal its base of leather straps. The headrest lay on its side under a short-legged chair.

A casket rested on its side by the bed. Rolled or folded papyrus lay scattered around it. Kysen picked up the documents and examined each of them. Unfortunately they were the same household records he'd seen before—records of expenses, several family letters, receipts, a copy of Unas's meager will. He stuffed the papers back in the casket.

Then he picked up a faience kohl tube and put it back in the cosmetic box. The box sat beside a tall, overturned stand that had once supported a water jar. The jar lay in pieces on the floor, forcing Kysen and Nebera to avoid stepping on jagged shards. The vessel had been painted—a frieze of blue lotus flowers on a buff background. Next to the shards lay an oil lamp, also broken, with its contents spilled over the plastered floor. Some of the oil had seeped into the plaster.

"Very well," Kysen said as he knelt beside the cosmetic box. "Tell me what happened."

Nebera dropped down beside him. "I was sleeping on my roof three nights ago and woke when I heard a crash. I knew Ipwet had gone to stay with her parents and plan for Unas's burial, so it couldn't be her. I thought it was a thief who had heard that the house was uninhabited."

"So you went to catch a thief alone? What if there had been more than one?"

"I—I didn't think. I was so angry that someone would steal from Ipwet when she was bereaved that I crossed from my roof to the other house. I went halfway down the inner stairs and listened. I heard someone moving around in the bedchamber, so I went all the way down the stairs and crept up to the door. It was dark, but I could hear someone moving around and cursing."

"Whoever it was must have stumbled into that stand

and dropped the lamp he was holding," Kysen said as he examined a perfume jar shaped like a fish. "You're sure the thief was a man?"

"Aye, lord. Though he kept his voice to a whisper, it couldn't have been a woman. He stumbled around in the chamber while I hid at the door. I think he was trying to find the way out, because he worked his way along the wall until he came to the threshold. I jumped on him as he came out of the room."

"And fought with him, I see."

Nebera gave him a pained smile. "I grabbed him from behind and got my arm around his neck, but the cur jabbed me in the gut with his elbow, and while I was bent over, he hit me a couple of times and then ran." Nebera touched his purple cheek. "By the time my ears stopped ringing and I could stand without growing dizzy, he was gone."

"So you never really saw him."

"No, lord."

"But you touched him," Kysen said. "You were close."

"Yes, but there was no light."

Kysen sighed. "When you grabbed his neck, did you have to reach down?"

"No. Oh, I see." Nebera sat back on his heels, and his gaze drifted blindly across the ruined room. "No, I had to reach up a little."

"You're sure."

"Aye, lord, the man had to be tall, taller than I am. And—and he was smooth."

"Smooth?"

"He wore only a kilt, and his upper body was well cared for. You understand. His skin wasn't that of a common laborer who works under the sun all day and cannot afford many baths and oils." Nebera's gaze came back to Kysen, and his eyes widened. "By the gods, he smelled of the perfume in skin oil. Not much, but some."

"Could you distinguish the perfume?"

"No, lord. But it contained scents I've smelled before—like scent-cone smell."

Kysen nodded. Scent cones were a common luxury. Placed on top of a person's wig, a shaped cone of ox tallow bearing herbs and spices melted, giving the wearer relief to sun-tortured skin and filling the nostrils with pleasurable scents. One of the most common was that which blended thyme and sweet marjoram. If the intruder had used a scent cone, some of the oil could still be on his skin.

"So," Kysen said. "This clumsy thief is tall and can afford oil or scent cones and labors not in the sun."

"And I know he wasn't a metalworker."

Kysen stared at Nebera, who rushed on. "Those who work over crucibles full of liquid copper or gold, their hands and body catch the bitter smell of the metals."

"Can you remember aught else? What of his hands?"

Rubbing his chin, Nebera lapsed into silence for a few moments.

"I don't know, lord. He was gone too quickly. Not a common thief, nor a practiced one. And now that I think upon it, perhaps not a thief at all. He must have been looking for something particular, although I don't know what."

"And you can think of no reason why anyone would have cause to secretly search Unas's house?"

"No, lord. Unas was so unremarkable, and of no great importance. He had no riches, no secrets, no power of any magnitude. He worked diligently. He was devoted to Ipwet, but in truth, he was more fascinated with sacred writings and dusty old texts than anything else."

When it was apparent that Nebera had nothing more

to tell him, Kysen rose and inspected the rest of the house. The cellar, kitchen, and roof seemed untouched. He even studied the oven where he'd found the pottery shards, all to no avail.

Nebera accompanied him, but remained silent. His remarks had solidified Kysen's opinion that Unas had been a man of honest tedium. And any man who thought that his diligence and store of mythical tales could rival the devotion of a strong young buck like Nebera was a fool. Or had Unas known about his wife and Nebera all along? If he had, would the knowledge have driven him to throw himself off the scaffolding?

He would sooner believe that Nebera had decided to eliminate the inconvenient husband. It was unfortunate that Nebera's innocence had been attested to by a dozen royal artisans, for although Unas hadn't been wealthy, Ipwet would no doubt inherit the house and its contents. Since Nebera had yet to establish his own household apart from his parents, such a windfall would save him years of labor. A sufficient reason for murder to some.

Nebera was familiar with Unas's habits. He might have lain in wait for the priest on the scaffolding and pushed him off it, then gone to his labors in the royal workshops. Nebera would have expected the death to be seen as an accident. Such misfortunes happened all across the Two Lands, where work on monuments to the gods and to kings comprised much of the labor of the empire.

How troublesome that the man couldn't have been a murderer. Nebera, however, seemed an honest man. His reputation among his neighbors and fellow artisans was good. He was a skilled worker, easy of nature, content with his lot. Kysen had formed a like opinion in his dealings with him.

Nebera was like many young men he'd known, satisfied to be born into a station at the behest of the gods,

who placed men in ranks from birth so that the[ ]
functioned in perfect balance. Few rose ab[ ]
birth, and when they did, it was according to th[ ]
the divine ones. However, sometimes people gre[ ] to re-
sent their fate.

He had to consider other possibilities regarding
Unas's death. There was the demeanor of Ebana and
Qenamun. Had they merely been taking advantage of
the priest's death to kick a hornet's nest into Meren's
face? Or were they hiding a greater secret?

When Unas's house had been invaded, where were
Ebana and Qenamun? Futile to ask them—they would
no doubt produce a gaggle of priests to attest to their
presence elsewhere. Too bad he couldn't send a swarm
of men to question their friends, neighbors, fellow
priests—but that would provoke a political furor.

Kysen left Nebera to close the house and stepped out
into the street. The last coolness of night had vanished
while he'd been inside. For a brief moment he was
alone. He lifted his face to the rays of the sun god, his
eyes closed, and watched the red glow on the backs of
his eyelids. Then he turned and began the trip back to
the quay, where he'd take a ferry across the river.

He hadn't gone more than a few steps when he was
forced to avoid a steaming pile of donkey droppings.
He slowed, then darted to the side, his shoulder brush-
ing the wall of a house. Unfortunately, he hadn't seen
the second pile. He cursed and leaped forward over the
noxious hillock. As he landed, he heard a loud thud and
turned to find a chunk of masonry the size of his head
embedded in the dung.

Kysen whirled, backpedaled into the open street, and
gazed up at the roof from which the masonry had fallen.
The only other occupant of the street was an old woman
asleep on her doorstep. Furious, he was about to charge
into the house when reason intervened. He was alone.

nyone, any number of men, could be waiting inside that house.

Launching into a run, he swept down the street, around an intersection, and down an alley that bordered the house. He shoved past a gaudily dressed Syrian merchant and his retainers while a man pulling a cart of wood scurried out of his way. The alley ended in a sharp turn that gave out onto the street he'd come from. Kysen searched the length of the alley and all the roofs. He was rewarded with the sight of a mother hanging out washing while screeching at several children, but little else.

The man with the wood was turning into Unas's street. Kysen stopped him.

"Have you seen a stranger rush from that house?" he asked, pointing to the one from which the masonry had come.

"Only yourself, good master."

Kysen nodded, dismissing the man, and fell to inspecting the house again. It was an old one, as were most in the neighborhood, and its mud brick was crumbling in many places. In a few years the owner might be forced to tear down the walls, level off the foundation, and build again.

He fought the urge to go inside alone. Tempting as it was, he'd been warned about such impetuous behavior by Meren and Abu. And he'd done something like it before and almost been killed. That had been at a deserted temple that served as a refuge for Libyan bandits. He'd nearly lost an ear, and his life.

He should have listened to Meren and brought charioteers with him. Now he'd hear about his recklessness from every captain, aide, and groom under Meren. He thought about not revealing the incident, but knew he couldn't conceal the truth. The falling masonry might have been an accident, but it might also have been an attempt on his life. Which meant that he shouldn't be standing in this alley by himself.

Kysen made his way west toward the riverbank and soon found himself in a market near the quay. He joined crowds of customers, vendors, and foreign merchants moving in small rivulets between stalls laden with Egyptian and imported goods. In the shade of a building a barber shaved and cut hair. A Nubian stacked elephant tusks in front of a stall along with small incense trees. Under awnings vendors hawked bread, fish, melons, onions. Kysen edged between the booth of a woman selling beer and a group of her customers, huddled around a common jar from which protruded clay drinking straws.

In the distance he could see one of the great royal trading ships coming to dock with a load of timber from Byblos. He worked his way between the beer vendor and her customers, his gaze fixed on the royal ship, his thoughts on that block of masonry. He shouldered his way through a group of shoppers, only to have one of them reach out and grab his arm. Kysen whipped around, yanked himself free—and came face to face with his adopted cousin, the priest Qenamun, and a bevy of lesser pure ones. They surrounded him, forming a wall of white kilts and bald heads.

"My noble cousin. How fortunate is this humble cup-bearer of the god to find you here."

Kysen wondered how was it possible to grow cold under the heat of the Egyptian sun. The hair on his arms almost stood up as he glanced around the circle of priests.

"I missed you as well, Ebana," Kysen said.

Ebana's raptorlike smile looked artificial. He drew nearer, coming within an arm's length while the priests tightened their circle.

"One would think," Ebana said, "that one of the Eyes

and Ears of Pharaoh would be too occupied with royal business to go shopping in the markets on this side of the Nile."

Kysen glanced around the circle of bald heads. There were five pure ones, none of whom looked as if they spent much time in scholarship. Thick necks, chests as wide as barges—they could have passed for mercenaries. They stood still in the middle of the market and formed an island before which waves of citizens parted. He knew better than to let them see his uneasiness. He'd been right in not chasing after whoever had dropped that masonry.

"How long have you been here?" he asked. It was a demand. Ebana's false smile vanished.

"Watch your tongue, boy."

"Someone just tried to drop part of a house on me."

"So you fled to the east bank?"

"It happened here," Kysen said. "After I left the house of your pure one, Unas."

He kept his gaze fixed on Ebana's face, but all he perceived was a brief squint of his eyes, quickly gone. Then Ebana smiled a smile of true pleasure and spoke in tones of spice and sweet wine.

"What say you, Qenamun? Is my cousin not unfortunate? You should perform a divination for him or study his birth day. After all, he should be warned of approaching dangers so that he can stay home and avoid them."

Qenamun fingered a pleat in his kilt. "It would do me honor to serve the son of Lord Meren."

The last thing he desired was a magician priest of Amun delving into his fate and fortune, performing spells about him, divining the future of his ka. A man like Qenamun could do great harm with his knowledge of the mysteries of the gods.

"I don't need magic," he said. "I need the truth."

Ebana lost his smile again. "Are you accusing—"

"There you are. I found her. Taste these and tell me I'm right. I have the best palate in Egypt, and these are the best honey cakes in Thebes." Rahotep pushed his way into the circle around Kysen, his arms full of round loaves covered with honey glaze.

"Kysen," Rahotep said. "What luck to meet you. Now you can settle a wager. I say Ebana should hire the baker of these honey cakes, for they're fit for the good god." He shoved a cake into Ebana's hands.

As the circle of priests loosened, then broke and dissolved, Kysen took one as well. To cover his relief, he bit into the cake.

"You've been in the market with Ebana?" Kysen said.

"Yes. You know me, always hungry, and these cakes come to me in my dreams. If Ebana doesn't hire her, I will." Rahotep tried to stuff an entire cake in his mouth.

"How long have you been with him?"

"How long?" Rahotep gave him a curious glance. "A goodly time, I suppose. What do you mean?"

"Oh, naught, my friend. It's just that I didn't know you and my cousin were such comrades."

"Ebana is going to sell me two foals from his black thoroughbred. You know I'm the best judge of horses in the Two Lands. They'll make a wondrous pair for my war chariot. We've agreed on a price, goods worth one hundred *deben* of silver."

Kysen had been watching Ebana while Rahotep boasted and swaggered, but the man revealed nothing. He stood with a honey cake in his hand and stared back at Kysen with his lips quirked in a half smile, unruffled as the golden Horus falcon, cool as the waters of the Nile at night. Taking up the challenge, Kysen listened to Rahotep, his gaze never wavering from Ebana's, and ate every bite of his honey cake. At last Ebana's voice cut across Rahotep's narrative.

"Perhaps you've had a warning from the gods, cousin. It may be that you should remain on the west bank. I would be grieved to find one day that you truly had gone into the west, to the land from which no man returns."

Kysen turned on his heel and walked away. "Fear not. If I do die, I promise to come back as the winged *ba* bird of the soul and take you with me."

9

▽

By the time Meren reached the palace precinct, the king had already finished his sacred duties and was at one of the practice areas near the royal quay on the west bank of the river. As he dismounted from his chariot, Meren surveyed the temporary encampment of the king's war band. Shields set into the earth formed a perimeter patrolled by the royal bodyguard. The fourth side of the rectangular enclosure was formed by the riverbank. Within the enclosure, grooms had unhitched horses from their chariots and tethered them to munch from feed baskets. An open tent had been erected where the king's campstool, armor, and extra weapons lay.

Near a stand of palms, two of the younger officers wrestled to the taunts and jeers of their fellows while others from the Valiant Bows regiment embedded five copper targets in the earth at the opposite end of the camp. Meren glanced over the riverbank. One of the royal warships had anchored offshore. Sailors stood watch on its deck for crocodiles and hippos, as did dozens of others in skiffs that formed a ring around one bearing the king.

Tutankhamun was standing between two older officers. He saw Meren, shouted, and waved the staff he was holding. Meren bowed to the king, then handed the reins of his chariot to a groom and walked to the riverbank to join Horemheb and Tanefer, who were among the king's advisers in attendance. Charioteers of the king's war band lined the bank on either side of this group to watch the coming contest.

Cheers rose from the group surrounding the wrestlers. One of the men had been pinned to the ground. Meren glanced at them as he greeted his friends. Horemheb nudged him with an elbow and nodded in the direction of three priests hovering at the edge of the water. Meren recognized the first prophets of the gods Ra, the sun falcon; Montu, god of war; and Set, who ruled chaos and the desert. The priests watched the king, their bodies arching out from the riverbank, noses almost twitching with unrest.

"Fools," Horemheb said under his breath. "Every time the king engages, they fall to praying as if they'll be blamed for each cut and bruise. They've already performed their sacrifices. What else is needful? The gods will watch over his majesty without their hovering."

On the water, a second skiff approached that of the king. Two men used poles to maneuver their craft in a charge at the king while a third attacked with a staff. The attacker was only a little over the height and weight of the king. Tutankhamun raised his own staff and blocked an overhead blow, then brought his weapon underneath to rap his opponent on the thigh.

The opponent swept his staff in an arc, aiming for the king's chest, but Tutankhamun used the momentum from his last blow; his staff swung up and cracked against the other. At the same time, the king leaned back, lifted his leg, and rammed his foot into his opponent's chest. The man overbalanced. His arms flailed, knocking one of his comrades with his staff as he lost footing and plummeted into the water. A cheer went up from the charioteers.

Meren smiled as the king waved his staff at them. The victory had been real. It would do the boy no good to allow him false accomplishments. Indeed, to flatter him unnecessarily would ruin any chance of his developing into a warrior who could lead the army and the kingdom. While the king's skiff headed for shore, the royal charioteers broke into groups for archery practice.

Meren turned back to Horemheb and Tanefer. "His majesty seems more cheerful than he has been of late."

"Ha!" Tanefer slapped Horemheb on the shoulder. "That's because we persuaded Ay to sit in judgment of Prince Hunefer's suit this morn instead of the king. His majesty hasn't seen a dispatch or treasury report or a foreign emissary since midday yesterday."

"Good," Meren said.

Horemheb grunted and sliced at reeds with his riding whip. "Enough of these pleasantries. I've let you be long enough, Meren, and you know why the king's majesty sent for you."

"Your mood is as foul as that of a wounded ox," Meren said.

Tanefer chuckled. "He's unaccustomed to someone disagreeing with him. He spends all day with soldiers who do nothing but agree and all night with a wife who sees nothing but perfection in him."

Meren held up a hand before Horemheb could retort. "I know my fortnight is up, old friend." He glanced at the river to see that the king's skiff was almost with them. "Where is Maya?"

This time Horemheb snorted like one of the chariot horses. "Hiding. You know how he dislikes proper argument. He sent word that the burdens of harvest recording would keep him away from the council for a few days."

Meren forbore from mentioning that Maya had invited him to his house for the afternoon meal. He was accustomed to the treasurer's wriggling out of situations in which he would have to directly confront more force-

ful characters than himself. And Horemheb was by far
the most forceful of the king's councillors, emphasizing
his points and views with growls, shouts, and hammer-
ings of any object within his reach. Yes, Maya disliked
such violent manners. If Horemheb was losing his temper frequently, Maya would bolt into a hole until the
warrior calmed a bit.

As the general opened his mouth to question Meren
again, the king's skiff came aground. Councillors,
priests, and officers bowed, but Tutankhamun ignored
them, leaped ashore regardless of water and mud, and
stomped toward the group that included Meren. As he
reached them, he signaled to Meren and kept walking.

"Lord Meren will attend my majesty. Tiglith, water."

The king's Syrian body slave darted forward with a
golden cup. Tutankhamun snatched the cup and kept
walking. Meren gave Tanefer and Horemheb an inquiring glance, but they shook their heads. He followed the
king to the shade of a palm tree, wishing he was with
Kysen inquiring into a simple priest's death.

"Well?" Tutankhamun said as soon as he reached the
tree.

"What is thy will, O golden one?"

"Don't pretend you don't understand what I'm asking, Meren."

The king emptied the cup of water down his throat,
and Meren took the cup from him.

"Very well, majesty."

"Then what's your answer? Do we campaign next
year?"

"It is necessary, divine one."

He saw the spark that glinted in the boy's eyes and
inhaled deeply. "However, I can't recommend that the
golden one lead the campaign without first giving him
at least some prior experience."

That spark fanned into a fire, and the king's jaw began to work.

"And just how does the golden one obtain battle experience without going into battle?"

"Indeed, majesty, thy heart guides thee to the crux of the question." Meren rushed on as Tutankhamun began to swear under his breath. "Therefore I recommend that thy majesty begin to attend small campaigns against the bandits and renegades that plague our villages from time to time, and perhaps the greater ones conducted against the barbarian tribes of Kush that threaten our southern forts."

The king burst into smiles, then laughed and clapped Meren on the back. "I knew you would change your opinion."

Meren held up his hand. "A moment, majesty. There is more."

"What is it?"

"If thy majesty excels in these maneuvers and encounters, all will be according to thy wish. But if not . . ."

The king made a rude gesture such as all boys make. "By my ka, Meren, you're a worrying grandmother. I'll do excellent well."

Meren felt a twinge of remorse for the way he closed in on the boy, but he did it anyway. "Then the divine one will deign to give me his word that, should ill befall him in these skirmishes, he will abide by my decision to keep him from battle for another year?"

The smile vanished. "You tricked me."

"No, majesty," Meren said. "Consider this a wager between the two of us. Against a year's delay, you wager that you'll gain the skill necessary to lead the army by the end of Inundation next year."

"Horemheb, Tanefer!" the king shouted.

The two men ran over to them while the king began

to stomp back and forth in front of Meren. When they arrived, he pointed at Meren and glared.

"He's tricked me. I must practice at war on thieves and barbarians."

Meren inclined his head. "The divine one has seen the wisdom of gaining experience in small skirmishes against bandits and the southern tribes before facing the trained armies of the Asiatics."

Meren could see that Tanefer was having difficulty suppressing his amusement, but Horemheb gave him a sharp look before he replied.

"Lord Meren but recommends the course of training followed by all great warriors, including himself, majesty. It's the path followed by Thutmose, the Conqueror, thy mighty ancestor."

He would have to thank Horemheb when they were alone, for Tutankhamun's anger vanished at once.

"The Conqueror, you say? I didn't know."

Tanefer slid into the conversation with the ease of the royal skiff floating on the Nile. "And of course it's the path followed by this humble subject and General Horemheb as well."

"There is more," Meren said. "Thy majesty must consult the records of battle contained in the House of Life, those of the Conqueror, of the great Ahmose who freed Egypt from the foreign Hyksos, and certain reports from my intelligencers regarding the practices of the Hittite armies."

His voice faded as an idea formed. He would send agents north to the outposts in Syria with instructions to capture Hittite officers alive; perhaps he would go there himself to question them.

"Excellent," Tutankhamun was saying. "At last we advance. This endless quibbling was about to drive me mad. What else must we do?"

"Thy majesty must issue orders for the calling up of

reserves," Meren said. "All the soldiers who have been allowed to return to their homes and lands must be summoned."

"And I must begin to recruit more men," Horemheb added.

"Which means," Tanefer said, "that the divine one will hold a great Enrollment of Recruits."

Meren nodded his agreement. "Then, of course, we must inventory all weapons and equipment and issue orders for more, and then all the troops must train even as thy majesty trains. There's much work to be done."

The king grinned and set out in the direction of his tent. "And after it's done, I will go to war."

Meren exchanged glances with Tanefer and Horemheb. None of them was smiling.

Ebana walked into the House of Life with Rahotep. Qenamun was a few steps ahead of them. Rahotep had returned with them to the temple to obtain a new book of dream interpretations from Qenamun, who was known for his power in interpreting the ancient scripts and magical signs. Rahotep was detailing his latest grievance, which was that the king hadn't given him an important command in Kush, the lands to the south of Egypt and the source of the rivers of gold that flowed into the royal coffers.

Qenamun paused to speak to one of the scribes in charge of making copies of the Book of the Dead. Ebana pretended to listen to Rahotep while he speculated upon the meaning of Kysen's sudden appearance in the quay market earlier. The boy had said that the house of Unas had been searched and disrupted. How had he found out? Meren must have alerted the city police of his interest in any matters pertaining to the dead priest. Or his spies had told him. Meren indeed had spies everywhere.

And now his cousin's attention had been drawn once again to the temple, and to the priesthood. Ebana called down the wrath of Amun upon whatever demon was causing his ill fortune. What was worse, Kysen now blamed him for that incident of the falling bricks. Why couldn't the boy simply realize that old walls crumble and masonry falls?

"So now I'm left with this paltry command in the Division of Amun," Rahotep was saying.

Ebana rolled his eyes. Rahotep seemed oblivious of the insult to the good god and to Ebana, but then, Rahotep had never been sympathetic to the feelings of others.

"Your burdens are indeed great," Ebana said with solemnity. "But come."

Qenamun had resumed his progress between the rows of columns. They followed him and turned down a corridor that led to the priest's workroom. Ebana disliked going into this chamber, where he would be at close quarters with so many magical implements. Qenamun's workroom tables groaned with the weight of grinding stones used to crush bones, herbs, stones, and other, less identifiable materials. Every corner was cluttered with jars and bowls filled with roots, wax, pigments, and pastes. One bowl seemed to be dedicated to growing a noxious mold Ebana suspected of being poisonous.

He allowed Rahotep to precede him. The priest went to a wall of shelves to the left and pulled out the casket containing his scribal equipment and his current commissions. The box was made of polished cedar edged with ebony so that the red wood stood out against the black. The gabled lid and side panels were all bordered with ebony inscribed with hieroglyphs. Carved in shallow relief on the cedar was the figure of Qenamun making offerings to the god of learning, Toth.

"I have but to inscribe the book with your name and titles, Prince Rahotep," Qenamun said.

Ebana paused at the threshold while Rahotep wandered to the first worktable and touched a wax figurine. Qenamun glanced at him as he set the casket on a work surface that projected from the middle of the shelves.

"The First Prophet has given me the task of cursing the rebellious Nubians who attacked that fort last month," the priest said.

Ebana pursed his lips. Qenamun was exactly the kind of man he would have forbidden to specialize in magic. How could Parenefer favor him so? True, the man could interpret dreams better than anyone, but so devious a heart should be kept from the power of great knowledge.

But he mustn't allow his thoughts to drive him, or they would show in his features. Ebana forced himself to give the lector priest a half smile as he watched him lift the cedar-and-ebony lid and reach inside the casket. He heard a hiss, then silence.

In the space of a breath, Qenamun's face went blank, then contorted as he screamed. His hand came out of the casket bearing dark, writhing tentacles. The priest's screams bounced off the stone walls as he threw the dark, wriggling mass away from his body.

Ebana saw the flare of a hood, horizontal stripes. Cobras! Ebana shouted at Rahotep, who was already running past him. Qenamun had jumped onto the nearest worktable, moaning and clutching his arm. Ebana darted out of the path of a fleeing snake and yelled at a group of priests who had come running at the noise. They turned as a body and fled back down the corridor as Ebana called to them to fetch a guard. He ran out of the room, turned, and clutched the edge of the open door. He searched the floor for cobras, but most of them had fled to dark corners underneath furniture and shelves.

Qenamun was still on the table amid vials, wax figures, and herb jars. He had curled into himself, still gripping his arm, which bore at least five strike marks. Ebana called to him, but he received only a moan in answer. He moved closer, but shrank back from the door when a long, narrow body rose up from behind a jar, hood flaring.

Down the corridor a guard arrived with spear in hand and was poking it into shadows as he inspected room after room. As the moments passed, he could hear Qenamun's breathing increase until it sounded like the pant of a dog. The guard reached him, and Ebana pointed to the cobra behind the jar.

"I think there are four others, maybe more."

The guard swallowed, then drew a knife from his belt, took aim, and threw. The knife hit the jar, and the cobra slithered behind a basket under the table where Qenamun lay. Ebana halted the man when he would have thrown his spear.

"Look." He pointed at Qenamun.

The priest's body had begun to jerk. His foot hit a jar and kicked it off the table. The crash sent the cobra slithering between two tall oil jars. They watched in horrified captivation while Qenamun's body twitched with violent spasms. Two more guards joined them with knives and spears while a servant came bearing three of Parenefer's hunting cats.

Ebana ordered the hunting cats released into the workroom, and everyone watched and waited while the creatures calmly set about stalking the cobras. There was no hurry now, for everyone could see the number of strike marks on Qenamun's body. A man might survive one, but not seven.

As the cats stalked and pounced, the priest lapsed into a stupor. By the time they were finished, so was the life of Qenamun.

10

▽

Meren leaned back in his chair and gazed up at a column shaped like a bundle of lotus flowers. Beyond the loggia where they were finishing the afternoon meal, real flowers, the blue and rose lotus, floated on Maya's pleasure pond in the glare of sunlight. He had arrived a short time earlier after watching the king at archery practice.

While he, Tanefer, and Horemheb had watched the king, Prince Djoser joined them and immediately mentioned the pottery shard story Kysen had begun to foster. While Tanefer and Djoser speculated on Meren's odd interest in pottery, Ahiram appeared, boisterous and in determined good spirits.

He'd been watching the wrestlers and now put forth the opinion that Meren saw plots and conspiracies in every shadow and whisper. The fool priest had probably tripped over his own kilt when he fell off the king's statue. Meren did his best to appear as if he knew more than he was telling and then turned his attention back to the king.

Tutankhamun had chosen a heavier bow than usual, and the practice hadn't gone well. With every miss, the boy's mouth had settled into a tighter line until it resembled the seam between two pyramid blocks. The tighter the line, the more quiet grew the warriors and officials around the king.

Ahiram had made things worse. At the last miss, he'd spoken up to say that the fault lay in whoever gave his majesty that bow, which was far too heavy for one so young. Tutankhamun had reddened and snapped the bowstring past his wristguard, causing a nasty burn. That ended archery practice. The priest of Montu had rescued everyone by divining in the remains of his sacrifice that today was not a good day for the bow and arrow.

With the king's young pride assuaged, Meren left the court. He'd noticed that the priest had offered his explanation after Tanefer had strolled over to have a quiet word with him. Meren decided to speak with Ay about Tanefer's diplomatic abilities. They could be of use in a position of greater authority, if the prince could be persuaded to accept the responsibility.

Now Meren lifted his silver cup to a servant, who hefted a wine jar out of its stand and poured dark, sweet liquid into it. He was stuffed with mutton and fresh bread, which meant that at any moment Maya would abandon inconsequential chatter about his family. He thrived more on the discussion of people's problems than on food, and had a habit of plying his confidants with rich victuals on the supposition that a full stomach encouraged a loose tongue.

Maya knew this strategy didn't work on Meren, but he tried anyway. He'd been trying for years. His latest interest appeared to be Meren's lack of a wife.

"It's been too many years, my Falcon. Sit-Hathor lives in the netherworld, and you're still here." Maya glanced at him sideways with heavy-lidded, tilted eyes. "Lady Bentanta, now, there's a woman worth marrying. As beautiful as the Nile."

"Change the subject, Maya."

"Very well."

Maya had agreed too readily, making Meren immediately wary.

"Don't you think that this argument about the king leading the army has been going on far too long?"

Meren glanced at his friend, said nothing, and lifted a brow.

"This incessant quarreling is giving me foul humors," Maya said when he realized Meren wasn't going to respond. "It disturbs my ka to have Horemheb shouting in my ear for several hours each day. I've been to war too, you know. I understand the risks, and that's why I recommend caution. But I tell you, I'm thinking of going to the king if my courage is questioned once more by that son of a commoner."

This time Meren straightened up in his chair. "There's no need. Today I suggested a plan by which the king can practice at war without actually engaging in it."

He explained his design to Maya, whose whole face brightened as he realized the compromise Meren offered.

"It won't please Ay, you know."

Meren nodded. "But he'll recognize the necessity."

"Nevertheless," Maya said, "Horemheb still disturbs me."

"How so?"

Maya dismissed the servants fanning them and scooted his chair closer to Meren. He continued in a low voice.

"I've heard disturbing talk—talk that says Horemheb chaffs at the constraints put upon him. He's furious at how the army and the empire have been neglected. They say he thinks Ay is too old, and the rest of us too cautious, and that Egypt needs a bold leader of prime years, not a b—"

"Meren!"

Maya jumped out of his chair at the shout, and Meren almost grabbed for his dagger as Tanefer burst out of the house.

"Pharaoh sent me to find you," Tanefer said as he snatched up a jar and gulped down water.

Out of breath, he wiped sweat from his brow and upper lip before going on. "The temple of Amun is in chaos. One of the priests has been killed—again. The one you questioned about the pure one who fell off the king's statue, that lector priest, Qenamun. Dead of the bite of the cobra, if you can believe it."

Meren knew they were watching him. He frowned and stalled while he thought.

"What can I do about a priest getting struck by a snake, Tanefer?"

Tanefer gave him a wincing smile. "Someone put five cobras in his scribe's chest. He stuck his hand in and came out with a fistful of them. Hardly a mischance, do you think? I know of few cobras that jump into chests all together and shut the lid."

"Five? Five?" Maya asked.

Meren ignored the treasurer. "When did this happen?"

"This morning some time," Tanefer said. He stabbed a piece of mutton with his dagger and began to eat it. Between chews he said, "Word spread over the city quickly, of course. I'll wager old Parenefer would have liked to keep the thing quiet, but it happened in the House of Life, and there were too many people, most of whom fled when the cobras got out. And now pharaoh commands you to inquire."

Tanefer swallowed another piece of mutton and grinned at Meren. "The divine one's words were: 'My majesty likes not this plague of death among my priests of Amun.' What he really meant was—"

"That he likes not this plague of murder among the

priests of Amun," said Meren, giving Tanefer a stern look. He turned to the open-mouthed Maya. "Thank you for the meal, my friend."

Maya waved him away. "Go, go. Five cobras, by the gods. Five."

"Don't you want to go along?" Tanefer asked him. "Perhaps they haven't killed them yet and we can help."

Color drained from Maya's face, which caused Tanefer to chuckle and Meren to step between them before Maya recovered enough to start a fight. He requested the services of one of Maya's servants, penned a note, and sent for Kysen, Abu, and a squad of charioteers to meet him at the temple. Parenefer wouldn't like him descending in force, but the time for diplomacy was over.

Two priests dead. Two who worked together. Not by chance. That he refused to believe. Something was wrong at the temple of Amun, more wrong than was usual, that is.

He drove his chariot to the ferry that would take him across the river to the temple. He would understand if someone were to kill Parenefer or one of the other chief prophets. The temple of Amun was the richest of all in Egypt, possessing wealth beyond imagining; its power almost compared with that of the king. The rivalry between the priests of Amun and those of the other great gods—Ra, Osiris, Set, Hathor, Isis—sometimes reached fatal dimensions. But these seemingly meaningless killings of a lowly pure one, and then a lector priest, this Meren couldn't understand.

Did Parenefer suspect both of being his agents? No, the old man was too clever to rid himself of spies so clumsily. Indeed, if Parenefer were behind these deaths, they would have appeared natural, or at the most, unquestionably accidental. Which meant that Parenefer wasn't behind them.

If this were true, he would have to look elsewhere for the culprit. Who else had the gall and the power to cause the deaths of two priests? Only someone with a great deal at risk, someone of power. Like a high government official—a nobleman—a courtier. No, his suspicious heart was running rampant. He didn't know enough to make such a conclusion. He would have to wait for the truth to show itself.

Priests and citizens scurried through the great pylon gate of Amunhotep the Magnificent in the ceaseless traffic that surrounded the house of the god. Artisans clambered up and down the scaffolding around the king's statue as if no word of violence had reached them. No doubt Parenefer had seen to it that none had.

Meren walked past the statue, glancing at the base, which stood almost as tall as he. Progress had been made, for a draftsman had drawn in the double cartouches of the king's coronation and given names—Nebkheprure Tutankhamun. The elongated ovals of two cartouches enclosed two sets of hieroglyphs, neither of which was finished.

On the left he could see the pointed end of a reed leaf at the top of the cartouche, and below the leaf, the beginning of a head of a bird. All that lay within the second cartouche was the circle of the sun and the beginnings of the outline of a beetle. When the drawing was complete a sculptor would carve the design in sunken relief.

He went inside the god's gate and heard murmuring. Priests of every rank clustered in knots and whispered. He turned left, went through a door, and took a path that led away from the sanctuary itself to the separate building called the House of Life. Like all the buildings within the temple enclosure, it was covered with carved and painted reliefs depicting the god, his wife Mut, and their son Khonsu. Before the door of polished cedar a crowd of priests, students, and servants milled, kept back by a pair of guards.

The group blocking his way parted and fell silent as he approached. He saw the guards exchange glances, trying to decide whether it was more dangerous to keep him out or let him in. They were disadvantaged, however; no nobleman of his rank would even stop to ask permission to enter. Meren passed between the two men and through the half-open door without a glance in their direction.

"Lord?"

He looked over his shoulder in surprise. The guard who had spoken cleared his throat.

"There be cobras within."

He nodded and left the man staring after him. Before him lay a columned central hall in disarray. Chests lay open, their contents strewn about where scholars had dropped them in their haste to escape. He listened to the hollow dripping of the water clock. He stepped over the scattered contents of a scribe's kit, avoiding the spray of ocher dust.

Beyond the thicket of columns was a doorway; he was walking toward it when he heard voices to his left. Entering a corridor that ran the length of the building, he found Ebana talking to several men outside the third room along the corridor. As he approached, Ebana glanced up, stopped in mid-sentence, then gestured to a guard. The man ducked inside the room and reappeared, followed by a servant holding three hunting cats in his arms. They bustled past Meren, who could hear a loud strumming from the cats as their tails lashed back and forth in contentment.

Ebana stepped in front of the threshold as he approached. Meren was surprised to see Prince Rahotep leaning against the wall outside the room. Rahotep was in shadow, but he moved into the light issuing from the room to reveal a face dewed with sweat. For once his bluster had been quelled. He wiped his forehead with a shaking hand. He ignored Meren.

"You're sure they're all in there?" he asked Ebana.

"All five of them, except for what the cats consumed. I told you it was safe to move."

"What if one of them escaped?" Rahotep peered down the corridor in the direction of the central hall. "It could be hiding behind a column."

"It's safe to go home," Ebana snapped. "By the gods, Rahotep, you weren't even touched."

"Don't go," Meren said.

Rahotep slumped against the wall and licked his lips while he goggled at Meren. "You saw more in the hall?"

"No, but I wish to talk to you."

Ebana folded his arms over his chest, still barring the entrance to the room, as Meren stood before him. "What do you here? This is a matter for priests, not charioteers and spies."

"I'm here at the command of pharaoh, cousin, so unless you wish to defy the king's wishes, stand aside. I want to see Qenamun before Parenefer arrives. You did tell that guard to let him know I was here, did you not?"

Ebana stepped aside, and as Meren brushed by him, he whispered, "Did you come alone, cousin? How brave of you."

Meren paused to meet Ebana's obsidian gaze. "I never fear to enter the sacred precincts of Amun. It seems that death stalks only priests here." He glanced at Qenamun's body and then back to Ebana, who scowled at him so that the scar on his temple seemed to leap into prominence.

Meren began to examine the chamber. Qenamun lay on his back on a table in front of a wall of shelves, his feet resting in a stone mortar and his head on the remains of a clay bowl. Beneath him and on the floor around the table lay plates of dried herbs, jars, wax figures.

Qenamun looked as if he'd fallen asleep. His nails and lips were pale, while his lower body had already taken on the purple hue Meren recognized. He'd asked Nebamun, his physician, about this color and received the explanation that without its soul, the body could no longer support blood, which then sank, as water flows down a slope.

He touched Qenamun's arm. It still bent. Along it on both sides were scattered the puncture marks of the cobra. Dried blood on his left thigh marked the site of another strike. Meren counted seven in all, five of which were concentrated on the upper arm.

He turned away from the body to glance about the workroom. Several heavy jars had been upset on the floor. Between two of them lay a basket with its lid askew. He opened it and beheld the remains of several cobras, their dark bodies ripped open to expose gnawed flesh. He counted five heads, then replaced the lid.

Turning to Ebana, he said, "You were here? How did this happen?"

"We'd just returned from the quay market," Ebana said. He nodded his head in Rahotep's direction. "Rahotep wanted a dream book he'd commissioned from Qenamun, and it was supposed to be in that chest. He stuck his hand in and found the cobras."

Meren went to a wall of built-in shelves, from the center of which projected a wide table. There lay a cedar-and-ebony casket. It was rectangular, its greatest side slightly more than a cubit long. He looked inside, but the box was empty except for a scattering of rush pens.

Rahotep's pale face appeared around the edge of the door. "Someone put the snakes in there on purpose."

Ebana rolled his eyes. "Gather your wits. Of course it was planned."

Meren was occupied with sorting through the stacks of documents on the shelves. One row was devoted to copies of chapters of the *Book of the Dead*. Another consisted of various theologies of the major gods—Ra, Osiris, Isis, Horus, and Set, as well as Amun. He found Rahotep's dream book under the story of the contentions of Horus and Set, along with an incomplete set of interpretations intended for Prince Ahiram.

"Qenamun's interpreting abilities seem to have found favor with quite a few of our friends," Meren said as he pulled several papyrus rolls from the shelf. He read the dedications of a few. "Here is one for Princess Hathor, another for Prince Djoser, and this one seems to be a dream divined for General Horemheb."

"How can you stay in there? It stinks of death," Rahotep said. "Gods, I need air!"

He clamped a hand over his mouth and fled. Meren watched him vanish without comment while he ran the tips of his fingers over a papyrus roll bearing the name of Prince Djoser. He plucked another roll from a shelf and found a scribe's palette beneath it. Pausing, Meren touched the palette's gilded wooden surface. His glance caught the gleam of alabaster behind another stack of texts. He pushed them aside to reveal ink pots.

He looked at Ebana. "Where did Qenamun keep his palette?"

"In that box." Ebana pointed at the cedar-and-ebony chest.

"Then someone removed its contents, concealed them, and put the cobras in their place, knowing that Qenamun would be likely to stick his hand in the box without paying much attention to what he was doing."

He turned back to the shelves and began filling Qenamun's casket with documents.

"What are you doing?"

"Taking what seems meaningful."

Ebana stalked over to him and grabbed Meren's wrist as he reached for Djoser's papyrus. Their gazes locked, and neither moved.

"This is a matter for the temple. I will investigate."

"Let me go, Ebana."

He felt the grip on his wrist tighten until his hand was almost numb. Sighing, Meren whipped his wrist back against Ebana's thumb and then yanked in the opposite direction, freeing himself. Ebana balanced on the balls of his feet, but Meren made no other move.

"Why are you so worried about my presence here?"

Ebana's body tensed, then the muscles in his face, arms, and legs seemed to slacken. "Because you transgress. It is for us of the temple to seek out the criminal responsible for this—this—"

"Murder," Meren said as he tapped the casket with a papyrus roll. He resumed filling the casket with papyri. "Do you know when Qenamun last opened this casket?"

"No."

Meren rested his forearm on the casket lid and contemplated his cousin. "You're not a fool. As soon as you realized this was murder, you began to make inquiries. My charioteers will be here soon to question everyone who dealt with Qenamun. Neither they nor I will leave until we get the answers we need."

They stared at each other, but broke off at the sound of tapping. The noise grew louder until the high priest marched into the room with his stick. Two guards lumbered in after him.

"What is this invasion of the sacred place of Amun!" Parenefer's bellow rebounded off the plastered walls.

"I've already sent word to Vizier Ay and his majesty of this misfortune. Presumptuous young barbarian, get yourself from here at once."

Parenefer's face had turned the color of red jasper as he leaned on his stick and paused to catch his breath. Then, at his signal, the guards gripped their scimitars, ready to draw them. Ebana backed away from him, and Meren took a step away from the shelves so that his right arm was unhindered.

Parenefer said more calmly, "I'm certain the divine one will agree that the priests of Amun are more capable of handling this matter than an outsider."

"And I'm sure that his majesty wishes to search out the evil that has taken place in the house of his divine father Amun himself—through me."

Parenefer walked over to the table where Qenamun's body lay and glanced at it. Yellow light from a lamp flickered in the depths of his eyes, but they showed no reaction to the sight of the dead priest. His voice slithered around the room.

"You're a Friend of the King, Meren, but make no mistake. You test your power when you tread upon the sacred prerogatives of Amun."

Out of the corner of his eye Meren watched the knuckles of a guard grow white on the hand that gripped the hilt of his scimitar. The air in the workroom was foul, and it suddenly seemed thick with the smell of malice.

"There has already been one untoward occurrence this day," Parenefer said.

He lifted his walking stick and touched the basket containing the dead snakes. Something inside shifted, causing the container to shiver, and Parenefer smiled at Meren.

"None of us want another misfortune. Do we, my lord Meren?"

11

▽

Parenefer directed a jackal's smile at Meren, and he felt the flesh on his back and arms prickle. He'd been certain none of the cobras had been alive. Hadn't he? The interior of the basket had been dark, but he would have seen movement. The shifting of the basket had merely been the settling of its contents.

But if the cobras were dead, why was Ebana watching the basket? He heard Parenefer chuckle as he worked the tip of his walking stick underneath the lid.

"You shouldn't evoke the wrath of the king of the gods, Meren."

Just as a gap opened between the lid and the container, a shout boomed at them from down the corridor.

"My lord Meren!"

Hoping his relief didn't show in his face, Meren smiled sweetly at Parenefer before raising his voice in answer. Footsteps pounded toward them, and in moments the room filled with tall bodies in leather and bronze armor. Six charioteers crowded into the chamber, came to a halt, and saluted him. From their midst emerged Kysen, followed by Abu. Kysen inclined his head toward the high priest, but addressed Meren.

"You sent for us, my lord?"

"Yes," Meren said. "By the word of pharaoh, we're commanded to inquire into the death of this priest,

Qenamun, which has defiled the sacred house of Amun."

Meren turned to Parenefer. "Perhaps I should summon more men, first prophet, for your safety. I could station a squadron about your residence, assign some of my own men to be your bodyguards, distribute charioteers in every part of the temple, to prevent further evil deeds until I discover who has done this terrible thing."

The high priest nearly strangled his walking stick. "I have sufficient guards for the purpose."

"But how do you know one of them isn't the criminal?" Meren asked softly.

Parenefer raised his arm and pointed at Meren with a crooked finger. "Someday you'll get too clever for your own well-being, boy."

The old man tapped and stomped his way out of the room, taking his guards with him. Meren told his men to question everyone who could be found to have entered the House of Life over the past day. They wouldn't find them all, but they had to try. Kysen was studying the body when Ebana broke his long silence and addressed Meren.

"So you've won this skirmish."

Meren dropped two more papyri into Qenamun's cedar-and-ebony casket. "I grow weary of your obstructions. Are you going to tell me who was here yesterday, or shall I tell pharaoh you refused to aid in the inquiries he commanded me to make?"

"It will do you no good, all this poking and prying," Ebana said. "Do you know how many people come and go from this temple every day? Hundreds, nay, thousands, from all parts of the empire. Worshipers, suppliants, stewards and officials from the estates of Amun, government officers, sacred singers, priestesses, students and their teachers, subjects in need of official wills or other legal documents. I could go on."

"No, just tell me who might want Qenamun dead."

Ebana walked over to Meren and leaned on the table beside the casket. "Qenamun was a lector priest. I suppose he might have offended someone in his practice of magic. Look on the table beside his body. That wax figure is of the Hittite king."

Kysen picked up the figurine and read the inscription. "He's right."

"A most secret request from General Horemheb," Ebana said. "So you see it could even have been a foreigner who put the cobras in Qenamun's way."

"I've found, cousin, that murder is often a crime of intimacy. In this instance, someone who was familiar with Qenamun's possessions and habits. Someone who knew his way to this room, knew when he could expect Qenamun to be absent from it and for how long. Someone like a priest."

Kysen wandered over to them. "And someone who had cause to hate him. Someone who, if I remember rightly, detested him because he created discord as lovingly as a spider spins a web."

Meren lifted a brow. "Ah, yes," he said. "How did you describe Qenamun, a scorpion? Did he do more to you than ruin one of your promising assistants? Was he a danger to you?"

With an abrupt lunge, Ebana stepped between Kysen and Meren so that his body blocked Kysen's view. He grabbed Meren's arm and twisted it to reveal the sun-disk scar. Only Meren heard his whisper.

"Dearest cousin, that scorpion was just as much a danger to me as the old king was to you."

Meren winced as Ebana's fingers dug into the flesh around the scar. Ebana knew the old heretic king had branded him with the symbol of his personal god. Was he merely telling Meren that there had been no danger, or was he implying knowledge of Akhenaten's death?

For a moment, the workroom faded as his inadvertent role in the old king's death flashed through his thoughts. He felt the sting of remorse, the shame of a defiled ka. Then he caught hold of his wits and jerked his arm free of Ebana's grip. But not before he saw satisfaction flicker across his cousin's face.

Meren turned back to the casket and lifted its gabled lid into place. "I'm not concerned with the past. My concern is that of pharaoh—the harmony and balance of the Two Lands. And most of all my concern is finding and destroying those who would threaten pharaoh, the living son of the god."

Ebana smiled with his mouth, if not with the rest of his face, as he walked away from Meren to the door.

"And since I serve Amun, father of the king," Ebana said as he left, "our concerns are the same."

Meren stood staring at the empty doorway for a while before uttering a quiet curse.

"Do you think he did it?" Kysen asked.

"I don't know," Meren replied. "It's as he says. Countless numbers of people pass into the temple each day. By the gods, Rahotep was here when it happened. But I won't believe that the two deaths have nothing to do with each other. They worked together, master and underling. Unfortunately, the secrets of the temple are as hidden as the underworld."

Kysen's gaze dropped to the tips of his sandals. "Rahotep. Ah, yes, Rahotep."

Hearing a reluctance in Kysen's voice, Meren turned to stare at his son.

"About Rahotep. And Ebana. And Qenamun."

"I'm waiting."

Kysen cleared his throat and embarked upon an explanation of his adventures at the house of Unas, his near-encounter with the masonry, and the meeting at the market with the priests and Rahotep.

"Damnation and fires of the netherworld! Did I not warn you never to go alone when making inquiries like that? No, don't speak." Meren expelled a long breath while silently reciting a prayer to Toth in an effort to govern his temper. Kysen knew his error, and he shouldn't be scolded like a child. "You're saying that any of them could have tried to kill you—Ebana, Rahotep, Qenamun, or one of the others."

"Aye," Kysen said.

"Rahotep," Meren said quietly. "I'd forgotten how belligerent he was while he was away so long with Tanefer. But perhaps he really has gotten worse— offensively boastful unto madness."

"He's much more hot-bellied than he used to be," Kysen said.

"I can't believe these two deaths are unrelated," Meren said, "but neither can I believe that Rahotep would have reason to kill them."

"We don't know why either of them was killed."

Meren walked over to the body of the lector priest. "Not yet, but I'm going to find out."

They examined the workroom silently for a while before Meren picked up the casket and prepared to leave. Kysen took the box from him, forcing Meren to meet his gaze.

"What was going on when we came in?"

Meren glanced over Kysen's shoulder at the basket containing the cobras. It hadn't moved since Parenefer last touched it.

"I'm not sure, but you may have saved my life."

He smiled at Kysen's slack jaw. "Those cobras in the basket aren't the only ones we have to worry about."

Two days after Qenamun was killed, Meren's men had questioned dozens of priests and visitors to the House of Life. Meren and Kysen had dealt personally with those of higher rank. After that first day, Parenefer had left them to their tasks while he kept to the high priest's residence and other parts of the temple complex, well away from the Eyes and Ears of Pharaoh.

Meren was in his office between the house and the charioteers' barracks, listening to Kysen read a list of those who had been at the House of Life the day before Qenamun was killed. Qenamun had left the temple for the last time that day an hour before sunset.

"Everyone knew he left early on that day of the week in order to receive private commissions at his home," Kysen said. "If you wanted to tamper with his possessions, you would wait for that day."

"I hadn't expected our shard rumor to produce such evil results," Meren said. "An ugly death, even for Qenamun. And—and, if indeed the rumor precipitated this murder, I've failed to divine its significance."

"It would take a god to understand the significance of a few pieces of pottery," Kysen said.

Meren sighed, set aside one of Qenamun's dream books, and rose from his chair. Both of them had spent hours examining the shards, to no avail. He went to a box inlaid with ivory, took out his leather juggling balls, and set them in motion.

"A lector priest of Qenamun's reputed power is privy to many secrets. And from what Ebana said, he was the kind of man to use what he knew to gain power and create discord." Meren followed the course of the balls as they whirled in front of him. As their speed increased, so did the pace of his thoughts. "If he was as Ebana says, he could very well have been the one who tried to kill you, which might mean he rifled Unas's house, and might mean he was Unas's killer."

"But we've found no indications of any of that at his temple workroom or at his house," Kysen said.

Meren weaved back and forth, trying to keep the juggling balls in line with each other. "Nor at anyone else's house. I'm tempted to ask pharaoh for permission to investigate Rahotep."

"Gods," Kysen said. "What a storm of fury that would bring."

"And I have no real evidence to present to the king when I request permission to treat a half-royal prince like a criminal."

Kysen snorted. "You might as well ask to throw Parenefer in gaol."

"I see you understand the difficulty."

Kysen threaded his fingers through his hair and then ran his finger down a list of names on the papyrus he was holding. "I've marked off those who seem to have no connection with Qenamun, which leaves us with over thirty others who either knew him or worked with him and were at the temple the day before he was killed."

Meren began walking around the room, tossing the balls ahead of him.

"Ebana was right. The temple provided perfect concealment. Someone could have conveyed the cobras in a casket or bag, and it would appear like any other offering meant for the god. Still, it would have to be someone whom the priests wouldn't question if he appeared at the House of Life. Another priest, or a nobleman, or a priestess."

"Abu says he still hasn't found evidence of cobras being kept at anyone's house or at the temple," Kysen said.

"They have to have been kept somewhere."

Kysen got up and went to a table where Qenamun's cedar-and-ebony casket sat. Its contents lay spread over the table, except for the rush pens, which had been left in the bottom of the box. He lifted a weight that secured a stack of papyrus rolls and leafed through them.

"There are texts here for Prince Djoser, Rahotep, General Horemheb, and Ahiram."

"I know," Meren said. "I've read them, but they're only dream interpretations and calendars that set out each day according to their portents, either good or bad. I can see nothing that would provoke someone to murder. Everyone has calendars and dream interpretations. Horemheb consults five or six lector priests each year."

Meren's juggling slowed. He listened to the soft pat-pat of the leather against his hands.

"Horemheb. I've been thinking about Horemheb."

Kysen glanced up from the stack of papyri, but remained silent, waiting. Finally Meren's hand fumbled, and a ball dropped and rolled under the table. Meren caught the remaining balls, but stood staring at nothing.

"I was at Maya's, just before Tanefer came to tell me about Qenamun. You know Maya. He loves to listen to intimate problems, and he was trying to get me to tell him mine. When I wouldn't, he began to talk. And he said something about Horemheb—that he chaffed at the constraints put on him. That he's furious at how the army and empire had been neglected. It's rumored that he thinks Ay is too old to be vizier, and pharaoh's councillors too cautious."

"We know this," Kysen said.

Meren glanced at his son. "Now it appears that the whole court knows it, and the army. And what worries me more is that Maya said Horemheb thinks Egypt needs—if I remember well—a bold leader of prime years. Tanefer interrupted us, but I think he was going to say, a leader of prime years instead of a boy."

Meren and Kysen regarded each other in silence. Outside, the sounds of the barracks could be heard—horses whinnying, the harsh laughter of the charioteers, the slam of a door.

"What do you think?"

Meren stooped to pick up the ball he'd dropped and began to juggle again. "Such rumors grow and spread like reeds in a marsh. Most are distortions bearing no resemblance to the truth."

"But when the rumor concerns General Horemheb . . ."

"Then," said Meren as he tossed a ball high above his head, "then we must find out how great is the distortion, and what was the seed of truth from which this flower of rumor sprang."

"But Horemheb? He fought beside you, and he's defended the empire against its enemies for years."

"I know," Meren said, hearing his own voice snap with temper. He stopped juggling and tossed the balls into their box. "I know, Ky, but pharaohs cannot afford to trust anyone blindly, and it's my duty to see that every hint of risk is investigated."

Kysen went back to his chair and picked up a closed leather dispatch case. "Have you thought that Maya might be lying?"

"Of course," Meren said. "But Maya has nothing to gain because he has no greater ambition than to be what he is. I'm more inclined to think of him as a furrow through which water carries the silt of rumor and intelligence, all jumbled together without regard to legitimacy."

Meren pulled his chair nearer to Kysen's, sat down and began to rub his forehead. "Gods, these endless intrigues and quarrels will drive me into madness one day."

He heard one of the epithets Kysen had learned from his training as a charioteer and looked up quickly. Kysen was holding a dispatch bearing the seal of one of the commanders at the frontier forts between the delta and Palestine and Syria. He handed the report to Meren.

It detailed an increase in activity, traffic on the desert

roads, raids by new groups of bandits—former soldiers of the armies of the fallen Mitanni empire had wandered south and were now reaching the frontier. They, along with outlaw nomads, were raiding isolated villages as well as attacking travelers, especially merchant caravans. Egyptian troops had clashed with the Mitanni and routed and pursued them, but lost their trail in the desert. The commander was concerned because of the unusually large number of these bandits. Some groups almost constituted a small army.

Meren handed the dispatch back to Kysen, thrust himself out of his chair, and walked back and forth between it and the table. "Curse it. Very well. Find Abu and have him make copies of the report. Then send him to Horemheb and General Nakhtmin. He is to see them personally and alone. They will reinforce the border garrisons." Meren stopped beside Kysen's chair and glanced down. "I may have to go north myself. I don't like this talk of renegades at our borders, and I've a need to question a Hittite, if I can find one."

"You're going to the frontier alone?"

"I don't wish to be noticed and have my presence announced to the Hittite king or his allies among the Syrian princes."

"But you can't go without protection! If you're recognized—"

They turned at the same time as a knock interrupted.

"Enter," Meren said.

Abu came in, only to glance over his shoulder in surprise as Tanefer sailed into the room after him. Abu gave Meren a startled look, but Meren shook his head.

"Your man told me to wait, but you know how I hate that," Tanefer said as he dropped into Meren's chair and glanced at the papers Kysen had left in his own.

Kysen stooped and picked them up, and Tanefer grinned at him.

"Fear not, young one. I'm not a spy. I'm a simple soldier, good at killing, but not skilled at intrigue and deceit."

"Tanefer," Kysen said as he handed the papers to Abu, "you're a walking scandal."

"An accomplishment at which I labor ceaselessly."

"You haven't come to give me news of another murder, have you?" Meren asked.

"No, brother of my heart. Ay asked me to try to keep the king distracted. The divine one is anxious to be off on his first skirmish, but the viceroy of Kush is due any day with a fleet laden with tribute, and the king must be here for the reception ceremony."

Tanefer rose and slapped Meren on the back. "So I have organized a hippo hunt. There's a rogue male preying just south of the city. Killed three fishermen today. So we're all to hunt tomorrow morning. The king commands your presence, both of you."

"I have much to do," Meren said.

Tanefer nodded. "Ah, the lector priest. Have you found out who killed him?"

"No."

Kysen threw up his hands. "It seems as if the whole city visited the temple of Amun on the day those cobras were put into Qenamun's casket."

"The answer may be simple," Tanefer said. "Was Qenamun bedding another priest's wife? Did he stand in the way of another's advancement or threaten a superior?"

"No doubt he did all of those things," Meren said.

Tanefer wandered over to the table bearing Qenamun's documents and began to peruse them.

Meren quickly walked to the door and swept his arm in the direction of the house. "Will you take the evening meal with us?"

Tanefer looked up, then preceded Meren outside.

"You're as secretive as a virgin with her first lover, Meren."

"And you're too curious for a simple soldier." As Tanefer walked back toward the house, Meren whispered to Kysen. "Give Abu his instructions and then follow."

Meren walked beside Tanefer on the path that led from his office, between the servant's quarters and through a small gate in the wall surrounding the reflection pool and pleasure garden.

Tanefer paused beside the pool to gaze at a blue lotus floating in a nest of deep green leaves. The fiery solar barque of Ra had passed its peak in the sky and was chasing the western horizon. Meren thought of these moments just before dusk as the golden time of day, because the sun's rays turned the air and water to gold. Tanefer knelt suddenly and reached out to touch the petals of the blue lotus.

"I come from a line of warriors, Meren."

"The Mitanni have always been great fighters."

"Unfortunately, my uncle and his lineage never learned when to stop and negotiate. That's why he lost his throne."

Tanefer dipped his hand in the water and looked up at Meren. His eyes held the sadness Meren had seen when he first returned home from Syria.

"The empire is crumbling. A rival lineage seeks the favor of the Hittite king Suppiluliumas, and now Egypt will soon feel the edge of the barbarian blade."

"Suppiluliumas isn't a fool," Meren said. "He won't attack Egypt directly yet."

Tanefer got up and wiped his hand on his kilt. "No, thank the gods. Egypt will be spared, and the Nile won't turn red with blood as did the Euphrates." He gave Meren a half smile. "But how long do we have?"

"It's not like you to be so low of spirit."

Gazing across the water, Tanefer shook his head. "I tried to make Ay understand, but he won't listen. You know the Hittites, Meren. You know their unparalleled appetite for carnage. How long can we sit in our palaces and squabble like spoiled children?" He sighed. "It's Ay's fault, you know, for allowing pharaoh and his advisers to cavil and pick at trifles while ignoring the rest of the world."

"You think Ay is too much like Akhenaten."

With one of his loose, easy movements, Tanefer plucked a lotus flower and twirled it in his fingers. "I think we've let whole cities perish in our blindness while we've grown fat and moribund on the fruits of the Nile."

"I'm not blind," Meren said.

Tanefer gave him a sad smile. "No—no, you're not." He tossed the lotus to Meren and laughed in an abrupt change of mood. "Come, old friend, have you not promised to feed me? Give me some wine, and I may be able to help you decipher this puzzle of the murder of the magician priest."

12

▽

Before dawn the next morning, Kysen sat beside the royal oarsman in the king's boat, shivering in the cool dampness of a marsh. Two priests had been murdered, but neither he nor Meren could neglect attendance at the hippo hunt arranged for the king by Tanefer. Pharaoh was whispering excitedly with the chief of the royal hunt, while all around them, hidden in the tall reeds and papyrus plants, noblemen and hunters steadied their skiffs. The boats were arranged on either side of a break in the reeds at the riverbank that marked the place where hippos came ashore.

The king's craft was wooden, larger and much more ornate than the skiffs, but Kysen wished he was in the one that held his father and Tanefer. The skiffs were far more maneuverable and would close in first on their quarry, but much less safe. The king would only be allowed to approach once the hippo had taken a few harpoons.

In truth, Kysen had never accustomed himself to being pharaoh's companion. He'd been born the son of a common artisan, and hunting with a living god was not something he did as easily as his father.

He watched Ahiram pole his float by and take up a position on the opposite side of the marsh from Meren and Tanefer. On shore a hunter signaled to Tanefer, and word was passed from boat to boat. The man next to Kysen began to whisper.

"Divine one, there's a group of three headed this way. They think the rogue follows them."

Quiet settled over the hunters as they waited. Hippos came ashore at night to do their grazing and caused great damage to crops in their wanderings. Kysen gazed over the black water and could barely make out the lighter shadows that indicated the kilts of Meren and Tanefer. They had dropped to a crouch, the long shafts of their weapons thrusting out over the edge of their skiff.

He glanced at the king, a slight shadow in a gold-and-lapis broad collar, but he couldn't make out the boy's expression. Tanefer had voiced the hope that this hunt would relieve the king's strain. Kysen doubted it would prove more than a temporary respite. The court still seethed with contention between those who advocated war and those who favored diplomacy. He'd seen the cost of this division in his father's face.

Meren hated war. He hated violence. When Kysen was much younger, he hadn't understood how a man so skilled with dagger, lance, and bow could detest their use except for the hunt. Then he'd grown old enough to assist Meren in his capacity as one of the Eyes and Ears of Pharaoh.

Now, finally, he understood that Meren commanded warriors in order to prevent violence. In the last couple of years Kysen, too, had had his fill of blood. There was no glamour in death, only waste. And it was this knowledge that separated Meren and Kysen from many men at court.

Meren was disturbed. Kysen could sense this, although he'd refrained from questioning his father. When Meren grew distant and sat staring at nothing while he rubbed the brand on his wrist, he was deeply troubled. He knew his father refused to believe that Unas's and Qenamun's deaths were unrelated. He also knew that Meren's confrontation with the high priest of Amun threatened to cause an open breach between the temple and the court.

Parenefer had complained to the vizier Ay and to the king. Ay was furious with Meren for causing more trouble than was already brewing at court. The king, always touchy when his authority was questioned by Parenefer, had insulted the high priest. And he refused to placate the old man. Now courtiers were jostling each other in their attempts to align themselves with whoever they thought would be the winner.

Meanwhile, Tanefer continued to press for a military campaign of monumental proportions. He advocated marching across Palestine and as far north as the upper reaches of the Euphrates to the homeland of Mitanni. Horemheb partially agreed.

What surprised Kysen was that Parenefer also agreed with them and threw his influence behind a new campaign. Meren said that the old jackal had caught the scent of plunder—the slaves, the rich estates, the booty that would flow into the coffers of Amun from conquered territories. Kysen had thought of another reason as well. If there was war, pharaoh would leave Egypt, and so would Meren.

Shifting his weight, Kysen settled into a more comfortable position. The sky was growing light, and still the hippos hadn't reached the bank. Soon the hunters would lose the cover of darkness. Tanefer must have been thinking the same thing, because he signaled across the water to Ahiram. The two craft bearing his father, Tanefer, and Ahiram skimmed out from the reeds and toward each other.

As the gap between the skiffs closed, the water beneath the king's boat churned. From shore he heard a hollow, buzzing noise that sounded like a laugh. Hippos. Kysen glanced over his shoulder, but he saw nothing that could have caused the shifting beneath him. He looked over the expanse of water toward Meren, who was saying something to Ahiram.

Without warning the Nile took solid form. The black waters churned, and a mudlike mountain with eyes rose up and growled. Kysen shouted an alarm. A hippo's yawning jaws gaped open to reveal pale, fleshy vastness and tusks as long as a child's arm. The maw snapped the prow of Ahiram's skiff in two.

Ahiram soared into the air and then dropped into the water. He sank, only to bob to the surface in front of the animal. Over his head, the mouth opened again.

At that moment, Meren hurled his harpoon. It jabbed into the hippo's shoulder, but not before the creature snapped at Ahiram, who cried out as a tusk gashed his arm. Meanwhile, everyone punted rapidly toward the fray. Kysen had snatched a pole and joined the royal sailors in stabbing deep into the riverbed, aiming the king's boat at Meren's.

Wounded and maddened, the hippo sank beneath the water again, only to hurtle to the surface once more, slamming Ahiram with its body. The violence of the wave it caused hurled Meren's skiff away from the fight and into another boat. The crash sent Meren plummeting into the waters. Kysen shouted at Tanefer, but the prince was already diving after his friend.

The king's boat gained on a skiff. Kysen recognized Horemheb and Maya, called to them, and poled himself down onto their craft. They skidded toward Meren, who had gone underwater and hadn't reappeared. As he strained to see in the dim light, he saw Meren and Tanefer break the surface near Ahiram, who was bleeding and trailing a useless arm in the water.

Kysen felt a stab of fear when the blackish gray bulk

of the hippo twisted and rammed downward under the water. Suddenly, tiny protruding eyes and flared nostrils appeared just above the water in front of the three men. Skiffs crashed into the hippo's body, but the animal ignored them. Its head rose out of the water. Those powerful jaws opened so wide a man could have fallen in and vanished. Kysen cried out again as a jagged tusk poised over Meren.

Ahiram flailed and thrashed with his good arm, but couldn't move quickly enough. The jaws began to descend even as Kysen grabbed Maya's harpoon and hurled it. The weapon hit the animal's neck but failed to sink into the thick flesh.

Then Meren lunged upward and grabbed for his harpoon, which still protruded from the hippo's shoulder. Tanefer cried out and threw himself at Meren. As he did so, his feet struck out and hit Ahiram, causing him to slide farther into the path of the raging animal. Tanefer collided with Meren, and his weight plunged them beneath the surface.

At the same time, the hippo snapped at Ahiram, and Kysen's skiff rammed into it. Harpoons and spears flew from the other skiffs as well. The hippo let out a bellow that sounded like a combination of a woman's scream and the trumpet of an elephant. With a last rumbling squeal, the creature dove under the boats and swam rapidly for the open river. Kysen shouted his father's name and searched among the litter of broken skiffs and floating weapons.

A dark head bobbed up out of the water; a second followed. Kysen lowered himself over the side as Horemheb and Maya slid the skiff in the swimmers' direction. He reached Meren, who was out of breath and shaking from exhaustion. Together Kysen and Tanefer managed to shove him up and aboard the skiff. Maya and Horemheb lifted Ahiram onto their skiff, where he lay cursing and fighting all efforts to attend him.

The king's boat drew alongside the skiff, and Tutankhamun ordered Tanefer, Meren, and Kysen to be brought aboard. Kysen scrambled up the side of the boat and dropped onto the deck beside his father. Meren lifted his head, chest heaving, and gave Kysen a wry smile.

"Outsmarted by a great, floating ball of lard."

Kysen said nothing, but his gaze scoured over Meren in unsmiling scrutiny.

"I fare well, Ky. Just a few bruised ribs."

Letting out the breath he'd been holding, Kysen refrained from any expression of relief. The king, who had been kneeling beside Tanefer, rose and approached them.

"What a fight," he said. "The cursed creature was in the water all the time. Tanefer says the hunters must have mistaken another male for the rogue."

Tanefer joined them, shoving wet hair back from his brow. "What a mischance."

"Divine one," Meren said. "What of Ahiram?"

The king stepped aside so that they could see Maya pressing a wad of cloth to Ahiram's arm. "They're taking him ashore to a physician, but he's furious."

"Aiieee!" Ahiram jerked his arm from Maya's grasp. "You're worse than the hippo." In the dim light, the whites of his eyes gleamed as he stood up and snarled. "I've no intention of becoming fodder for hippos and crocodiles, me." He gasped, clutched his arm, and sank to his knees, still glaring at them. "No creature, beast or man, catches me unaware and lives. Do you hear?"

The skiff continued on its way to shore, Ahiram glaring at the king's boat until the two craft passed out of viewing range. Around them nobles were retrieving weapons and preparing to sail back to the city as well.

"Why is he so furious?" the king asked.

Tanefer chuckled as he squeezed water from his short kilt. "You know Ahiram, majesty. Always taking offense where none is offered. He's ashamed at the way the hippo bested him, and fears that we're laughing at him."

"But it wasn't his fault," the king said. "The rogue outwitted us all."

Meren sighed and grimaced as he got up from the deck with Kysen's assistance. "Thy majesty is possessed of logic and a sense of balance that Prince Ahiram has always lacked."

Tutankhamun frowned as he glanced over the drenched forms of his councillors. "What foolishness. It was but the luck of the hunt. I shall tell Ahiram so when he comes for guard duty tomorrow. If he's well enough to stand his watch."

"He'd rather stand guard than remain home within reach of a physician," Kysen said.

Ahiram's cowardice in regard to medical treatment was well known. The king smirked, then lost the battle to refrain from laughing. A little contrite, Kysen couldn't help but smile. Meren, however, seemed to feel no guilt about laughing at his absent friend, nor did Tanefer. As the sun blazed into radiance over the eastern desert, the sound of merriment floated over the water and lapped gently at the banks of the river.

The morning after the hippo hunt, Meren lay among the cushions of a couch set beneath the low-spreading branches of a fig tree in his orchard. His physician had wrapped bandages around his ribs so tightly he had a difficult time breathing. And they itched.

He scratched beneath the linen while Kysen read the reports on the inquiry into Qenamun's death that had come while they'd been in attendance upon the king.

"Qenamun's wife and five children are visiting her parents on their farm near Edfu," Kysen said as he paced in the shade of an incense tree. "The only person at his house except for servants is his aged mother, who's sick with grief."

"And those clients Qenamun went home early to meet?" Meren asked.

"One was Princess Hathor, who worries about being barren, and another is an overseer of royal surveyors, who suffers from swollen joints. Both have sought the aid of numerous physicians and priests beside Qenamun."

Meren maneuvered himself to a sitting position, waving Kysen away when he would have helped. "I'm only sore, Ky, not dying. Ah, here's Abu. I told him I wanted to review that report listing those who were at the temple and who also carried objects in which cobras could be hidden. What have you found, Abu?"

The aide sat down on a mat before Meren's couch and crossed his legs so that his kilt stretched out as flat as a table. On this surface he spread a roll of papyrus.

"A wealthy farmer from Abydos stopped at the House of Life before presenting a casket full of offerings at the sanctuary. He wanted to visit with his son, a scholar priest training under Qenamun." Abu pressed his palms down on the paper to hold it flat. "Three relief painters were in and out of there all day carrying boxes and baskets of brushes, plaster, paint, other tools."

Abu paused and glanced up at Meren. "Both Prince Rahotep and Prince Ahiram visited Qenamun. To talk about dream interpretations. And their servants carried boxes containing offerings. Of course, no one looked in the boxes."

"Of course," Meren said as he got up and lifted his

face to the breeze that had whipped up abruptly. "Now go on and say it, Abu."

Kysen looked up from his own reports. "Say what?"

Abu released the papyrus roll and began gathering it into a tight cylinder. He said nothing.

"There are at least two more names on that list," Meren said. He paused and glanced at his son. "One of them is Ebana, who brought numerous documents to the House of Life late in the day before Qenamun was killed—in great leather document cases. And he was busy in one of the record chambers until after dark."

Meren carefully spread his arms wide in a stretch as Kysen appeared to think over the implications of this news. He smiled at his son.

"I knew you'd be interested. Can you guess the other name?"

"Parenefer," Kysen said at once.

"Very good."

"You thought I wouldn't consider a high priest?"

"The first prophet of the king of the gods," Meren said. "I wouldn't blame you for failing to consider him."

"Oh, I'd consider him, but what good will it do?"

Meren poured water into a cup from a jar suspended from the fig tree and drank. "You're right, Ky. Parenefer lives within the temple complex. He could have had someone put those cobras in Qenamun's casket. But why?"

"That's the difficulty with both deaths," Kysen said. "There seems to be no reason for either."

"Aye," Meren said, "and it seems that the only way to make progress is by force." He sat down on the couch again and gave Abu and Kysen a pained grin. "Do either of you look forward to attempting to put priests to the cane and whip?"

They lapsed into silence at the suggestion, for no one

had ever done such a thing. Priests disciplined their own. And if the high priest or other high functionaries of the temple were involved, the only power that could bring them to account was that of pharaoh.

"There is one other," Abu said as he tied his papyrus roll. "Prince Tanefer was there on that day, but he carried nothing and came to visit your cousin, lord."

"Curse it," Meren said. "I should have asked who did not go to the temple. The list would have been shorter." He rubbed his chin. "I'm going to have to ask pharaoh for a special commission that enables me to question the princes and the priests of high rank." Such a commission would mean that he could force Parenefer, Ebana, and Rahotep to answer questions they didn't want to answer.

"I have another message, lord." Abu rose. "Cook waylaid me on my way here and said to tell you if you don't break your fast now, she's going to throw her spiced roast ducks in the river."

Meren jumped up from the couch and headed for the house with Kysen and Abu close behind. "By my ka, I spend my life rushing to and fro trying to please everyone—visiting royal statues, attending water tournaments, archery practice, dinners, murders at temples, hippo hunts, and now my cook commands my presence at my own table."

Tables awaited them on the loggia that stretched along the back side of the house. Meren had just finished half a duck when a royal guard arrived with a summons from pharaoh. He met Kysen's gaze.

"Don't look so amused," Meren said, "or I'll take you with me."

"Someone has to remain here to supervise the Qenamun and Unas inquiries."

"Very well. But if the king has found some bandits to hunt, I'm sending for you. I'm not riding into the desert after criminals in the heat of the year without sharing the experience with you. Come along, Abu."

His aide insisted upon an escort, so Meren arrived at the palace with Abu, four other charioteers, and several personal servants, as befitted a man of great consequence. From the moment he neared the royal residence, he noted the presence of more guards than usual.

A troop of charioteers raced by him as his chariot clattered down the long, wide avenue leading up to the palace walls. Growing more and more uneasy, Meren snapped his whip above the heads of his thoroughbreds. They galloped between arching palm trees and swung the chariot around in front of a line of royal guards.

Leaving his men and servants before the palace gates, he sought out the king in the chamber next to the privy apartments where Tutankhamun conducted many of his day-to-day government affairs. Rahotep stood outside the room talking to the chief of the city police and an officer of archers who served under Prince Tanefer. They stopped talking as Meren entered the king's office and stared at him.

Inside, Tanefer was gazing out at the city from a balcony. A great map of the delta was spread out on a table. Maya and Ay were pointing out survey lines to the king when Meren entered and bowed.

"Ah, Meren." The king left the map, motioned for the men to follow, and joined Tanefer on the balcony. "Tell him," he said to Tanefer.

"Ahiram failed to come to guard duty at the palace this morn," Tanefer said.

So this was the reason for the additional guards. He began to feel stabs of apprehension. Raising a brow, he noted the lack of expression on Tanefer's face. "His wound has festered perhaps?"

"He's not at home," Tanefer said.

The king rushed on. "He's not anywhere in the city.

Tanefer searched and found that he sailed north before dawn."

Meren tried to read Tanefer's expression, but his friend had resumed his perusal of the flat rooftops of the city with his back to the room. Princes did not flee the capital without reason.

"Damnation, Meren," said the king.

"Yes, majesty."

"What has he done that he runs away in fear?" the king asked.

"Aye, majesty," Meren said. "This is a question that must be answered."

Tanefer looked at Meren at last, his face still blank. "I've asked to be allowed to pursue Ahiram, but the divine one's word was to send for you."

The king began to pace back and forth on the balcony and bang his fist into his thigh. "He's done something, and he fears to remain in my presence. Which means I can't trust his men."

"Thy majesty speaks well," Meren said. "You've dismissed them?"

The king nodded. "I've called Tanefer's men and my whole war band to duty. You know what I want, Meren."

"Aye, majesty," Meren said, even as he turned to leave. "I will try to capture him alive."

Suddenly, Tanefer knelt before the king. "Please, divine one, allow me to go with Meren. I know Ahiram well, and might be able to persuade him to surrender."

The king met Meren's gaze over Tanefer's head. "No. There's too much strife here at court, and I need men here I can trust. This act of recklessness requires Meren's particular skill. Indeed, I'd be willing to wager some secret machination of his may have caused Ahiram to run. Am I right?"

Meren wasn't about to admit how confused he really

was, so he merely bowed to the king. "Thy majesty's perception is divine, as always."

"Farewell, Meren. Next time, before you scare one of my guards into fleeing, you might consider telling my majesty about it."

13

▽

Kysen strode around Ahiram's bedchamber while Meren questioned the only servant left behind by the prince, a porter. Their men were searching other parts of the house. Ahiram's family, a wife, her three small sons, and a daughter, had been sent to the country several days ago, while the prince remained in Thebes. The trip had been sudden, and one for which his wife had been unprepared. Ahiram had insisted that most of the servants go as well. In less than a week, Ahiram had emptied his house of nearly anyone who might have observed his activities.

This knowledge had roused Meren's suspicions to even greater heights, so much so that he'd delayed his departure. There wasn't much time before he would have to sail. Tanefer had questioned the man earlier, but Meren was doing it again. As he walked across a finely woven mat, Kysen watched the man shake his head, bow, and leave. Tanefer hadn't mentioned those abrupt departures, but then, Tanefer wasn't accustomed to making inquiries for pharaoh.

Ahiram's house wasn't as large as Meren's, but it was richly furnished. Kysen paused by the bed of polished cedar. Its lion's-paw legs and footboard were trimmed with gold. The chamber itself bore a frieze of lotus flowers around the top of the walls and along the bottom as well. Clothing chests lay open, their contents strewn over the floor, chairs, and bed. Ahiram had packed and left so hastily there had been no time for his servants to put the house in order.

A box had been overturned near a recess in the wall opposite the bed. Within the recess sat a small statue of the foreign goddess Ishtar. Someone had picked up the belts, bracelets, and other contents of the box and set them in the recess and in the lid of the box.

Kysen picked up a belt of gold and turquoise, then replaced it in the niche near the statue, alongside a reed pen holder shaped like a papyrus-bundle column. His hand strayed to a bracelet, a wide, hinged band of gold upon which had been applied a decoration in the form of a stylized boat. Within the boat rested the round, blue disk of the moon, which sailed across the sky each night. Meren interrupted his inspection by dismissing the porter and joining him.

"The porter knows little, since his post offers him no intimacy with his master," Meren said as he picked up the moon bracelet. "He says Ahiram sent his family away before Qenamun was murdered. Only three servants were left in the house, including the porter.

"After the royal physician tended to him yesterday morning he came home much disturbed. What interests me is that he ordered the house guarded the moment he came home. All three servants were set to keeping watch, although he didn't say what they were supposed to guard against."

"He was frightened," Kysen said.

"From the moment he came home, and I can't divine a reason for it." Meren lay the moon bracelet aside and propped his back against the wall beside the shrine. "You've found nothing?"

"It's as Tanefer says. He left hurriedly, without putting the house in order. Food is still in the kitchen, although all of it has been put away." Kysen swept his arm around. "And if there was ever anything to find here, he took it with him. There aren't any papers."

Meren's gaze darted around the chamber, taking in the discarded clothing and other personal possessions. Disorder, but a disorder that arose from haste rather than violence. He rubbed his chin and gave Kysen a sideways glance.

"I asked the porter if he'd noticed any cobras about the house."

"Well?"

"No," Meren said. He folded his arms and studied the frieze of lotus flowers. "It's just that I can think of no other happening of import which might cause Ahiram to flee, and he was acquainted with Qenamun."

"If you'd caught a bunch of snakes, where would you keep them and how?" Kysen asked.

"I'd keep them in baskets somewhere isolated," Meren said. "But not for long. They'd be hard to conceal because they would need feeding . . . rodents."

"And in a prince's house, there are few places of concealment because of the number of servants."

Meren shoved away from the wall and began walking toward the chamber door, with Kysen close behind him. "Aye, so if I wished to conceal my collection of cobras, I would want to find a deserted place, something hard to find in a city like Thebes. Therefore I'd catch them quickly and get rid of them quickly. And the need for haste would mean I would have to find a convenient nearby hiding place."

"One of the storage rooms," Kysen said as his father led him to the kitchen.

Abu and another charioteer joined them. Meren walked across the kitchen to a stairwell that led down into darkness. Kysen found a lamp and preceded his father and the others downstairs. Below they found the usual evidence of household activities—the making of bread dough, weaving, and storage of oils, wine, and spices.

"No cobras," Kysen said.

Abu whirled around to face him. "Cobras!"

He and his assistant were gazing at him, brows lifted to their hairlines. With caution, Abu began opening any jars that weren't sealed, as did the other charioteer. Meren walked past a mortar and pestle sitting on the floor along with a stack of trays and pottery cups, rounded a group of oil jars, and stopped. He signaled for Kysen to join him, and they stood looking at seven wicker boxes, a row of three stacked on top of a row of four against one wall. Meren drew closer, reached out, and shook one of the top boxes.

"I think it's empty."

"I hope you're right," Kysen said.

"I will open it, lord." Abu's tone as he stepped between them and the boxes bore no hint that he was asking permission. The second charioteer drew his dagger. Abu lifted the lid of the box, taking care that it opened away from his body. He flipped the box on its side and jumped back at the same time. Nothing. He shook the next box. Something rattled, but it sounded like pottery. Inspection revealed pieces of a broken tray.

Abu glanced at Meren and Kysen, wet his lips, and proceeded with his examination. The rest of the boxes were empty except for clumps of dried rushes which could have been used for packing—or nesting.

"Damnation," Meren said. "And I must sail soon."

"We'll continue here," Kysen said as he followed his father upstairs.

Meren was on his way out of the reception hall when he stopped abruptly, almost causing Kysen to run into him.

"Wait." He glanced back into the main hall. "Reia."

The charioteer left the hall to join them. "Yes, lord."

"You looked at the refuse pit behind the house?"

"Aye, lord."

"Anything unusual?"

"No, lord. Only the usual—offal, wasted food, vermin."

"Vermin?" Kysen asked, looking at his father.

"Aye, lord. It looks as if the prince's cats have been busy. Someone dumped a bag full of dead mice into the pit."

Kysen exchanged glances with Meren. He turned and beckoned to Reia.

"I'll attend to it," he said to Meren. "Come, Reia, we're going to look at these mice again."

Meren stood at the bow of the fastest river craft in his fleet, *Wings of Horus*, and lifted his face to the north breeze. Nearby, the pilot searched the lapis-blue waters of the Nile for the next sandbar while thirty oarsmen rowed in time to a chant. Long, low, and sleek, the ship was one of the largest private vessels on the Nile. Its hull was painted black, the railing red and gold, and every other boat on the river gave way before its dark menace, skiffs and barges alike scattering like cattle before a leopard.

Meren had ordered the ship manned with a double crew. He had to catch Ahiram, even if it meant risking sailing at night. Behind them came supply vessels bearing food, weapons, chariots, and horses.

His hands almost twitched with impatience. He'd stirred a scorpion's nest at court and at the temple of Amun because of a dead priest, and the result had been a second murder and the flight of a prince. Until he'd seen those baskets and found out about the mice, he hadn't been certain all three events were connected. He'd thought he'd become too suspicious from all his years at court. Now, however . . .

He glanced back at the stern, where a helmsman manned the giant rudder oars attached to tillers. To port and starboard he could hear the stocks of rowing oars creak against the ropes that held them lashed in place and the sound of oar blades cutting the water. Over the rhythmic chant of the oarsmen blared the notes of trumpets blown by three sailors in warning to other craft.

He hadn't had time to change from his court regalia after leaving Ahiram's house, and the sun felt as if it were beginning to melt the gold bands at his wrists. Abu and his officers had orders to watch for Ahiram's yacht. Charioteers lined the railing and searched each landing, every small islet and marsh, for the prince's distinctive red-and-yellow craft.

Because of the house search, Meren hadn't gotten under way until several hours after he'd left the king, and now the sun had long since passed its apex. Village after village had receded in their wake, nestled in the green of vegetation. In the distance the bare mountains and cliffs of the desert loomed, ready to encroach on the slim ribbon of blue that was the Nile.

Meren had ordered the ship slowed as it passed Gebtu, a town that stood at the crossroads of the river and one of the routes that crossed the eastern desert to the Red Sea coast. This road connected with trails to the gold and copper mines and stone quarries that lay along its path. If he himself were running away, he might try to reach one of the Red Sea ports rather than take the obvious route to the delta and the great sea. But there had been no red-and-yellow yacht in sight.

Now *Wings of Horus* sped north toward the town of Iunet, the site of one of the great temples dedicated to Hathor, goddess of love, music, dancing, and pleasure. If the chase went farther, he would pass his own country home without being able to stop to see his daughters. Curse Ahiram.

Why? Why would he kill the lector priest? And what of the pure one? Only a shadow of suspicion linked Unas with Qenamun and Ahiram. Meren had admitted this to himself. He had no knowledge that the three had ever conversed together, although Qenamun and Ahiram had known each other.

Ahiram had been touchy and on edge lately; this Meren had noticed. But then, who was not, with the controversy going on at court? Meren hadn't given any sign that he suspected Ahiram of murder, so why had the prince lost his courage? Something frightening had to have happened to make Ahiram run away. Something more than just an accident at a hippo hunt.

Meren was beginning to suspect that one of the priests at the House of Life might have discovered Ahiram's guilt and threatened him. After all, Ebana had been present at Qenamun's death. He'd been at the House of Life at the same time as Ahiram on the evening the cobras must have been put in Qenamun's casket. All Meren could do was pray to the gods that he caught Ahiram alive to answer his questions.

Meren walked back to the deckhouse that sat in the middle of the ship. Inside the cabin he went to his quarters, where his body servant relieved him of his court raiment. He lifted the long, hot wig off his head and thrust a hand through thick locks cut short in the manner of most warriors. He washed, then donned a simple kilt.

When his servant would have crowned him with another heavy wig and bracelets, he refused them in favor of a gold-and-malachite headband. He wasn't going to chase after an experienced soldier in the hampering garb of a courtier. He went outside to stand between the two slender columns that supported the awning before the deckhouse. A cook named Thay, who had been with

Meren since he was a youth, rose from his kneeling position before a brazier and thrust a plate of beef at him.

"The lord has not eaten all day."

Meren took the plate, wishing he weren't surrounded by people who felt it their duty to supervise his habits. Thay clapped his hands, and a boy appeared from the deckhouse bearing a chair. The lad set the chair down beside a table bearing a flagon and a goblet. Then he stood beside it.

The boy watched Meren. The cook watched him. Meren sighed and went to the chair. He glared at Thay and took a huge bite of beef, chewing with resentment. The cook nodded his satisfaction, retrieved bread from a basket, and thrust it at Meren.

While he ate, he tried to think of a reason Ahiram would want Qenamun dead. They'd only been acquaintances, as far as he knew. How could Qenamun have been a danger to a royal prince? He didn't know enough yet to answer that question. Meren had almost finished his meal when a cry went up from the bow. Gulping down the last of his wine, Meren thrust the goblet at the boy and strode across the deck toward Abu and several charioteers.

"Lord, look!" Abu pointed at a yellow-and-red yacht pulling away from the quay on the east bank.

Meren shouted at the pilot, who in turn yelled his orders to the oar master. He felt a surge as oars dug deep into the water and the speed of the strokes doubled. The helmsman swung the rudder oars. *Wings of Horus* veered around a cumbersome barge loaded with limestone blocks, then cut around a sandbar and directly into the path of the yacht. Behind them Meren's supply boats glided into place, blocking their quarry completely.

In a short time a plank dropped between the *Wings of Horus* and the yacht. Meren and several of his men

boarded the smaller craft, only to find a confused and
frightened ship's master and crew. Another, smaller boat
belonging to Ahiram had sailed earlier with servants
and slaves. Ahiram had disembarked not long ago on
the east bank. The ship's master had been ordered to
sail north, to the delta, to a small estate owned by a
friend of Ahiram.

Leaving those on the supply ship behind to deal with
the yacht, Meren went ashore with Abu, sending forth
his men to scour the quay. A short time later one came
back, saying Ahiram had set out on the desert road with
a band of men, all in chariots. Meren waited with impatience as his own chariot and horses were unloaded. He
gazed across the river to the west. The sun was dying,
its glare turning from almost white to a deep gold as it
sank. They would never catch Ahiram before nightfall.

The moment his groom finished harnessing his thoroughbreds, Meren stepped into his chariot. Abu shoved
an arrow case into the side compartment and handed
Meren his dagger. While Abu gathered the reins, Meren
checked his lances and scimitar. Then he glanced over
his shoulder at the fourteen chariots ranged in a double
column behind him and shouted the order to move out.

They launched into a trot followed by a full gallop. The docks vanished behind them; one after the
other, groups of travelers dashed out of their path. A
scout on horseback guided the company around great
caravans slowly moving east toward remote mines and
quarries and those headed west with foreign cargo.

Meren gripped the side of the chariot and braced his
legs as the vehicle jounced over ruts and stones. Dust
and grit flew in his face, but his gaze swept back and
forth across the horizon as they scaled barren hills and
raced across the rocky surface of the desert. Soon all
evidence of travelers vanished.

There was still no sign of Ahiram, and the sun was

quickly disappearing behind them. If it hadn't been for the speed of *Wings of Horus*, he would never have closed the distance between them as much as he had. Now he had to trust in the superiority of his horses. His constant training with them would show in their stamina and speed. The question was, did Ahiram have better animals?

The outrider slowed. He suddenly pointed, cried out, and swerved off the road to the north. Jumping off his horse, he bent over something in the desert floor. Light was growing dim as Meren's chariot pulled alongside the outrider.

"Lord, a group of chariots left the road here."

Meren examined the shallow marks made in the creamy dust. A group of at least seven chariots, not a caravan of pack animals and drivers on foot—Ahiram. The tracks had to be fresh, or the wind would have obliterated them. No one left the road and headed into the desert at night unless forced. Had Ahiram lost his wits, or had his courage failed? He might have seen bandits coming at him. Or was he meeting someone?

"Follow the tracks," Meren ordered.

He jumped into his chariot again, and Abu slapped the reins on the backs of their team. To either side of them, his men spread out. Whips cracking, they headed away from the Red Sea road.

If they didn't find Ahiram soon, they would have to stop for fear of losing his trail in darkness. They were going at a trot now. Meren was about to call a halt when a sound floated to him on the night breeze. He knew that sound, that high-pitched, wordless blare— part scream, part *ching* of metal against metal—the sound of distant battle.

He glanced at Abu, then turned and shouted an order, sweeping his arm out, over his head and in the direction of the sound. A war cry went up from the charioteers, and the company burst into a gallop that took them over the crest of a hill. Halfway between the hill and the horizon he spotted the skirmish.

A group of men crouched behind overturned chariots and dead horses fought off what appeared to be bandits. As Meren and his company sped toward them, the attackers broke off. Some clambered into abandoned chariots, while a few vaulted onto the backs of horses that had escaped harness and fought the animals until they launched into a gallop. Others waited long enough to release a volley of arrows.

Meren reached over the side of the chariot for his shield, shouting a warning. He heard the angry buzz of arrows. Hefting his shield so that it covered Abu and himself, he gripped the chariot with his free arm.

Three missiles hit the shield before he risked a look. The attackers had broken off and were retreating. Around him he saw charioteers releasing a return volley at those still within range, while their drivers aimed their chariots at the enemy. With the ease of years, he grabbed his own bow, strung it, and let off an arrow.

Like all charioteers, he'd been trained to fire while being rattled by a charging chariot. He released quickly, hearing the flat, thwacking sound of the bow. The arrow shot up in a low arc and stabbed into the chest of a bandit who had lingered too long. Meren put the bow back in its case and grabbed his scimitar, but by the time they arrived at the scene, the last of the robbers had vanished.

Meren bolted from his chariot before it stopped. No one was left standing, so he signaled to his men to pursue the bandits. Two chariots remained behind. With Abu at his side, Meren walked from body to body. Most of the victims seemed to be Ahiram's guards.

There was one unarmed man, a servant by the roughness of his dress, no doubt one of those Ahiram's porter had mentioned. Meren walked by the servant's body. He pointed to a wounded horse. One of the charioteers drew a short sword.

Meren turned away from the sight, only to come upon the cloaked body of a bandit. He was about to pass it by when his thoroughness made him stoop and pull the cloak. The body rolled over; the edges of the cloak fell back.

The bandit had died of an arrow in his neck. He wore his hair in plaits bound by leather thongs, and, unlike an Egyptian, he had a beard that had been twisted into complex, curling ringlets. But what disturbed Meren was his body armor, a shift of bronze scales. He knelt and studied the short sword that had fallen beside the man's hip. Then he lifted the bandit's right arm. The right wrist was thicker than the left, the right forearm heavier of muscle and crisscrossed with scars.

Rising, Meren rubbed his chin. He heard a moan and whirled to face what he'd thought was another dead man. As he drew close he recognized the familiar short figure lying facedown next to an overturned chariot. He knelt beside Ahiram and turned him on his back. Face, curly hair, and pointed beard coated with dust and blood, Ahiram gasped and clenched his stomach. His other arm was supported in a sling. Meren tried to pry the man's hand from a bleeding wound in his gut, but Ahiram's eyes flew open, the whites standing out against his dark skin.

"Mer-en." Ahiram struggled to breathe, and his bloodied hand clutched Meren's arm. "Be wary. He'll betray you too."

"Who will? Did you kill Qenamun?"

Ahiram was staring up at him, his breath coming after long pauses.

Meren put his hand over Ahiram's. "Did you kill him? Why did you flee?"

He heard a long, gurgling intake of breath. Meren swore; he'd heard that sound too many times. He wasn't surprised when the life vanished from Ahiram's eyes and his body relaxed.

Meren stood and moved away, his gaze raking over the dead man, taking in the loose, torn robe of dark brown. Ahiram had changed from an Egyptian kilt to the wool clothing of an Asiatic, as had his companions. The attackers had robbed their quarry of jewels and weapons. Little was left to inspect. Ahiram was barefoot; had they even taken the sandals of the dead?

Meren was contemplating the strange chance that the man he'd been chasing had come upon bandits, when the sun dipped below the horizon. A last burst of fiery light glinted off the gold foil on a sandal lying upside down a few paces from Ahiram's body. Meren stared at it, still intent on who the attackers could have been. Then he blinked and strode toward the sandal. Holding a torch in one hand, Abu joined him.

"The bodies have been looted," Abu said as Meren slowly picked up the sandal. "But I think most are officers who served under Ahiram. Shall we make camp for the night, lord?"

Meren didn't answer. He turned the sandal over and ran his fingers across its surface—wood overlaid with a marquetry veneer of bark, leather, and gold foil. Expensive. Prince's sandals.

He was about to toss it away, but hesitated. Something about it seemed too familiar. Holding it nearer the torchlight, he examined the design on the sole. Two captives, an Asiatic and a Nubian, were bound with stems of Egyptian lotus and papyrus. Above and below the figures were groups of bows.

This device, the representation of Egypt's traditional enemies, meant that the wearer trod his foes underfoot.

Few men wore such a device. It was usually reserved
for royalty, but not for foreign princes like Ahiram.
With growing alarm, Meren searched his memory for
the last time he'd seen this sandal.

It was too large to be the king's, and most of pharaoh's footwear was gold. Some of it resembled this
one, but none bore the lozenge pattern in red-and-gold
foil on the strap across the instep. But Meren had seen
this sandal once, long ago. He closed his eyes and
strained for the memory, one he had deliberately thrust
into the darkness of his ka.

He had been in a cell, enduring whippings ordered by
Akhenaten because he wasn't a believer in pharaoh's
chosen god, the sun disk Aten. He was on his stomach,
his cheek pressed to the packed earth of the floor. The
air stirred, and he opened his eyes to see a foot beneath
the hem of transparent linen, a foot encased in this
gilded sandal. A foot that trod upon the enemies of
Egypt—that of the ruler of the Two Lands.

"Bloody demons and everlasting fire," Meren murmured.

"My lord?"

Meren grabbed Abu's arm and pulled him farther
away from the others. He thrust the sandal at Abu, who
examined it.

"This isn't Prince Ahiram's."

Abu was looking at him now, wary and alert. "Yes,
lord?"

"The last time I saw this sandal, it was on the foot of
the old king."

"But . . ."

They stared at each other, each thinking back over
five years. Akhenaten had died without warning, a victim of one of the plagues that had swept the kingdom
out of Palestine, Syria, and the kingdoms of the Tigris

and Euphrates. That is what the court knew. That is what Ay had told Meren. Akhenaten had been struck down shortly after naming Tutankhamun's older brother, Smenkhare, coregent so that he could share the burdens of governing with a younger man.

The whole of the Two Lands had grieved—if not deeply or long. And then Akhenaten had been buried, contrary to tradition, in a tomb east of his heretic capital rather than on the west bank of the Nile, soon to be followed by one of his daughters and the young Smenkhare as well. The crown of Egypt had gone to the sole male heir, the youngest of the three brothers, Tutankhamun. Meren might have believed that Akhenaten's death had been caused by the plague if he hadn't seen the results of the real sickness in Smenkhare. Akhenaten's death had been much more sudden, with no fever, no lingering, nothing.

But the kingdom needed stability, not strife caused by suspicions of regicide. Tutankhamun, a child of nine, had needed his support, his vigilance, his protection. So he attended the burial of Akhenaten, king of Egypt, and watched the priests and attendants pack away all pharaoh's possessions in rich caskets and boxes. These had been placed in the tomb Akhenaten had designed for himself but never completed.

Necropolis officials had sealed the tomb for eternity after the funeral. Time passed. The old gods of Egypt clamored for restoration and repair of the damage wrought upon them by the heretic king. The decision was made to abandon the parvenu capital and return to the royal city of Thebes.

The court quit the heretic city, leaving a skeletal staff in charge of the royal tombs in which were buried the fanatical Akhenaten, his incomparable queen Nefertiti, and several of their daughters. And it was there, in the deserted capital, deep underground in the royal tomb, that this sandal should have been.

"The king's sandal," Abu said in a whisper.

Meren's thoughts were leaping ahead, searching for explanations. "You know what I'm speaking of. We both know the virulence of the hatred borne for Akhenaten. So many had their livings taken, their lives ruined. Ahiram's own father died because of Akhenaten."

Abu shivered as he looked at the sandal. "He had the names of the gods stricken from their temples and brought the wrath of Amun down upon all our heads. Plagues, famine—"

"The wrath of Amun!" Meren stared at Abu.

"Lord," Abu said, "are you saying—"

"Don't speak of it," Meren snapped. He thrust the sandal at Abu. "Put that somewhere out of sight and say nothing of it to anyone. Not to anyone. We're leaving."

"But, lord, the others haven't returned."

"Abu, look at that bandit. He's no peasant criminal. He's a warrior who hasn't taken much care to conceal himself. Leave one man to wait for the others. They're to bring any prisoners to the docks. We're going back to the ship at once."

"At night?"

Meren wasn't listening. He turned and raced back to his chariot. Abu ran after him and jumped in as Meren slapped the reins across the horses' backs. While Abu shouted instructions at the men still at the skirmish site, Meren turned the chariot in the direction of the desert road they'd abandoned.

Abu nearly fell out of the vehicle when it bounced over a stone. He landed on his knees and clutched at the sides of the chariot.

"Where are we going, lord?"

"To a place I thought I'd never see again," Meren said as he pulled the reins to the right to guide the team south. "To a place of great beauty, and of death— Horizon of Aten."

14

∇

Six days later, at dawn, Meren drove his chariot up a side valley of the royal wadi outside the heretic's city of the sun disk, called Horizon of Aten. Charioteers, priests, and guards followed him at a trot, their faces contorted more from fear than from exertion. Meren stopped at the entrance to Akhenaten's tomb, a hole guarded by four men who stood gawking while he threw his reins at a puffing priest.

He didn't expect to see anything, but he strode past the sentries anyway and down a series of steps, into darkness. The chief mortuary priest followed him inside, fumbling with a lamp. Meren waited, his whip slapping against his thigh as the man lit the wick. Then he turned and resumed his descent.

After a few steps, he came up against the blank face of a wall over which plaster had been smeared. The seal impressions of the necropolis. Tracing the impressions of a recumbent jackal over nine captives, and the cartouche of Akhenaten. None had been broken. The impressions were as clear as the day he'd watched them being pressed into the wet plaster.

"You—you see, lord," said the mortuary priest. "Untouched. I am most diligent, er . . ."

Without a word, Meren turned and ascended the steps. The entrance to Akhenaten's tomb faced east and the rising sun, his god. Meren blinked as he emerged from the tomb and surveyed the valley and the surrounding hills. Pharaoh's tomb lay at the end of a long passage that descended into the hillside. A foot track led up the side of the hill.

His appearance was greeted with a sudden silence from the men who waited outside. Abu separated himself from a group of anxious priests as Meren went to his team of horses.

No one spoke until Abu asked, "All is well, lord?"

Meren whispered to his mare and let her nuzzle his cheek. "The seals are unbroken, but that means nothing. We'll see what's behind the hill." His ka knew he was too late.

Leaving the chariots, Meren and his men scaled the slopes above the tomb until they came out of the wadi. Stones clattered down the side of a hill as their feet slipped on the uneven surface. Meren looked across the expanse of rock and scrub—deserted, lifeless, with no sign of robbers or of excavation. Behind him the sun was climbing rapidly as charioteers spread out in a line to either side of him and surveyed the expanse of wasteland that stretched to the horizon.

Meren shook his head. "We may have to open the tomb."

"Open—lord, are you certain?" Abu asked.

Glancing at his aide, Meren heard him mutter a charm against demons and desert monsters. He returned to his survey of the desert.

"Do you think I want to do it? I tell you I've seen that sandal—"

He stopped as he noticed a shadow, a long one that seemed to grow from behind an irregularity in the desert floor. He started walking, then picked up speed until he was running.

"Lord, wait!"

Abu pounded after him, as did his men. He raced

around a large rock and came to a halt. Abu careened to a stop beside him. They both stared down at the shadow, thrown by a wide, almost flat stone that wasn't large enough to hide the hole underneath completely. Meren held up his hand as several men crowded around him, and they stepped back. He examined the ground around the hole, but there wasn't enough dirt to take footprints.

"Move it," Meren said.

Abu and two other men shoved the stone aside to reveal a shaft. It descended at an angle, east, in the direction of the tomb. Meren looked from Abu to the other charioteers who stood around the entrance, taking in their set, taut features. Then he glanced past them to find several mortuary priests stumbling toward them.

"Have you found something, lord?" panted the chief priest.

The charioteers stepped aside to reveal the shaft.

The priest shrieked, while a cry went up among his assistants.

"Silence!" Meren bellowed. He had never seen a priest quiver like a startled hound. "You," he said to the chief priest, "find one of your staff who's slim enough to fit into this shaft and send him in. Also send to the temple for laborers. The tomb will have to be opened."

The priest stared at him, jaw set adrift by horror.

"Don't gape at me. Obey!"

While priests scrambled back to the royal valley, Meren nodded in their direction and spoke to Abu.

"I'm going to leave men here to make sure none of them flees. This tunnel couldn't have been dug without some in the mortuary temple collaborating, especially guards. Before we leave, we'll bring the chariots around and search to the west, but we're going to have a difficult time finding looters."

"Why, lord?"

Meren gazed down into the dark shaft. "Because I

suspect Ahiram sent most of what was stolen out of Egypt when he began to lose his courage weeks ago. And because some of them are already dead. Someone killed them a few days ago near the Red Sea road before I could find them and question them. And now I'm left wondering why a prince like Ahiram would rob the grave of a king."

Over a fortnight after he left, Meren walked into the reception hall of his house in Thebes. He was so weary that he hardly noticed when the porter took his chariot whip. In the half-light cast by alabaster lamps he could see Kysen coming toward him. Behind him he heard Abu murmuring instructions to servants. He leaned on a slim column and pressed his forehead to it.

"Father?"

He straightened and smiled at Kysen. "A long journey. I passed Baht and couldn't even stop to see your sisters."

Kysen studied his face, then dismissed the servants. Abu vanished without being told, and Meren followed his son through the house and out onto the loggia that overlooked the pleasure pool. Moonlight cast a spray of silver across the water. He sank onto a couch with a sigh while Kysen poured a cup of wine and handed it to him. His eyes felt as dry as the floor of a desert valley.

"You look like fiends of the netherworld have been feasting on your ka," Kysen said as he dropped to a cushion on the floor beside the couch.

"I think they may have."

"What's wrong?"

"I found Ahiram. He's dead."

He told the story of finding Ahiram and the royal sandal.

"So you went to the tomb."

Meren didn't answer at once. A maid appeared with

a tray of food, but he waved her away, and they were left alone. Someone's pet baboon screeched, and he heard a heron's call as it flew overhead toward the river. Meren lifted his cup and drank until it was empty before he continued.

"Akhenaten's tomb has been desecrated." He didn't want to go on.

Kysen swore under his breath and then swallowed. "By Ahiram?" He made a sign against evil.

Meren could hear the startled disbelief in Kysen's voice.

"Ahiram," he said. "The looting must have taken place weeks ago, because he was wearing the king's sandals. No doubt he had his men bring some of the riches to him in Thebes where he could make use of them. But we found none of it at his house, which makes me think he's hidden it somewhere. He'd hired mercenaries and bribed a few guards and priests. I left some of my men in charge at Horizon of Aten until pharaoh can send a commission there, and soldiers to search for the looters and their spoils."

"But why? Why would he do such a thing?"

Meren rubbed his face and sighed. "I've been thinking about that. You know Akhenaten refused to help Ahiram's father when he was being attacked by those rebels in the pay of the Hittites. He never forgave, and I suppose he thought he could avenge himself on pharaoh's spirit by destroying his body."

"Destroying it?" Kysen's voice had grown rough with apprehension.

Meren nodded. They lapsed into silence again. Of all the fates dreaded by an Egyptian, the destruction of the body was the worst. The body was necessary to the survival of the ka, the spiritual double. Everyone knew that the ka needed the things the body needed—food, drink, clothing, an eternal home, the tomb. With these things one went equipped into the netherworld. But without the body, the soul perished.

Meren closed his eyes against the vision of plastered and painted walls showing the king and Nefertiti. He had stepped on torn bandages and bits of gilt wood from the shrines that had once surrounded Akhenaten's coffin in order to look at the body. The disconnected remains had been gathered and replaced in the stone sarcophagus. Bandages soaked with resin intermingled with bits of hair and bone.

He had turned away on the pretense of inspecting what remained of the tomb's once-luxurious contents. Few portable riches remained, not even the gold finger stalls from the king's hands. Most of the royal jewelry and regalia had been taken, but not the tall jars of oil and wine. Ahiram's hirelings had been interrupted, for they'd left caskets full of fine linen, furniture, and chariots covered with sheet gold.

Meren set his wine cup down on the floor. Slipping his finger inside his belt, he withdrew an object and handed it to Kysen. It was an openwork gold buckle showing Akhenaten worshipping the stylized sun disk, its rays directed toward the king's face and ending in small hands.

He sat up. "I have to tell the king. He'll believe me when I show him that. The thieves dropped it when they fled."

Kysen put a restraining hand on his arm. "You can wait a few hours. You need rest. Look at you. You have hollows in your cheeks and there are shadows under your eyes that look like bruises."

"I can't wait," Meren said. "Ahiram's last words were for me to beware, that 'he'll' betray me too. That means someone we know has conspired with Ahiram in the desecration of a royal tomb."

"Gods," Kysen said.

Meren stood and paced back and forth. "Someone here sent foreign mercenaries disguised as bandits after Ahiram. Someone who saw Ahiram's loss of courage, knew he fled before we did, why, and where he would go. Someone who had been his ally and couldn't afford to have Ahiram captured and questioned."

"Parenefer," Kysen said. "Everyone knows the malevolence the priests of Amun hold for Akhenaten. Who else would have the influence to persuade Ahiram to undertake the desecration? Why else would Ahiram kill Qenamun unless they'd fallen out and he feared the priests of Amun would kill him first?"

"Yes, but why Ahiram? The reach and power of Amun is great enough without enlisting an outsider. Oh, don't tell me. Parenefer planned to blame Ahiram alone if he was discovered. But I don't see the relationship between Ahiram, Qenamun, and poor Unas. By the gods, Ky, I can prove nothing other than Ahiram's guilt."

"We think Ahiram killed Qenamun," Kysen said. "Most likely because they'd fallen out over this tomb desecration. If the priests have done this evil, then perhaps Unas found out and was killed. If Qenamun was the one who ransacked Unas's house and tried to kill me, then . . ."

"Then Ahiram may have decided to rid himself of Qenamun before he exposed both of them," Meren said. "And we can prove none of it."

He cursed and stalked out to the pool, where he stood scowling at a frog as it hopped along the flagstones. Kysen joined him and dropped down to sit by the water's edge.

"After I tell the king, we must meet and go over everything we know. Without unquestionable proof of Parenefer's involvement, we can do nothing. He's too powerful, powerful enough to raise an army against the king."

"What about those mercenaries who killed Ahiram?" Kysen asked.

"Dead or escaped." Meren lowered himself beside Kysen. "You've had Ahiram's house sealed?"

"Yes, and I've saved the bag of mice and the baskets. But how can we prove him guilty of Qenamun's murder with such objects? You say his servants are being questioned as they return."

"Their words will be much better proof to bring before pharaoh. If they know anything." Meren sighed. "I have to go."

"If you go now, the whole city will know something's wrong."

Meren rubbed his face with his hands again. "You're right. I must be tired not to have considered the stir I'd cause hauling pharaoh from his bed at this hour. Very well. I'll go in the morning."

Kysen jumped to his feet and offered his hand. Meren took it and pulled himself upright. Together they went inside through Meren's bedchamber, and Kysen left him. Meren's body servant awaited him with fresh water in the bathing chamber, and he luxuriated in his first full shower since he left. By the time he was dry and crawled into bed, he'd come awake again.

He'd been this way since he'd divined the significance of Ahiram's stolen sandal—weary and yet unable to sleep for fear of demon-haunted dreams. If he slept, Akhenaten came to him dressed in his finest raiment, wearing the double crowns of Upper and Lower Egypt. Once he'd dreamt that the king had suddenly appeared in his chamber while he was sleeping, carrying a white-hot sun-disk brand that he forced into the flesh over Meren's heart.

He had hated Akhenaten. Did the dead king's ka know it and seek revenge? Did Akhenaten know how he'd suspected a plot to kill him and allowed himself to be sent from court rather than try to stop it?

He tried sleeping with a headrest. He'd suffered from

a headache since looking at Akhenaten's desecrated body, but the pain had receded to a dull thud. Now it spiked through his skull again. He moved the headrest to the floor, turned on his stomach, and groaned. How could he sleep, knowing the priests of Amun had conspired with courtiers to ravage the tomb of the heretic? Not easily frightened, he nevertheless kept listening for the flap of wings that would signal the appearance of the *ba*, the aspect of a soul with the body of a bird and the head of the dead man.

Someone knocked, and he called for them to enter. It was Kysen, carrying a small cup of eggshell-thin pottery. He handed the cup to Meren.

"Abu sent this."

"I don't need it."

"He said you would say that. I could call Mutemwia and have her perform a spell to help you sleep."

Meren groaned. Mutemwia was nurse to Kysen's son and a collector of magic spells for all occasions. Her charms usually ended up hurting more than they aided.

He took the cup and downed the potion in one gulp. Tart and peppery, it burned down his throat and into his chest, but in a few moments the ache in his head faded. He lay back and closed his eyes. Then he heard Kysen's voice.

"Don't worry. Abu set guards all around the house and your chamber. I know how you hate being dosed senseless, but you can't go on without sleep."

Meren nodded without opening his eyes. "Be careful, Ky. There's more afoot than just murder. And anyone who would loot the tomb of a pharaoh, the living god's brother, wouldn't stop at killing both of us."

Meren arrived at the palace before the king began to dress and found him listening to Ay read a list of the day's tasks. He sensed among the guards and servants an uneasiness he attributed to the sudden change of the duty assignments. Ay had relieved all of Ahiram's men, an entire squadron of royal guards. These men were now being questioned. He entered the royal apartments to pharaoh's cheerful greeting.

"Ah, Meren, Ay tells me you found Ahiram," Tutankhamun said. Lounging sideways in an ebony-and-gold chair, the boy was finishing a meal of spice bread and fruit.

Meren glanced at Ay, but as usual, the old man's faded brown eyes revealed nothing. The vizier's swollen fingers curled around his walking stick like gnarled grapevines. Meren had sent a message to Ay with news of Ahiram's death, but had committed nothing else to writing.

He studied Ay's face. It was a long one, with folds and creases like cracks in the mud of a sun-baked canal. He owed Ay his life, for the vizier had interceded with Akhenaten for him when the old pharaoh would have killed him for having a father who defied him.

"Prince Ahiram is dead, golden one, set upon by bandits on his way to one of the Red Sea ports."

The king dusted bread crumbs from his hands. His body servant Tiglith produced a moist cloth.

"And did you find out why he fled?" Tutankhamun asked quietly.

Meren glanced at Tiglith. "The garden is still cool, majesty."

Tutankhamun had been wiping his hands. He looked up quickly at Meren as he continued to ply the damp cloth. After a short silence, he tossed it to Tiglith, turned on his heel, and left the bedchamber. Ay followed him, but hesitated, allowing Meren to catch up as they entered the king's pleasure garden.

"You look like you haven't slept since you left. Was it that terrible?"

"I have slept, and it does no good. No, don't ask. I want to tell this tale of evil only once."

They joined the king beneath an ornamental trellis, festooned with grapevines, that sat in isolation in a part of the garden reserved for it. Around it were low-growing flowers and shrubs, but there were no high walls or trees nearby, lessening the chance that they could be overheard. Tutankhamun sat on a folding stool and motioned for his guests to sit. Ay took another stool, but Meren drew near the king and knelt on the woven mat beside him.

He'd tried to think of a way to tell this news that would lessen the king's fear. He decided simply to tell the story from the point where he set sail. The king listened in silence until Meren came to the discovery of the looters' tunnel. Then he interrupted.

"How bad is it?" he asked, his gaze fixed on a row of incense trees.

Meren felt the corner of his mouth jerk in a downward spasm. "They meant to destroy the body. They almost succeeded."

Tutankhamun turned wide, startled eyes in his direction. He wet his lips and spoke in a faint voice.

"What you mean is that Ahiram's hirelings looted my brother's tomb and then ran away. They violated the eternal house of pharaoh?"

Hearing the disbelief in the king's tone, Meren produced the belt buckle and dropped it into the boy's hand. Tutankhamun stared at it, turning it over and over while shaking his head. Meren waited.

Tutankhamun had been the youngest of three sons born to Amunhotep the Magnificent, far younger than Akhenaten. He'd lived with his mother, the great and powerful Tiye, and only went to Horizon of Aten when he was five. Smenkhare, a youth, had watched over Tutankhamun at the heretic's court. Akhenaten had been much too preoccupied with his sun-disk god to pay much attention to the boy. However, he'd been kind when he remembered Tut.

Still, Meren realized that Tutankhamun's greater distress arose from the horror of sacrilege, and a realistic fear for himself. The king recognized how short a distance it was to sail from doing violence to a dead king to doing violence to a living one. When the king asked, Meren went on to detail his suspicions regarding Qenamun, the priests of Amun, and the death of Unas.

"I'm not sure who else may be involved. Qenamun seems to have had dealings with several of thy majesty's chief servants."

"Who?" Tutankhamun snapped.

Meren hesitated, but when the king asked a question, one answered. "Rahotep, Djoser, and then there are the priests, especially Ebana. Ahiram's servants are being questioned. I should know more by the end of the day."

The king jumped up from his stool and circled a support post of the trellis. "I should arrest them all!"

Ay spoke for the first time since they began. "Tut, I have sent soldiers in pursuit of the desecraters, but you can't arrest princes and priests without great consideration and proof of their crimes. There would be riots."

"Who would dare riot against me?"

"Parenefer would arrange it," Ay said.

Tutankhamun pounded his fist into his palm. "I'll arrest him too."

Standing, Meren went to face the king, blocking his harried pacing. The boy stopped short and glared at him.

"It would be better to wait until we have unquestionable knowledge of what happened and who was responsible, divine one."

"We know already," the king said.

"No, majesty, we suspect. At the moment, the only

persons who we know committed this evil are dead. But there is at least one other person involved, the person who sent those so-called bandits to kill Ahiram. Remember what he said, 'he'll betray you too.' "

"Which means," Ay said, "that we must take care to find this man, for no doubt he's the leader of these traitorous criminals."

Tutankhamun pounded on a trellis post. "It has to be Parenefer!"

Meren's voice cut through the king's muttering.

"What if we're wrong?"

Boyish curses faltered. "Then I'd let Parenefer go."

"Yes," Meren said. "But he would hate you."

"He hates me now."

Ay pulled himself to his feet by bracing against his walking stick. "The wrath he cultivates and hoards for Akhenaten spills over onto you. If you humiliate him, the greatest priest in the kingdom, he'll hate you for yourself, and then he will begin to plot your death."

Tutankhamun turned on Meren. "So you wish to risk my life so that Parenefer isn't offended?"

"No, majesty, I—"

"Oh, never mind. If I must wait out this threat, at least I'll distract myself. I'll go on a raid against these bandits that plague the village of Long Shadow."

Meren wanted to groan. "Thy majesty should delay such outings until I've had time to solve this mystery."

"Damn you, Meren, this is another trick to keep me from becoming a man!"

The gods should protect him from young bulls anxious to test their horns. Meren thought of all the logical reasons why the king shouldn't leave Thebes and knew Tutankhamun wouldn't listen to them. So he only had one choice left—the most unpleasant.

"Forgive me, divine one, but thy majesty has forgotten an urgent problem that requires royal attention."

Tutankhamun folded his arms over his chest. "Oh?"

"Thy majesty must repair the damage to his brother's body and then find another house of eternity for him, Queen Nefertiti, and all the other royal family who are buried at Horizon of Aten. And this must be done in secret, so that his enemies do not attack him again, and so that none ever learn of this unspeakable transgression. I'm sure thy majesty realizes how dangerous it would be if his subjects were to learn that a pharaoh's tomb had been violated."

A startled glance. A dazed silence. Then curses, a loud, resentful string of them. The king understood. He would comply, and he was blaming Meren for his sudden disappointment and for his renewed fear. Nevertheless, Meren was startled when Tutankhamun darted at him. So abrupt was the movement, he did nothing to avoid the blow when the king backhanded him.

"May the gods curse you, Meren. Get out, get out!"

His jaw stung, and he tasted blood. Meren straightened, raised his arm, and touched the corner of his mouth with the back of his hand while he gazed at the boy. Tutankhamun was breathing hard. His gaze dropped to Meren's hand as it touched his mouth, then to his inner wrist.

Meren stiffened; he had forgotten to wear a bracelet or wristband to cover the sun-disk brand. Ay was remonstrating with the king, but neither pharaoh nor Meren heard him. Tutankhamun narrowed his eyes as he stared at the scar. Meren dropped his hand to his side. The king's gaze met his.

"I'd forgotten," he said.

Ay fell silent.

Tutankhamun went on in a suddenly flat voice. "Parenefer isn't the only one with cause to hate my dead brother."

15

▽

Meren tried not to stalk out of the palace.

Imagine that you're walking out of your own house, he told himself. Imagine that it is Remi who has just indulged in a fit of temper. Only for a while. Just until you're out of the palace precinct.

He fixed all his attention on walking without haste, easily, as if he were slightly drowsy because of the early hour. All the while, deep in the recesses of his ka, he was furious. Furious at the son of the god. The obstinate young fool.

Passing into the great reception hall, Meren entered the growing crowd of courtiers and officials who had business with pharaoh this day. A young man separated himself from a group of army officers and hailed him while digging his little finger in his ear. Meren cursed in silence, then turned to greet Prince Rahotep.

"Ah," Rahotep said. "You've returned. Did you find him? I could have found him in half the time you've been gone."

"Of course I found him," Meren snapped.

The prince took a step backward and held up both hands. He shook his wide head. Meren reflected that it looked like it had been flattened under a falling obelisk.

"Don't bark at me," Rahotep said. "I only asked what everyone else will."

He'd almost given himself away. Touching his forehead as if weary, he smiled.

"Forgive me. It has been a long and unhappy journey."

"So you found Ahiram. Where is he?"

Meren hesitated. "He's dead."

"Dead! But how?"

"All the circumstances of his death aren't clear."

"What do you mean, not clear?" Rahotep's voice began to rise. "Either he's dead, or he's not. Did you kill him?"

This last had been said in a loud voice. Silence fell over those nearest them, and Meren saw a priest of Ra and several officers of the infantry look their way. Rahotep had clamped his mouth shut and was gawking at him as if he couldn't believe he'd blurted out the accusation. Meren directed a regal stare at the prince.

"You're overexcited, Rahotep. Maybe this is an inauspicious day for you, and a sacrifice to Amun or Toth would aid your disposition." He paused while he watched Rahotep try to shrink into himself. "Or perhaps you should just go home."

He left the prince standing in the small clearing his outburst had created and continued to weave his way through the crowd toward the tall double doors in the palace entryway. These portals were of cedar of Byblos overlaid with sheet gold, which showed scenes of the king in his chariot making war on the nine traditional enemies of Egypt. He forced himself not to glare at the image of Tutankhamun.

So great was his concentration that he almost ran into Tanefer and Maya when they appeared in front of him. They fell in step with him as he walked outside to the courtyard and called for a groom to bring his chariot. When the groom had gone, both men faced him.

"What have you done, Falcon?" Maya asked in a

whisper. "We just came from the king, and he's furious with you. I've never seen him furious with you."

Tanefer gave Maya an irritated glance. "You know he's not going to tell you, nor should he. Did you find Ahiram?"

All this interest in Ahiram was only natural. Still, Meren watched both men as he responded. "I found him."

Both men gazed at him with frank interest, which told him nothing.

"Well?" Maya said. "What was his reason for fleeing the court? Have you made him talk? Gods, Meren, you'll have to tell us sometime, and if you don't, we'll find out anyway. I'll get it from Ay."

"Ahiram is dead."

Maya fell silent, staring at him, while Tanefer sighed.

"What did you think would happen?" Tanefer asked the treasurer. "Only the guilty run away. The innocent have no reason to flee. Therefore Ahiram was guilty of something, some great evil. He wouldn't take flight for a lesser crime."

Tanefer paused and glanced at Meren, who kept his expression benign.

"Did you find him dead somewhere, or did you kill him?" Maya asked. "Were you able to question him?"

The treasurer still regarded Meren with anxious curiosity, but Tanefer smiled as he directed an assessing gaze at him.

"He's not going to tell you," Tanefer said. "Peace, Maya. You'll have to wait, for something of great import must have happened, or our divine one wouldn't at this moment be storming about the royal apartments in a temper and refusing to begin his royal duties. I'll wager Meren found Ahiram and learned something none of us is going to like."

"Look at him," Maya said to Tanefer. "I might as

well try to talk to a stela for all I can read in that face. Has someone turned you to granite, Meren?"

The golden doors of the palace swung open, and Ay appeared from the shadowed interior, followed by a flock of scribes and servants. He waved them back inside and joined the three men in the courtyard. At the same time, Meren's chariot arrived. The groom hopped out of it and stood holding the reins.

"There you are, Maya," Ay said. "The golden one has summoned you again. Tanefer, go with him."

"What's wrong?" Maya asked the vizier. "I should be told, you know. I'm a king's councillor too."

"Then go council the king," Ay said.

Maya was growing red with annoyance. Meren remained silent even though he knew his friend was taking offense. But the risk was too great. He wanted no one to know how much or how little Ahiram had said before he died. And if everyone assumed he had killed the prince, well, it didn't hurt for people to fear him. Not if there was some plot against the king brewing between the court and the temple of Amun.

Tanefer pulled Maya away toward the palace. Meren took the reins from the groom and dismissed the man. Ay clutched his arm and they began to walk across the courtyard, the horses pacing slowly beside Meren.

"You mustn't be angry with his majesty," Ay said.

Meren glanced around the courtyard, but all the sentries and grooms and arriving courtiers were out of hearing range.

He spoke to the vizier without glancing his way. "Gods, spirits, and fiends preserve me from your admonitions."

"I know he's being unfair, but he will calm. You see, he's heard the rumors about Horemheb."

Meren slowed, then stopped and turned to face Ay. "What has he heard?"

"That Horemheb thinks he'd make a better pharaoh.
That he could lead the army now, march all the way to
Carchemish, and kick Suppiluliumas back to his frozen
Anatolian mountains. So you can see why Tutankhamun
is fearful. If his generals are dissatisfied, he is indeed in
danger. And he thinks the only way to fight this threat
is to make war himself."

The rumor hadn't died as he thought it would. Most
flew about the court like a desert breeze and then vanished; this one hadn't. Instead, it had grown, whirling
around, gathering intensity, feeding on the refuse it
picked up in its wanderings. He glanced at Ay, who was
examining the golden head of his walking stick.

"Horemheb is a commoner," he said. "He'd never
even imagine himself on the throne."

"Any man who marries the royal heiress can come to
the throne. You know that. It has happened."

Meren shook his head. "He saved my life when we
were youths in the charioteers. It was a skirmish against
Libyan rebels at the el-Kharga oasis. I fell from my
chariot when it hit a rock, flew up like an arrow, and hit
the ground like a boulder. Got the wind pounded out of
me, and while I was dazed, a Libyan pounced on my
chest and would have slit my throat if Horemheb hadn't
chopped his head off."

A squad of infantry marched toward them, parted,
and flowed around them as Meren and Ay stared at each
other.

"I don't want to believe the rumor either," Ay said.
"But neither of us can afford to ignore it."

"He would never betray the king."

"We must discover what is going on soon."

Meren patted his horse's muzzle as he thought.
"Look at what's happening."

"I have been," Ay replied.

"No, I mean, what the result has been. Pharaoh no

longer trusts two of his most intimate advisors." He brushed his cheek against the softness of a big muzzle. "Horemheb, and me. Someone is trying to separate the king from his closest and most trusted friends. Why? Not just to gain influence over a boy who is king, but possibly to render him—"

"Vulnerable," Ay said.

Meren nodded. "And to force him to put his trust elsewhere, in the wrong people, who will then betray him."

"Which is why I've warned Karoya and put the king's war band on guard duty at the palace. I've asked Tanefer to stay in Thebes and add his men to those at the palace. He was going to his estate near Bubastis. Hasn't been home in nearly eight months and wanted to see his wife before he was sent away again on some campaign. But he'll stay as long as we need him."

"Good." Meren got into the chariot and leaned down to Ay. "I can do no good here while the king is so unreasonable."

"It's only the fear."

"Nevertheless, it's as if Kysen had accused me of trying to kill him. No, don't say anything more. Since the king no longer listens to me, I'll work on solving these murders. Someone powerful has committed this great evil, and I'd better find out who it is before he strikes again, at the king, directly."

The man spoke only the language of the Mitanni.

Kysen studied the prisoner. Although near him in age, the prisoner wore a beard and curled locks. A once-fine robe of red and green, interwoven with gold thread, was wrapped around his body, but it had been torn in combat. It was stained with sweat and blood from a gash in the young man's upper arm.

He had been called to the barracks, a long, low building with a central hall, cells, and quarters for the charioteers. Two weary men had brought the prisoner in after chasing him down the Red Sea road. Evidently, after the skirmish he'd circled around and tried to reach the coast. They had tried to question him, only to find that he spoke no Egyptian.

Kysen walked back and forth in front of the man, impatient and worried. This man might know who was responsible for Ahiram's death and for the desecration of Akhenaten's tomb, and he couldn't understand him. The longer they remained in ignorance, the greater the danger to pharaoh and to the Two Lands.

His guards had thrown the Mitanni to the floor at Kysen's feet. Now he was crouched there as if ready to spring. His date shaped eyes reflected the golden light and black shadows created by a lamp sitting on a wooden stand that reached almost to Kysen's shoulder.

High rectangular windows let in little light to aid that cast by the lamp. The prisoner darted glances at the guards standing to either side of him and at Kysen. Abu and Reia waited near the columns between Kysen and the door.

"The lord Meren was right," Abu said. "Mercenaries. We had heard that soldiers of the Mitanni were fleeing in the face of the Hittite invasion."

"Send to the office of the vizier for a scribe who can talk to the man," Kysen said to Reia. "But not one who only knows how to translate written documents. And Reia, hurry."

As Reia left, Kysen studied the prisoner. His lips were cracked and swollen. Dried blood had gathered at the corner of his mouth.

"You're sure he was one of these so-called bandits who attacked Prince Ahiram."

"Aye, lord," said one of the guards. "We followed him from the skirmish, but his horses were swift, and he outran us until one of them went lame."

Turning away from the prisoner, Kysen poured a cup of water from a jar by one of the columns. He approached the prisoner, who watched him, his body growing more tense as Kysen closed the distance between them. Kysen stopped a pace from the man and held out the cup. The young man didn't move. Sighing, Kysen took a sip of the water, then offered the cup again. A hand snaked out and grabbed it.

Gulping noisily, the prisoner drank the entire cup and held it out to Kysen. Kysen almost smiled at the gesture. Few prisoners found the courage to make demands. But then, this one looked at his captors with contempt. Kysen could see it in the way he almost smirked at his guards.

As he refilled the cup, the Mitanni spoke for the first time. He spat out unintelligible words like invisible javelins. Kysen understood none of it, and only caught one word that made sense—Saustatar. Saustatar had been a great Mitanni king, a conqueror who had battled the ruthless and bloodthirsty Assyrians and looted the royal palace at Ashur. Furrowing his brow, Kysen contemplated the young man. Of what relevance could a dead king have to this soldier, who most certainly should be worrying about his impending death?

Kysen turned to Abu. "Why—"

The door opened before he could finish. Reia ushered Rahotep and Tanefer into the hall.

"What have you here, Ky?" Tanefer asked. "Reia said you had need of my eloquent tongue." He then said something in Mitanni and bowed mockingly to Kysen.

"A bandit?" Rahotep asked as he went over to inspect the crouching prisoner.

Reia said, "You were in haste, lord, and I met Prince Tanefer in the street."

Trying not to glare at Reia, Kysen hesitated. How was he going to refuse without offending? Before he could think of something, a stream of chatter burst from the prisoner. Tanefer's head came up. He went still and stared at the Mitanni, then he said a few words to the man. The prisoner responded with an avalanche of babbling in which Kysen could only make out the word "Saustatar."

"What is he saying?" Kysen asked as they both walked over to the Mitanni.

"He's speaking too fast," Tanefer said. "You have to remember, Ky, that only my mother spoke our language to me, and she's been dead for years. Let me ask him to slow down."

"Don't trouble yourself," Kysen said, but Tanefer was already speaking.

He said a few words, quietly and slowly, while Rahotep walked around the prisoner and inspected him as if he were a sacrificial goat. Suddenly the Mitanni launched himself at the lamp stand, sweeping it aside with one arm as he dove for Rahotep. The lamp crashed to the floor. Oil spilled, flamed, and went out, leaving the hall in near darkness.

At the prisoner's first move, Kysen and Tanefer had sprung at him, but he'd darted away quickly. Then the darkness engulfed them. Kysen stopped abruptly to gain his bearings. He listened to the sounds of a scuffle and a scream of foreign words that rose higher and higher. Someone barreled into him. He fell as hands fastened on his neck and squeezed. Then the door opened, shoved by Reia, and he looked up at his attacker.

"Abu, get off!"

"Forgive me, lord. I thought you were the mercenary."

They got to their feet and beheld a pile of bodies. Rahotep shoved himself off the mercenary, then pulled the prisoner off Tanefer. The prisoner rolled on his back, gurgling, to reveal a dagger in his chest. His hands were wrapped around the hilt of the dagger as he died.

Kysen dropped beside Tanefer, who was moaning. He pulled his friend to a sitting position. His broad collar and chest were wet with blood.

"Are you hurt?" Kysen asked.

"I hit my head," Tanefer said. "I think he fell on me."

They both looked at the dead man.

"I should have warned you," Tanefer said. "But he was too quick for me. He was saying that he wouldn't allow Egyptian dogs to torture him and then kill him. He wanted to die a warrior, but I didn't think he'd kill himself."

"Nor did I," Kysen said as he gave Tanefer a long glance.

He went to the dead man and pulled the dagger from his body. It was a fine one with a gold hilt. Not the ordinary weapon of a charioteer on duty. He had his own still, as did Tanefer. Kysen turned to Rahotep, who was staring at the blood on Tanefer's broad collar.

"This is yours."

Rahotep glanced at the dagger and nodded. "When he jumped on me, he must have taken it."

"And did you fight him for it?"

"Of course, but we ran into the column, and then Tanefer. But I didn't have the chance to kill him. If Tanefer didn't, then he must have done it himself."

Cursing under his breath, Kysen gave orders for the body to be removed to a cell. He should never have allowed Rahotep and Tanefer in the barracks. Furious at himself and at Reia as well, Kysen wondered how he was going to tell Meren he'd lost the only living witness to this tangled series of crimes.

And where was Meren? He'd been gone since morning, and it was now midday.

16

$\triangledown$

Meren left the offices of the vizier, directing his team of horses down a street that twisted back on itself due to the accretion of government buildings over the centuries. He'd accompanied Ay here so that they could confer about the reliability of the men now guarding pharaoh. Now, without this distraction, his suppressed anger and grief at the misunderstanding with the king surfaced.

Only a short time ago, during the investigation of the murder in the place of Anubis, he remembered Kysen making a remark about those foolish enough to steal from a dead member of pharaoh's family. Better to steal from royalty long dead, whose very names had been forgotten. Yet now the unimaginable crime had been committed. Why now?

Ahiram had long hated Akhenaten for his failure to support Egypt's ally of many years, the prince of Byblos. But as the years passed after Akhenaten's death, Ahiram seemed to put aside his wrath and accustom himself to his new life. Having come to Egypt as a youth to be trained with the other royal children, he'd been back and forth between the rich trading city and Egypt for years, until one day the trouble with the Hittite-backed raiders made it too dangerous to return home.

Ahiram had lingered at court, receiving more and

more harried and desperate messages from his father.
He had pleaded with Akhenaten to intercede, to send
the fabled Egyptian army to his father's aid. But
Akhenaten preferred the isolation of peace to expensive
warfare. Meren remembered the king telling Ay that he
could trade with whoever won, for Byblos needed
Egyptian gold no matter who ruled it. And so Ahiram
had been unable to help his father Rib-Addi, longtime
friend of faithless Egypt.

Had Ahiram's fury caused him to seek vengeance
upon Akhenaten? Had he even taken a role in the king's
death? A pointless speculation, given how little Meren
knew of the circumstances of that event.

He guided his chariot through an intersection
crowded with the stalls of vendors of fruit, beer, fish,
and other commodities. One man had even leaned his
awning against an obelisk erected at the crossroads by
some long-dead king. Pedestrians gave way before
Meren while several vendors tried to catch his attention,
but he was too caught up in his thoughts to do more
than wave them away.

Why try to kill Akhenaten's soul now? And what
about Qenamun and the other priests of Amun? Without
evidence of their complicity, he couldn't accuse them of
conspiring with Ahiram in the desecration of the royal
tomb. They had been behind it, though. He would have
wagered anything on that. He needed to question Ebana,
Parenefer, and Rahotep, but without pharaoh's confidence he lacked the power to intimidate them into answering him. However, he could talk to Tanefer
privately, for he knew all these men and Qenamun as
well.

Why desecrate Akhenaten's tomb now? Had Parenefer finally succumbed to his craving for vengeance?
Perhaps Tutankhamun had provoked this retaliation, offending the old man with his youthful arrogance. Plant-

ing that colossal statue in front of the god's gate hadn't improved Parenefer's temper either.

Or had the high priest simply fed his feelings of maltreatment and resentment until he lost all sense of caution? Parenefer's appetite for riches had grown since Amun had been restored. No matter how many of his vast estates pharaoh allocated to the god—Amun had more farmland than anyone except pharaoh, several hundred orchards, almost half a million head of cattle, countless villages, ships, and workshops, and almost one hundred thousand laborers—the priest was never satisfied.

He was jolted out of his musings when a woman on the roof of a house he was passing hurled a rug into the air and flapped it, showering him with dust. He cursed and coughed at the same time. Gripping the side of the chariot, he dusted himself as the horses slowed, then stopped. She looked down at him, put her hand over her mouth, and vanished down an interior stairway. Rushing into the street, she threw herself to the ground, babbling apologies.

"It was naught but an accident, mistress." He nodded to her and slapped the reins.

Soon he turned down a wider street, taking care to stay in the middle, out of reach of tidying women. Slapping the reins again, he urged his team into a trot. Threshold after threshold passed. The street seemed deserted. The sun was directly overhead. Heat rose from the packed earth beneath the chariot wheels and flowed toward him from the high, uneven walls of houses that rose three and four stories above his head.

The horses were lathered and had suffered from the heat while he mused. Berating himself for his negligence, Meren urged the team to gather speed. He wasn't far from home now. As he reached the end of the street, he saw a flash of bare skin and a white loincloth.

Shouting, he hauled on the reins hard as a child dashed in front of the horses. They hardly slowed, then rose on their hind legs, screaming in alarm as they saw a blur of movement in their path. The chariot swerved to the right. It tipped on one wheel while Meren fought to regain his balance and control the horses at the same time.

His shoulder hit the side of the chariot. Then he shoved his feet against the floor and threw himself to the other side of the vehicle. The reins slipped from his hands as he hit, but the chariot settled on both wheels. Not waiting to regain his breath, Meren jumped to the ground, intent on grabbing a harness, only to find himself surrounded by soldiers. Long kilts, scimitars, spears.

Foot soldiers, not charioteers. Meren counted nine men. He hadn't a chance. Two of them grabbed his team and calmed them. He heard the snort of another animal, and glanced up to see a chariot coming down the street. Horemheb stood beside his driver, his face blank. He jumped out of the moving vehicle as it passed Meren.

Meren scowled at him. "What are you doing, damn you?"

"Come with me."

Glancing around the circle of soldiers, Meren shook his head.

Horemheb's lip curled. "What ails you? Don't you trust me? No, I can see you don't. Then come because you have no choice."

Meren watched Horemheb turn and vanish into the black depths of the house by which he'd stopped. Three men took a step toward him. He gave them one of the looks he reserved for callow recruits who have committed some inane error. They halted, and he followed Horemheb into the house. As he left the street, he glanced over his shoulder. Except for his escort, all the soldiers and both chariots had vanished.

A woman turned into the street, leading a donkey. Meren hesitated, estimating the chances of escape, but a hand grabbed his arm and pulled him into darkness. He gripped his dagger, but the hand released him.

"Let go of it, Meren," Horemheb said. "You're against spears."

He held his hands away from his body. Someone closed the door. Another soldier appeared from the interior holding two lamps. Horemheb's rough features and crooked nose appeared in a flickering shower of light. The yellow flame seemed to lighten his already sun-bleached hair. Then, abruptly, they were alone.

"I want to talk to you," the general said.

Meren whirled, marched to the door, and put his hand on the latch.

"So you believe the lies too."

He released the latch, turned, and put his back to the door.

"What lies?"

"I may be common, Meren, but I'm not stupid. You above all hear rumors, so I know you've heard the ones about me. I'm dissatisfied, afraid Egypt will fall under Hittite rule. I think the kingdom needs a strong leader, and that I'm the one."

"We've been friends since we were youths."

"Aye."

"You saved my life."

Meren didn't move as Horemheb came nearer, never dropping his gaze.

"Aye, I did that," Horemheb said.

"And we've served pharaoh together."

"What are you saying?"

"And in all that time," Meren said, "you've never abducted me and forced me to do your bidding."

Horemheb cursed, stuck his thumbs in his belt, and studied the floor. After a while, he raised his gaze to Meren again.

"Forgive me, old friend. These rumors have driven me near to madness. Even Maya looks at me with suspicion, and today the king refused to give me an audience. Ay says to be patient, but I know what happens to men who lose the confidence of pharaoh."

"Have you left the city in the past fortnight?"

"What?" Horemheb gave him a confused glance. "How could I leave? We've been making plans for this campaign you hate so much."

"So you never left Thebes."

"I said so, didn't I? What are you talking about?"

"Ahiram is dead."

"Dead! I thought he'd run himself into debt or fathered a child on a virgin princess. Why dead?"

Meren continued to stare at Horemheb. "Someone hired mercenaries to track him down and murder him."

Nothing. Not a flicker of an eyelid, not a twitch of a muscle.

"A powerful enemy, had Ahiram," Horemheb said.

"Yes. One who could send soldiers after him. Not unlike what you just did to me."

The quiet was broken only by the sound of their breathing.

"There's one difference," Horemheb said softly.

"What is it?"

"You're still alive."

Meren lifted his chin. "Am I going to stay that way?"

"Not if you don't quit snarling suspicions at me, damn you. How could you ask me that? I've come to you for help, may the gods curse your hide. Now I think I'd rather beg it of that old mound of vulture's dung, Parenefer."

At last Meren smiled. Curbing his temper and asking

for help, two accomplishments that came hard for Horemheb.

"I might not have the power to help you for long. I too have incurred the disfavor of pharaoh."

"You? How?"

Meren didn't answer at once. If he confided in Horemheb, he might be trusting the traitor Ahiram had warned him about. However, if that were true, it was already too late. He couldn't believe that his friend was behind whatever plot was fermenting around him. Had Horemheb wished to seize power, he could have done so at Akhenaten's death, when Tutankhamun had been a child and the government in disarray.

Did not a man's actions speak of his character? Horemheb had saved his life, had devoted himself to protecting the Two Lands. Sometimes one had to take risks, trust one's friends. Slowly, Meren began to tell what he knew of the deaths of Ahiram, Qenamun, and the pure one, Unas.

"So I think Ahiram put the cobras in Qenamun's box, but the servant who helped him was killed with his master. So far there are no others who witnessed his actions. The porter only knows that he and one other servant were told not to go near the wicker baskets."

They were sitting on the floor with a lamp between them. Horemheb had dismissed his men. The general handed Meren a cup of beer and grunted.

"So, you think all three deaths and the discord at court are connected."

"Aye," Meren said. "But I can't weave the pieces into whole cloth. No one would admit to having seen anything on the morning the pure one was killed. We never found the boy who carried the message for Unas to go to the temple before dawn. When nothing happened, I almost decided that the death was an accident.

Then Unas's house was ransacked by a tall, shaved man who smelled of cone scent."

"It could have been the lector priest."

"You'd never make a good inquiry agent, Horemheb. You assume too much."

"What do you mean?"

"I mean the description is too vague and could fit many men, even you, or my cousin Ebana, or that too-friendly neighbor, Nebera. So we spread the rumor that Kysen had found those pottery shards."

"To flush your quarry," Horemheb said.

Meren nodded. "But if it succeeded, it succeeded too well, for when Kysen went to examine Unas's house, someone tried to kill him."

"By the gods! Did you catch him?"

"No, and I thank the gods Kysen wasn't hurt. I had questioned Qenamun earlier. He seemed honest, open, ingenuous."

"Doesn't sound like a priest of Amun."

"No," Meren said. "And what's worse, it was shortly after this questioning that the attempt on Kysen was made. I like it not that Qenamun, Ebana, and also Rahotep were nearby when someone tried to drop part of a wall on my son's head. Kysen was so furious that he confronted them about the attempt on his life."

"Rahotep. Our prince who knows all, who never quibbles at telling us so, who thinks he's more royal than he is."

They stared at each other quizzically.

"Later that same day, Qenamun was killed," Meren said.

"The cobras," Horemheb said. "I didn't do it. If I want to kill a man, I use a more direct method."

"But you had dealings with him."

"Qenamun gave good dream interpretations."

Meren smiled at his friend. "So think Djoser and

Rahotep, and Rahotep was with him when he was killed. So was Ebana, again. It was just before I heard of Qenamun's death that the rumors about you began."

"By the balls of Set, I've done nothing!"

"Calm yourself. I accuse you of nothing. Anyone who knew Qenamun's habits could have entered the temple on the day he left early and concealed the snakes. Of those with such knowledge, several are of high rank—Djoser, Rahotep, Ahiram, and you, among others."

"Me again."

Meren sighed. "Will you allow me to continue? How can I think if you're barking at me? I should have gone home to do this."

"No, no. I'll be quiet."

"And all this while you and I and pharaoh's other advisors have been arguing about the unrest in Syria and Palestine, about the Hittites, and about whether the king should campaign. You know fugitives from the Mitanni empire are reaching our borders, renegade soldiers. Tanefer warned me that trouble was approaching, and now he's proved right."

"But what does that have to do with these murders?"

"Nothing. It's just that the court was already unsettled, seething with rumors and unrest, and then Ahiram vanished. After the hippo hunt. I think he killed Qenamun and then lost his courage."

"That doesn't sound like Ahiram."

"I know, but considering what he was hiding, it makes sense. Perhaps he thought the gods were angry, and that was why he almost got eaten by the hippo."

"Aye," Horemheb said. "Even I would lose my wits if I'd robbed and desecrated a pharaoh's eternal house."

"And before I could reach him, he was murdered by disguised mercenaries." Meren stared at the lamp flame. "And this last murder opens the whole affair, because whoever killed Ahiram must have done it to keep him from exposing his fellow criminals, especially whoever is their master. That person has a long reach, long enough to chase down and kill Ahiram, and the boldness to risk all to strike at a dead king."

"We both know who that is. Parenefer."

"I told you not to assume, my friend. There are too many gaps, too many things we don't know. Who killed Unas and why? It could have been Qenamun, or Ahiram, or another. If he was guilty, what was the real reason Ahiram killed Qenamun, and why did he run away when I gave no sign that I suspected him?"

"Meren—"

"Yes, Horemheb."

"Your job is much harder than mine. I only have to fight wars. You have to peer inside men's souls and foretell the future."

Meren gave him a wry smile. "Your words are a great comfort to me."

"You say Maya is behind these rumors about me?"

"No, he heard it from someone else, but Tanefer interrupted us about Qenamun's death before I could ask him from whom."

Horemheb rose and offered his hand to Meren. "I think I'll go find Maya."

"He's at court." Meren gripped his friend's hand and pulled himself to his feet. "But don't jump out at him as you did me. He'll shriek so loud the palace roof will fall in."

He went outside to find the boy he'd almost run over holding his chariot in the shade of an awning. He drove home slowly this time and tried not to lapse into thinking until he was there. He arrived to find the house quiet.

Even that small terror, Remi, was quiet, but that was only because he was napping. Meren grabbed bread and

meat from the kitchen and went to his office. Grooms
hurried into the stables. Charioteers fell to sharpening
javelin points and swords as he passed them. His scribe
ducked into the records room.

He was wary by the time he saw Kysen waiting outside his office. After a few moments of listening to his
son, he was furious.

"What fiend put it into your head to allow Tanefer to
translate?"

"It happened before I could stop it. I was going to
refuse, but he started without my permission. I should
have been more alert."

"By the gods, you should have."

Meren stalked over to a table where a jar of beer and
its strainer rested along with cups. He grabbed one, then
thought of the danger to which Kysen had exposed himself in that fight in the dark. Something cracked. Kysen
cried out, and Meren blinked. He'd thrown the cup
against the wall. A splinter of pottery had ricocheted off
the wall to hit Kysen in the cheek.

Swearing, Meren grabbed a cloth from the table and
went to his son. "No, remove your hand and let me
see."

He found a tiny piece of the glazed cup embedded in
a cut high on the jaw. "Hold still."

Drawing his dagger, he carefully used the tip to remove the splinter, then dabbed the cut with the cloth.

"Forgive me, Ky."

"You didn't do it on purpose."

"I don't care. There's no excuse for hurting you."

"What's happened?" Kysen took the cloth and held it
against the thin line of blood on his cheek. "Something's gone wrong. I can tell."

Meren related the morning's events. Kysen's eyes
filled with dread at the tale of the king's wrath. He tried
to say something, but Meren went on to speak of

Horemheb. Kysen's brow furrowed as he heard the story of his father being waylaid.

"You said someone with power is behind these deaths and the—the great crime." He set the cloth aside. "Forgive me, Father, but it could be Horemheb, and he could have been trying to deceive you."

"He isn't."

Meren looked away from the blood on his son's cheek. On that day long ago when he'd seen Kysen's scars and bruises and bought him from his blood father, he'd vowed never to use brutality against the boy.

"Don't," Kysen said.

"What?"

"It was an accident."

Meren tried to smile. "I need time to think. We have to talk to Ebana, Parenefer, Tanefer, and Rahotep, but carefully, since I've no formal commission of inquiry for any of them."

"We can talk to Tanefer without one," Kysen said.

"I know, and I will, but Rahotep concerns me. He's shown up in all sorts of odd places at significant times—the quay market after someone tried to kill you, the House of Life when Qenamun was killed, and now here, where our only witness to sacrilege and murder dies."

"I'll find him," Kysen said as he walked to the door.

"Take Abu and his men with you."

"I won't need them against Rahotep."

Meren swept to the door and caught Kysen's arm. "That was not a request, my son."

Kysen gave him a lopsided smile. "As you command, O great one, O Eyes of Pharaoh, my lord. Only I wish you'd be on guard as well, even against Horemheb."

"Go away, Ky. And be careful this time. Anyone who would kill a prince wouldn't stop at killing my son."

17
▽

After Kysen left, Meren decided to sort through the papers in Qenamun's casket again. He was reading an interpretation of Rahotep's dreams, the most numerous of which seemed to consist of various creatures whose sole desire was to eat the prince's entrails. In others, Rahotep's dead mother came to him to prophesy greatness for her son. Had Rahotep believed the prophecies and acted upon them? While Meren was reading, Remi marched in, dragging a toy hippo on a string and carrying a hand mirror in his other hand.

Meren thrust the interpretations aside, snatched the boy up in one arm, and took the mirror from him. Its handle of polished silver bore the image of the goddess of beauty and fertility, Hathor.

"Where did you get this, small fiend?"

"Don't know."

"Don't know, or don't want to tell?"

Remi began to wriggle in his arms, so he set the child down. A ray of light from the high windows flashed a beam into his eyes and he winced. Setting the mirror on the table next to him, he turned his back on it.

It had belonged to Sit-Hathor. Years ago he'd put away many of her possessions for the time when his daughters were old enough to make use of them. The most precious of these, the ones that reminded him of her the most, these he kept in his chamber in a chest.

Mutemwia must have been distracted for a moment. If she turned her attention away from the boy for more than the space of a breath, he scuttled away and got into trouble. He heard Mutemwia call Remi, who grinned and put both small hands over his mouth and crouched on the floor. Meren tried not to laugh but failed, and the sound brought the nurse into the room.

"Disobedient, wretched little baboon." Mutemwia picked Remi up. "Forgive me, lord. I but paused to speak to the cook, and he was gone."

"A welcome interruption, Mut. But please, no more escapes this afternoon. I've much to do."

"Aye, lord."

Left alone, Meren again noticed the mirror. He'd forgotten to give it to Mutemwia. When he looked at it, he remembered being fifteen and so in love with his long-legged, untouchable wife that he would scandalize the household by going to her room and watching her use the mirror while applying her cosmetics. At first she'd been furious with him for the intrusion, so furious that she screamed at him. In spite of his hard training at letters and war, her rage at his small transgression had hurt.

Even nineteen years ago, he'd known to conceal his pain behind an emotionless mask that made him feel like one of those figures carved on temple walls, well-made but frozen, inert. And all the while, beneath the facade, the pain hadn't gone away. Because she hadn't loved him then, and he'd expected the euphoria that harpers sang of, that he'd read about in poetry.

He closed his eyes for a moment while he drove out the memories. Then he looked for some place to put the mirror. Some place where he couldn't see it. His gaze fell on Qenamun's casket resting on the table. He began to lift the lid and stopped, remembering the cobras.

"Fool," he said to himself.

Still, he tipped the lid so that it opened away from his body. The box was as empty as before, except for the scattering of rush pens at the bottom. His fingers brushed the slim implements as he placed the mirror in the casket. Leaving the lid off, he picked up Rahotep's dream interpretations again. Line after line of cursive hieroglyphs covered a long rectangular strip of papyrus— the text of the dream in black ink, the interpretation in red.

He perused the contents for some time. On the surface Rahotep's dreams portrayed him as an unacknowledged hero, but the magical interpretation often contradicted the dream. If Rahotep dreamed of success, Qenamun prophesied increased taxes, the death of a wife, a robbery. Rahotep was a prince, but he disliked parting with his wealth. And try as he might, Meren couldn't understand why either he or Ahiram would risk their lives by robbing the tomb of the king's brother.

Vengeance seemed an insufficient motive for either of them, as did the riches contained in the tomb. But what other reason could there be? What other purpose would be served?

Two things resulted when one robbed a pharaoh's tomb—one got rich, and one deprived the dead of sustenance. Vengeance ended with the destruction of the soul. But the riches lasted longer. And a pharaoh's riches provided enormous revenues, which could then be used for any purpose. What purpose needed secrecy?

"Crimes," muttered Meren as he rolled up the dream interpretation. "Secret riches provide funds for deeds one wishes to conceal." His hands stilled on the papyrus roll. "Like treason."

He dropped the roll on the table and rubbed the back of his neck. Like a water snake at night, a vague idea slithered through his thoughts, dark, slippery, not quite perceived. Cursing under his breath, he realized he wasn't going to catch this idea by chasing it. He decided to go to the place where this mystery began, the statue of the living god Tutankhamun.

Meren could hear the rhythmic grinding of stone against stone as he approached the colossus. He'd taken a ferry across the river alone. Abu would scold him for not taking an escort, but he often felt the need to pursue his inquiries by himself. His deliberations fared better if he didn't have a hulking charioteer or an entourage of servants hovering over him.

He knew his friends thought this craving for isolation unusual. Great men walked about the world with servants going before them and trailing after them—the greater the man, the more numerous the gaggle of retainers. But Meren needed no entourage to announce his consequence, no minions to help him look at a statue.

Most of the surfaces of the colossus had been polished now. He stood at a distance watching workers scurry up the scaffolding. At the base, the inscription of the king's names was complete. A master stonemason seemed to be inspecting the carvings. He was wiping one of the hieroglyphs of the king's name, Tutankhamun.

His cloth slid over the sign of the reed leaf that resembled a feather, and over the top of the leaf, which formed a raised notch. Then he moved on to the next cartouche. The cloth worked over the top symbol, the curved surface of the disk that rested above the beetle in the cluster of signs that spelled the king's coronation name, Nebkheprure. Then it traced the outline of the oval cartouche just above the disk.

Meren's gaze traveled up the length of the statue's leg and beyond, high above the ground, where the platform still surrounded the statue's head. He estimated the spot where Unas had fallen. Kysen had been right to question the fall, for Unas would have had to throw himself away from the ladder to land on that spot.

Musing over this puzzle, he passed through the pylon gate of the god and worked his way through swarms of priests, laborers, and supplicants to the House of Life. He attracted attention as he approached the building, but he wasn't surprised. A murder had heralded his last visit, and once here, he'd faced down the high priest. A novice sidled past him and darted into the temple. On his way to one of the prophets, no doubt, with word of this intrusion.

He brushed aside the obsequious attentions of one of the chief scribes of the House of Life, requested a lamp, and went alone to Qenamun's room. Shoving open the door, he held up the lamp to dispel the darkness. Someone had put the chamber in order.

Scraps of papyrus, broken pottery, and wax figures had been swept away. The documents that had been scattered about the room had been rolled and tied into bundles. Several such bundles rested on end on the floor.

To his left sat the shelves of texts against the wall. Before him lay the table on which Qenamun had died. Someone had placed his scribal equipment there. Meren glanced at pots of ink, a knife used to trim rush pens, the indispensable scribe's palette. Of wood overlaid with ivory, this palette was a luxurious version of an everyday instrument. A thin oblong box, it bore two hollows in which red and black ink were kept. Thousands of scribes carried humbler versions of such palettes in the city.

A sliding panel covered the slot used to store pens, but it was empty: Ahiram, in his haste to replace the scribal equipment with cobras, had dumped over fifty pens in the bottom of the casket that now resided in Meren's office.

No one had removed the incomplete wax figure of the Hittite king with its curse. The inscription called down every evil plot, deed, fate, and monster upon Suppiluliumas, whose name was enclosed in a cartouche. Meren set the figurine aside. He glanced at a stack of bowls behind it. They were clean, unused. Passing on, he continued to search the chamber.

He held little hope of finding anything. Qenamun was too clever to leave signs of his guilt where they could be found, and he'd already searched the place once. He was bending over a leather document case when a shadow fell between him and the lamp. He turned to face Ebana.

Closing the door, his cousin placed himself between it and Meren. "I didn't think you'd come here after our last encounter."

Meren straightened and leaned against the table.

"Did you know, cousin, that you're one of the few people whose first words haven't been to ask if I caught Ahiram?"

"Would you tell me if I asked?"

It was like balancing on the tip of an obelisk. He couldn't bring into the open the destruction at Horizon of Aten, and yet he had to know if Ebana was involved.

"Shall I tell you?" Meren asked. "I'll relate what appears to have happened. Ahiram ran away out of fear that some crime of his had been discovered, and was killed by bandits before I could reach him."

Ebana didn't look away. He met Meren's stare with a lifted brow. "What crime?"

"I've given you the surface, upon which lilies float. Are you certain you want the unwholesome substance that sinks beneath?"

"You've become accomplished at subtly building suspense and hinting at evil to come," Ebana said, "but your artistry goes for naught if the victim understands your strategy."

Picking up a stone used to smooth the irregularities from sheets of papyrus, Meren sighed. "Very well. Ahiram had committed acts of great evil. He lost his wits and fled when he thought I was nearing the truth." He tossed the stone in the air and caught it, then smiled at Ebana. "How incongruous that I only discovered the truth through his carelessness and alarm."

Ebana had always been adept at playing parts in the great plays that told the stories of the gods. His acting skill had served him well in making his way at court and in the temple. Meren couldn't help admiring it now, when it was used against him. Brows drew together to indicate confusion.

"I still don't understand," Ebana said.

Meren kept tossing the stone slowly, as if he intended to remain in this dead man's room indefinitely. "*Wings of Horus* is the fastest ship on the Nile, Ebana. I caught up with him before those mercenaries you sent could finish him."

He watched understanding dawn over Ebana's face. He stopped tossing the stone; he hadn't expected to startle his cousin out of his composure. A wave of concern washed over those features that so resembled his, and then was gone. Dread crept into Meren's soul.

"If you had him, or anything else, to prove that I'd committed some transgression, we both know you'd have taken me prisoner the moment you docked."

Meren was shaking his head. "Even after all this time, I don't think I believed you'd go so far. Why? Pharaoh has decreed a restoration so complete that Amun is more powerful than ever."

"If I were to speculate upon the matter, I might reply with a question. Can evil be erased by one who shares the blood of a heretic?"

"So you believe that an innocent should suffer for the crimes of his brother."

Ebana came nearer, within a pace of Meren, and spoke in a low voice. "You would pry into my soul? You who served the sun disk that brought blasphemy and plagues to Egypt. That was your statement, not mine. But since we're speaking of innocents, I would remind you of my wife and son. How would you feel if someone took your son and dashed his head against the flagstones until it burst? Ah, did that frighten you?"

"Are you threatening Kysen?"

"I but asked a question."

"Damn you, Ebana, if you harm him, I'll hunt you from here to the netherworld. You'll wish the Devourer had taken your soul after I've done with you."

"You're no longer great enough to utter threats, my dear cousin. Everyone knows what happened at the palace, how you've angered pharaoh and lost his favor. What did you do to make him so furious, when he dotes upon your words and admires you as if you were the god and not he?"

Meren said nothing. He hadn't expected the rumors of his downfall to spread so quickly. If they had reached the temple, his power to serve the king was threatened, for no one would respect his authority. Ebana smiled at him and let out a long breath like the hiss of a cobra as it flared its hood. He opened the door and stepped to the threshold.

"You'd better take care, sweet cousin, or pharaoh will send men to murder you and your son and his son in your beds as his brother did to me." Ebana laughed. The sound reverberated down the hall as he closed the door behind him, leaving Meren alone in the chamber where Qenamun had been murdered. His hand hurt. He looked down to find it strangling the hilt of his dagger. He had to summon his thoughts and dampen his rage before he could direct his fingers to uncurl and loosen their grip.

The walk out of the temple seemed unending, and yet he reached the colossus without hindrance. He'd half expected Ebana to waylay him in some dark corner of the House of Life. He returned home certain that Ebana had had a role in the looting of Akhenaten's tomb, but with no way to prove it to pharaoh. Not that Tutankhamun needed proof to believe the priests of Amun had committed the evil.

What was he going to do? He couldn't tell anyone he suspected his own cousin of the crime. What proof did he have? An expression on a face, a silence. Ebana had said nothing to betray himself or anyone else. The only way to get more from him would be by force.

This last thought occurred to him as he entered his office. It was late afternoon, and he felt as if a century had passed since his confrontation with pharaoh. How had it happened, this fall from grace? No, he wouldn't harass himself with such musings. He found his juggling balls and began to toss three of them.

Casting his thoughts back, he remembered how frightened Unas had seemed when he last saw the man. Unas had been such an earnest little snail, concerned with accuracy, quality, detail. So why would he break a bowl and then try to burn it? Such an extraordinary act for a man who, in his heart, was so very ordinary.

He watched a leather ball as he tossed it in the air. It was of dark leather, almost as dark as those burned shards. He remembered that fragment of inscription on one of them. Which cursive hieroglyphs might they represent? Those curved lines above each fragment of a letter annoyed him for some reason, but he couldn't think why.

Darting forward, he managed to catch a ball he'd thrown badly as his thoughts moved on to the three dead men. Try as he might, he couldn't produce a tangible connection between them. That trip to the temple had been useless, and it had exposed him to danger. He'd almost expected Ebana to try to overturn the king's statue on him. What a fate, to be crushed by the image of the pharaoh he'd worked so hard to serve, to lie beneath the carvings of his names . . .

Meren continued to toss and catch leather spheres. Carvings. Two cartouches, curved lines encircling hieroglyphs. All at once, two unrelated pieces of knowledge slipped into place—the curved lines on the inscription on the shards, and those carved in relief on the statue's base. Two curved lines side by side; the encircling ovals of two cartouches. And beneath them, the tip of a reed leaf and a portion of a disk. Two cartouches drawn on the colossus—and on the rim of a bowl.

A bowl inscribed with the king's name. Pharaoh's name, on a common pottery bowl found in the house of a dead priest. Why place such an inscription on a bowl?

Oil jars bore the year of the reign, as did wine jars. No, this was a small bowl like those in any common kitchen. Then Meren caught his juggling balls and stood holding them in the middle of his office. He'd seen bowls recently, but not in a kitchen—in a room, Qenamun's room.

There had been a stack of them next to the wax figure of the Hittite king, the one with the curse on it. The curse! There was a special instance in which bowls were inscribed—when they were to be used as cursing bowls. Of course Unas had no reason to burn a bowl, unless it was a cursing bowl, and then only if the curse were heinous. If it bore the name Nebkheprure Tutankhamun.

Magic. And who of all those involved in this mystery was connected intimately with magic? Lector priests specialized in sacred writings and magic, and Qenamun would have possessed the knowledge necessary to imbue the vessels with magical curses. He must have been making bowls bearing curses against the king. A lector priest would break them to bring about evil and precipitate the magic.

Meren shivered as he held the leather spheres. Those bowls must have been part of Qenamun's collection of magical implements, to be used for some fell purpose. Qenamun needed those curses to protect himself while he was doing evil, betraying pharaoh.

Had the priests of Amun been protecting themselves against pharaoh discovering their crimes? If Qenamun knew that Unas had found the bowls, he would have killed the priest rather than risk betrayal. But what if the curse against pharaoh was meant for use in a greater, more far-reaching evil?

Placing the juggling balls on the table in his office, Meren sank into his chair, growing more and more uneasy at the direction his thoughts were taking. Qenamun simply might have been protecting the priesthood against pharaoh with these cursing bowls. But such an explanation didn't account for why Ahiram, who wasn't a priest but a warrior and courtier, had become involved in the first place. Nor did it necessarily explain why someone had sent foreign mercenaries to kill Ahiram. Unless the looting of the royal tomb served another purpose besides vengeance.

If Ahiram had suddenly become more wealthy, he, Meren, would have noticed, would have made inquires. He must have wanted the valuables from the royal tomb for some other purpose. Another visit to Ahiram's house might help him think. Distracted by his deliberations, certain that he'd caught the scent of an unseen and dangerous animal, Meren left without telling anyone where he was going.

18

▽

The same porter stood watch over Ahiram's house when Meren arrived. Since the prince was dead and the place had been examined, there had seemed to be no further need to guard it. Like most houses of the nobility, it was set behind a high wall, with gardens, a reflection pool, and service buildings. Meren was interested only in the places Ahiram might have left signs of his evil acts.

Leaving the porter at the front gate, he went to Ahiram's chamber again. Once more he rummaged through the covers of the polished and gold-trimmed cedar bed. He kicked aside scattered clothing that had been taken from chests.

He came across a small casket by the bed that contained writing supplies, a palette with rush pens, pots filled with red ocher and black soot, and one for water. An ebony-and-gilt-wood case for spare rush pens rested on top of unused papyri, yet there were no letters, no accounts, no personal writings of any kind. Ahiram must have destroyed any correspondence he didn't want found.

What had he expected? Kysen was thorough, and he would have found anything significant remaining in this room. Still, Meren eyed the frieze of lotus flowers along the walls near the floor, looking for concealed niches.

Bending over, he moved along the wall, running his fingers over the lotus design, until he came to the recess containing the statue of the goddess Ishtar. His sandal hit a belt. He straightened and kicked it aside. His gaze caught another belt, the one with gold and turquoise beads that Kysen had left beside the pen holder at the base of the statue.

Then he looked at the goddess, with her pleated and tiered skirt and rounded eyes. Ahiram had felt the need to propitiate a foreign goddess, and yet when he most needed her favor, he'd strewn his possessions all over her altar. Meren shook his head at such conduct. There weren't any offerings that he could see. No food or wine or incense, and he didn't think Ishtar would be satisfied with a pen holder. A pen holder.

Slowly, his hand reached out to the tubular case. It was of wood shaped like a bundle of slender papyrus stalks and overlaid with gold foil. He picked it up and shook it. Empty. But hadn't he just seen another equally as rich in the casket by the bed?

Meren rolled the columnar case between his palms and stared at the wall. Few warriors such as Ahiram had need of enough rush pens to fill two elegant holders. He rested his shoulder against the wall near the statue and examined the pen holder. A sudden image came to him, of many rush pens spilled in the bottom of Qenamun's casket. Ahiram had Qenamun's pen holder.

The man had been a fool to purloin the case from Qenamun, as he had Akhenaten's sandals, but Meren could see that he'd grown more and more distraught after Unas was murdered, until he lost all sense on the day of the hippo hunt. Even on the water waiting for their prey, he'd been anxious, querying Tanefer about how long they should wait for the animal, fussing about the delay, and then nearly getting himself killed.

Meren's hands stilled on the golden case as he remembered the struggle with the hippo. Tanefer's huntsman had told them the hippo was ashore, not in the river. Therefore the creature had taken them by surprise, rising up out of the water like a mountain with eyes and toppling Ahiram.

He and Tanefer had tried to help Ahiram, but the hippo had knocked him into the water as well. He remembered plummeting into the blackness, the breath knocked out of him, nearly losing consciousness. Tanefer had come after him.

When they broke to the surface, the hippo was attacking Ahiram again. He had thrown himself at the creature to grab the harpoon sticking from its shoulder, and then Tanefer had lunged at him. Lunged at him and at the same time kicked out, shoving Ahiram beneath those long, yellow tusks.

Shoving him. Meren closed his eyes. *No.*

"Put it down, brother of my heart."

Tanefer was standing in the doorway, a dagger strapped to his upper arm, a straight sword in his hand. The blade was wet and red. Soldiers followed him into the room, bearing spears, and took up positions surrounding Meren at a distance.

"Put it down," Tanefer said.

Laying the pen holder back in the niche, Meren walked toward his friend. "You weren't trying to save me from the hippo. You were trying to kill Ahiram." He thrust his sudden grief into the dark pit of his soul as he approached Tanefer.

"Stop. I'm not a fool, to let you get too close."

Meren glanced at the bloodied sword.

"You killed the porter." He shook his head and couldn't keep the broken quality from his voice. "Oh, Tanefer, not you."

Tanefer's gaze held bitter amusement. "I knew you were close, damn you. You've forced me to move too quickly."

Meren took another step, but Tanefer jabbed at him

with the sword. Spears aimed at him. He halted and lifted his arms away from his body. He remained calm without, while feeling as if his heart had been sliced in half.

"None of this has been about revenge upon Akhenaten, has it?"

Tanefer smiled. "You always were the cleverest of us. No, vengeance was an added but unnecessary sweetness. I needed gold for my men."

"The Mitanni prisoner," Meren said as he thought rapidly. "You killed him to stop us from questioning him."

"Yes, but when my men reported to me that you'd gone to the colossus and to Qenamun's office, and then here, I knew you were close to the truth. So now I must do what I'd wanted to put off until you were more isolated at court, when you were desperate."

"What is that?" Meren moved to the side, but Tanefer moved with him, keeping himself between Meren and the door.

"It's like I've been telling you, my friend. The empire is threatened by the Hittites. Without a strong leader, Egypt could fall to them just as my country did. Can you imagine proud, rich Egypt under the whips of those barbarians?"

"No."

Tanefer moved closer and rested the tip of the bloodied sword on Meren's broad collar. Meren remained motionless and stared into the too-calm eyes of his friend.

"None of you ever really understood what it was like. My mother was the daughter of a king, sent to a foreign land where she was tossed into pharaoh's palace and ignored. She should have been chief queen and I the heir, and year after year she endured the insult of giving place to those of less-royal blood. But she raised me in the secret knowledge of the superiority of my heritage."

"But you've had great honors. You never—"

"After she died, well, there was no one to remind me of my heritage, and I was so young. I was content."

Tanefer's breathing quickened. "Until I saw my mother's homeland for the first time. Great cities ravaged, armies defeated, women and children carried into slavery. And the warriors—proud, brave men brought low because of the cowardice of pharaoh. It took me a long time, but I finally realized that I had to act. I tried to tell you that time by your reflection pool. Weren't you listening to me?"

Meren surveyed his friend, the way his brows drew together, the brightness of his eyes, like the lakes of fire in the netherworld.

"I was listening, but I don't think I heard the inner meaning of your words."

"No, you didn't, or you would have remembered that had Egypt come to my uncle's aid, he wouldn't have lost his throne. I could have been king after him, if not for that. With the support of Egypt, I could have had my own empire. But Akhenaten helped destroy Mitanni. His brothers have been no better. A line of kings that could allow such destruction deserves to perish."

"Egypt will never accept a foreign king."

"Only half foreign," Tanefer said. "And she will, if I'm married to the Great Royal Wife, and if I have the support of the great ones of the land—if I have your support, Meren."

"You ask my support while you hold a sword to my heart?"

Tanefer lifted the blade, and Meren turned away from him, pretending to consider what had been said to him.

"I'm giving you a choice, brother of my heart, because of all of them, I can least bear killing you."

Meren couldn't bring himself to reply to that. Horemheb would laugh at him if he were here, at his failure to pry deeply enough into Tanefer's soul. He'd been so furious at Ebana for stoking the fires of their enmity that he had been distracted from perceiving danger in other directions.

Finally he said, "You and Parenefer have been planning this for a long time."

"Parenefer? That old fool knows nothing of me. I had Ahiram approach him through Qenamun about looting Akhenaten's tomb. He thought the aim was vengeance upon the spirit of the king."

"So the foreign stragglers and refugees have come to Egypt at your invitation."

Tanefer nodded. "I planned well, and yet some evil fiend cursed me when that priest overheard Qenamun and Ahiram at the temple discussing plans for the disposition of the tomb goods."

"Unas," Meren said.

"Aye. And when I heard you'd discovered fragments of Qenamun's cursing bowls, I had Ahiram dispatch the lector priest. Unfortunately, you alarmed him with your constant inquiries and your reputation for discovering crimes."

"So you arranged to kill him at your hippo hunt."

Tanefer gave a wave of dismissal. "Necessary. In his state, sooner or later he would have broken."

"But you failed, and he ran, so you sent some of your Mitanni mercenaries after him."

"They followed him the moment he left the city. Did he live to tell you anything?"

"Only that you would betray me as you did him."

Tanefer smiled. "That's not true. You and I have been friends far too long. We admire each other. And after all, I did save you from being eaten by a hippo."

Meren shook his head. "You can't succeed."

"You don't know how long I've been suborning royal guards and building companies of renegade Mitanni soldiers."

"You've been stocking the military with your minions. That's why Rahotep has so many under his command. And your renegades, where are they?"

Laughing, Tanefer lifted his sword again, and Meren backed away.

"You can't think I'd tell you. Not yet, not until you've committed yourself to me."

He had to delay, pretend to be swayed, or Tanefer would kill him. Abruptly, a small detail flitted into his mind.

"Saustatar," Meren said. "That captured Mitanni kept mentioning Saustatar."

"Ah, yes, my name among my people. I've taken one more suitable than my Egyptian one. You see, Meren, I intend to be as great a conqueror as my ancestor. Greater, for my empire will stretch from Egypt to the Euphrates and beyond. And I hope you'll consent to join me in creating it."

"You know how I feel about pharaoh."

"The boy who has just cast you aside like a soiled loincloth?"

Now was the time. Meren turned his back and lowered his head, hoping Tanefer would take his gesture as resentment against Tutankhamun. He couldn't fight nine men, especially not if one of them was as good as his friend was.

Tanefer had come close again. "You have great influence and power, brother of my heart, and you command the respect of the royal charioteers, the infantry. And you can help me with Ebana."

Meren's head came up.

"Ebana?"

"The priests of Amun have begun to suspect me. Too many deaths. They may balk at the need for my small palace revolt. But if you talk to Ebana—"

"No."

"Don't decide in haste, old friend, for your life depends upon your answer."

He couldn't appear to capitulate too easily, for his affection for pharaoh was too well known. Time was what he needed, time to be missed. He cursed himself as he realized Tanefer's men were guarding pharaoh. He and Ay had trusted Tanefer. Biting the inside of his cheek to keep from losing governance of his rage, he shook his head gently, as if wavering because of Tanefer's forceful arguments.

"I shall give you a few hours to think," Tanefer said.

He pointed the sword at two of his men. They approached Meren and bound his hands in front of him. Tanefer prodded him out of the room.

"No one will think to look for you here, especially not in the cellar."

Meren was shoved downstairs and into the black depths of the subterranean room. Tanefer left him there and paused in the doorway at the top of the staircase.

"You have a day, my friend. Consider well. You could be my vizier. I'm going to need one after I kill Ay and Maya."

"You can't kill everyone."

"I grow weary of argument. It's as well you have a son. As long as you know I have him under my hand, you won't buck too hard at wearing a harness. A good evening to you, brother of my heart."

The door closed then, leaving Meren in darkness. He had a few hours at most. During that time, he must accustom himself to the idea of killing an old friend.

* * *

Kysen strode into the house followed by Abu and Reia. Servants passed him bearing freshly roasted meat and new bread.

"Mut," Kysen called.

The woman paused on her way to the great hall with a tray of food.

"Where is Lord Meren?"

"I haven't seen him, lord. He went out earlier, then returned and shut himself in his office."

Kysen and his men made their way out of the house, through the pleasure garden, and to the offices. He was tired and disgruntled. He'd spent hours tracking down Rahotep and belaboring him with questions. Hot-bellied with resentment at Meren's treatment of him earlier at the palace, Rahotep had sparred, jousted, and lashed him with words. Finally he'd refused to answer any more questions. Kysen had lost his temper. If Abu hadn't stopped him, he would have punched the flat-faced, vain fool.

He shoved open the door to Meren's office. "Father, you'll have to talk to that arse Rahotep—"

His steps slowed as he realized the room was empty. Abu came in after him, followed by Reia, and they all glanced around.

"He's gone out again," Abu said.

"I thought he said we'd meet here at mealtime," Kysen said.

Reia nodded. "Aye, lord, he did."

"He'll be back soon, then," Kysen said as he plopped into a chair.

He was up again immediately when his gaze fell on the table bearing Qenamun's casket. Papyri were strewn over its surface. It was unlike his father to leave important materials in disarray. He went to the table and picked up one of the leather juggling balls that lay on top of the papyri.

Meren was always careful to conceal them, for only common entertainers juggled, not a hereditary prince and Friend of the King. Kysen peered into the casket.

"What is this doing here?" He lifted the silver mirror and turned to show it to Abu and Reia.

"I don't know," said Abu. Reia shook his head.

"You've never seen it?" Kysen asked.

Abu came closer and examined the mirror. "I think it belonged to the lord's wife. But if it's the same mirror, it's usually kept in the lord's bedchamber in a chest."

Kysen set the mirror on the table and glanced at the juggling balls again. Meren had left hurriedly, or he would never have left the juggling balls out. He would have put the mirror away, too. Tapping his fingers on the back of the mirror, Kysen thought for a while.

"Abu, search the house, grounds, and barracks, everything. See if my father is at home after all."

While he waited, he put away the juggling balls and placed the dream interpretations and other documents back in the casket. Abu returned with Reia.

"Lord Meren isn't here."

"Very well, we'll eat while we wait, but first send men to the offices of the vizier, and to the houses of Unas, Qenamun, and Ahiram, to see if Lord Meren has gone there."

By the time the sun was setting, his messengers had returned with no news of his father. No one had seen him, and the houses of the dead men appeared deserted. Kysen walked outside with Abu along the path in front of the house.

"I don't like this sudden disappearance," Kysen said.

"He took no men with him."

Kysen nodded and then grimaced. With word of Meren's fall from favor spreading, someone might have decided to rid himself of a rival at court. Meren's duties and place in Tutankhamun's affections had gained him enemies—Prince Hunefer, some of the army generals, now Rahotep. And Parenefer. And Ebana, who had once loved him, possibly hated him most of all. If Meren had discovered proof of the priests' role in the royal tomb desecration, his life would be in danger.

"Ebana," Kysen muttered.

Abu turned to him and shook his head. "That way lies danger, lord."

"Which is why you're coming with me. Get the men. We must make haste if we're to find him before he leaves the temple."

Kysen had Abu and the other charioteers follow him at a distance as they left the quay and approached the temple. Pure ones, laborers, scribes, and Servants of the God streamed forth between the pylons. Boys carrying their student scribe kits over their shoulders chased each other down the avenue and across the long shadow cast by the statue of pharaoh. Kysen approached the temple entrance from a side street and lingered just beyond the avenue at a tall stela inscribed with the great deeds of pharaoh's father, Amunhotep the Magnificent.

A bread vendor nearly bumped into him because he was standing concealed behind the tall slab of stone. He motioned to Abu, and the charioteers parted, distributing themselves at intervals along the avenue. One even leaned against the base of the king's statue.

Kysen watched as the flow of priests, servants, and slaves crested and then ebbed. Across the river the horizon was catching fire; a brilliant carnelian haze lit the cliffs that marked the beginning of the dead land. Glancing back at the temple gates, he saw two men emerge from their shadow.

Ebana must have had an engagement that required formal dress, for he'd donned a transparent pleated robe over his kilt. Kysen hadn't recognized him at once, for he wore a long court wig along with a belt and arm bands of electrum and turquoise. A matching broad collar covered his shoulders. The man with him was Tanefer, who rivaled Ebana's splendor in gold, lapis, and red jasper.

At his side, Abu stirred. Kysen put his arm in front of the charioteer.

"Wait until he's alone."

The two men had walked out of the temple in silence. Neither looked at the other. A chariot and driver appeared, rolling up to Tanefer. Tanefer leaned close to Ebana and said something. Ebana shook his head.

Tanefer laughed and held out his hand. His driver placed a whip in it. Tanefer touched Ebana on the arm with the coiled lash, and Kysen drew in his breath as the priest turned on the prince. He couldn't hear what Ebana said, but whatever it was caused Tanefer to laugh again as he mounted his chariot. The whip flicked out to tease the pleats in Ebana's robe. Jerking out of reach, Ebana hissed something at Tanefer, who executed an elaborate bow from his chariot, cracked the whip, and drove away.

Ebana walked down the avenue swiftly. Kysen waited until the priest was almost opposite him and slid out into the street. As he moved, charioteers left their positions and surrounded the priest.

"Greetings, adopted cousin," said Kysen.

Ebana stopped when Kysen stepped into his path, then glanced around as Abu and the others closed in on him. His hand dropped to the gold hilt of the dagger in his belt.

"What do you mean by this display?"

Kysen said, "Do you know where my father is?"

"No," Ebana said. "Where is he?"

"You haven't seen him?"

Ebana narrowed his eyes, then smiled. "Have you

lost your father, common cousin? How negligent of
you."

Kysen stepped nearer, which caused Ebana to grip his
dagger and the charioteers to stir. "I've no time for di-
versions and antics. Have you seen my father or not?"

"Earlier this afternoon, but fear not. He left me in
good health. Why are you so agitated, boy? Your father
needs no band of armed governesses trailing after him."

"Meren is missing, and you hate him enough for me
to come to you first now that I'm trying to find him."
Kysen dropped his voice. "And if he's harmed and
you're to blame, I'll find you, hack you into chunks,
and feed your carcass to the crocodiles."

Ebana met his gaze steadily, then smiled. The scar on
his face stretched as the muscles in his face moved.

"You truly fear for him. Tell me, plain-blooded
cousin, is it because of me, or because you're afraid that
pharaoh has turned away from him and had him done to
death?"

"I'm going to reach down your throat and pull out
your heart," Kysen replied. He almost jumped at the
bark of laughter that answered him.

"By the good god, you're a fierce whelp." Ebana
raked his glance over Kysen. "I don't know where
Meren is, but Tanefer mentioned him just now."

"Why?"

Ebana shrugged. "He had much to say to me, and
part of it concerned the quarrel between your father and
pharaoh. Where are you going?"

"To find Tanefer," Kysen said over his shoulder. "He
might know where my father has gone."

"May the good will of Amun be with you. You may
need it if your father has run afoul of one of his enemies."

Kysen wasted no effort in replying to the taunt. He
left Ebana standing in the avenue staring after him and

raced away through the streets in the direction Tanefer had taken.

Ebana's voice called after him. "Tanefer was going home, down the Street of the Golden Lion."

Kysen dodged around carts, donkeys, priests, and women carrying water. The charioteers ran in his wake. He hurtled down zigzagging alleys and streets, knowing that Tanefer's chariot wouldn't be able to go quickly in the narrow streets and crowds. He reached the Street of the Golden Lion and glimpsed Tanefer's chariot as it passed through the gateway—and he stopped. Abu plowed into him, and he careened into the wall of a house.

"Stay back."

"Lord?"

Kysen pointed at Tanefer's house. "Look."

Servants were trudging back and forth from the house to carts laden with boxes. Several chariots drove away from the house bearing women. Kysen shrank into a doorway, then motioned for his men to follow him. He edged along the street until he found an exterior stair. Abu waylaid a perplexed householder, and Kysen slipped upstairs to the roof.

As Abu joined him, he knelt behind the front wall and gazed out at Tanefer's house. Why was Tanefer vacating his house? Had he been ordered afield? If there had been some word of trouble at one of the frontiers, his friend might be sent to handle it. Still, the move was sudden.

"Abu, have you heard of this move?"

"No, lord, but events are happening swiftly at court."

Kysen scolded himself silently. He'd grown too suspicious, and he'd allowed his concern for Meren to override his good judgment. He stood up. All he need do was go to Tanefer and ask him what he was about. Then his eye caught the gleam of red jasper set in gold.

Tanefer was leaving the house by a side door, alone. He kept his back to one of the walls surrounding the house until he slipped through a small gate that let out into an alley. Once outside, Tanefer walked swiftly down the alley and into a crooked path that wound away from the Street of the Golden Lion. Without a word, Kysen left the roof, raced to the alley, and dodged along the path until he caught sight of Tanefer again.

Abu appeared at his side as he peered around a corner at Tanefer's retreating back.

"Lord, what are you doing?"

"It's not like Tanefer to skulk around the streets like a starved hyena. I don't like it. There's something wrong."

"But Prince Tanefer and your father are old friends."

"Shhh! I know that, but there's something wrong, and I'm going to find out what it is. If it's nothing, we'll go back and take a whip to Ebana."

They flitted after Tanefer like a shadow after a hawk in flight. Soon Kysen began to recognize streets and houses. His conjecture turned to certainty when, after surveying a deserted street, Tanefer walked quickly to the entryway of the house of Prince Ahiram. Kysen flattened himself against the wall beside the gate and looked toward the house.

"Why has he come here?" Abu asked.

Kysen shook his head as the charioteers who had been following them arrived to conceal themselves in doorways and against the wall. It was growing dark. Kysen waited for a few moments, but Tanefer failed to reappear. Then from behind the house came a man, a soldier by his appearance, leading a chariot. He tethered the team to a stone on the ground near the door and disappeared behind the house again.

"Abu," Kysen said. "Remain here with the others."

"Lord, this is foolish. You know what your father said."

"He's in a dead murderer's house, Abu. I have to know what's going on, and I can't sneak in with all of you stumbling after me. *Stay here.*"

Kysen raced across the street and planted himself against the wall that ringed Ahiram's house. He ran around it to the side wall, only to find that Abu had followed him.

"Forgive me, but the lord Meren gave me orders."

"Damn you. Very well, then boost me over the wall."

He sailed up and onto the top of the wall. Lying flat, he peered into a front garden in the fading light. It was deserted, so he lowered himself to the ground and darted behind a sycamore. He heard a slapping sound and a grunt. Abu's head appeared over the wall. The charioteer struggled atop the wall, then dropped over the side and joined him.

"Gods, you're tenacious as a goose after a fly."

"Thank you, lord."

Kysen watched the front door, but it was growing dark. He and Abu moved to the concealment of Ahiram's chapel. Looking around the corner of the building, he saw Tanefer come out the front door.

"He's coming. I think we're close enough to hear— gods!"

Kysen fell silent, then drew his dagger, for behind Tanefer, flanked by two men carrying spears, came his father.

19

▽

Meren allowed the two guards to shove him out of the house after Tanefer. If he was forced to fight, he'd rather do it in the open, and Tanefer didn't fully believe his professed decision to join him in treason. He had tried to be convincing, seeming to waver between loyalty to pharaoh and Tanefer's passionate ambitions for Egypt. Yet his hands were still bound.

He had tried to accustom himself to what must be done, but most of his time had been spent wondering at the mysteries men kept hidden in their souls. He had known Tanefer for so long. He'd trusted him in battle with his life, caroused in beer taverns with him, even been with the same woman. Yet each of them reserved a part of himself—a part rich in secret wounds and corruptions—sheltered in the depths of the ka.

It was that time between dusk and darkness when pale objects seemed to brighten with the last vestiges of the heat of Ra. Meren glanced around the forecourt as he was pushed toward a chariot. He'd been gone long enough for Kysen to miss him. He could only hope the boy was trying to find him, but he couldn't think of any signs he'd left that would make Kysen search at Ahiram's house.

Then he heard a wiry screech, and another—the sound of two cats fighting. Meren fought hard not to show his relief. When his guards shoved him again, he balked and knocked aside a spear. Tanefer turned, drawing his dagger at the noise.

"Where are you taking me?" Meren demanded. "I've said I would join you. Release me now."

Tanefer strolled back to him, slapping his palm with the flat of his dagger blade. "I think not. I've had time to consider, and despite your so-graceful submission, I think I'll feel better if it's accompanied by a complete estrangement from pharaoh."

Meren stared at his friend. "So you're going to make him hate me."

Tanefer laughed. "Perhaps. But first I'll keep you awhile. If you vanish from sight without warning, pharaoh will have good cause to look upon you in a manner like to Ahiram. After ten days or so, I'll release you. Then, no matter how dear you are to him, he'll never be able to trust you again."

"And he won't believe me if I tell him about you," Meren said.

"Also, if you betray me," Tanefer said, "your interference will come too late. In ten days I'll have my men gathered outside the city." He stopped and glanced around. "Enough of this chatter. It's almost dark. I couldn't risk moving you in daylight, you know. Your face is too well known."

Meren felt the tip of a spear poke him in the back. From somewhere beyond the high walls that blocked his view of the street, the din of cat fury began again. He took a step toward the chariot, moving away from the guards. As he moved, he heard a familiar twang and hiss. The guard behind him grunted and toppled as an arrow took him in the chest. Another arrow flew past, just missing the second guard.

At the same time, Meren twisted around and grabbed the second guard's spear. Before the man could respond, he'd yanked the weapon from his grasp. The guard

drew a knife from his belt. Hampered by his bonds,
Meren jumped back, hefted the spear, and shoved it.
The tip caught the man in the thigh. He screamed and
dropped to the ground. Around him he heard the war
cries of his charioteers and saw men scaling the guard
walls.

The second guard's knife was lying beside him.
Meren dropped to one knee and reached for it with his
bound hands. The edge of a blade descended in front of
him and pressed into his neck. As it did, he heard Kysen's voice call a halt to the charioteers. He heard Tanefer whisper in his ear.

"Don't, old friend. I don't wish to kill you."

The edge of the dagger sliced into his skin, bringing
a searing sting. Blood seeped between his flesh and the
blade, trickled down his neck. He drew his hands back
from the knife as his regret at having to fight Tanefer
vanished in his fury.

"Now," said Tanefer, "rise slowly."

"Damnation to you, Tanefer."

"I know, brother of my heart. This grieves me as
well. Forgive me."

Tanefer's arm slipped around his throat and shoved
his chin up, further exposing his neck. Meren stood and
Tanefer turned him so that they faced Kysen and half a
dozen charioteers scattered between the house and the
guard walls. The chariot was standing by, but only because the horses had been tethered.

Tightening his grip on Meren, Tanefer called out.
"Well done, Ky, but you should have killed me first."

Kysen began to walk toward them, and Meren felt
the blade sink deeper into his flesh. Charioteers started
closing in on them. He set his jaw, refusing to cry out
as Tanefer wished. Then the blade lifted, swiftly. Like
the strike of a hunting cat, Tanefer's blade jabbed.

Meren felt it pierce his flesh high on his shoulder. He heard Kysen shout.

This time he couldn't prevent a cry from escaping as the dagger embedded itself and then withdrew. Stunned, Meren felt his body stiffen. His hands came up to press against the wound. Blood wet them. Figures rushed at him, but Tanefer stopped them by returning the dagger to Meren's throat.

"Forgive me, Ky," Tanefer was saying, "I do regret causing Meren pain, but this is the most efficient solution to my dilemma. Now you must allow me to go to my yacht unhindered, for that's the only way your father will live. If you try to prevent me, I'll simply delay, and if that happens, the way Meren's bleeding . . . Well, do you wish to risk it?"

"No."

"I thought not. Now drop your weapons. All of you move back to the wall. Meren, we're going to my chariot. You will drive. That's why I kept your wound shallow."

"You've lost," Meren said through clenched teeth. "Don't make things worse."

"You're mistaken. Look at your son, he'd hand me the sun boat of Ra if it would save your life."

Tanefer began to drag him sideways toward the chariot. It was almost nightfall now, and he could hardly see Kysen or anyone else. His thoughts raced while he fought the pain of his wound. He was fast losing strength. If he was going to fight, it would have to be now. He was about to grab Tanefer's dagger arm when he heard a sound—*phhhht*. Tanefer jumped and gasped as an arrow grazed his arm.

This was his chance. Meren grabbed Tanefer's dagger. He shoved it away and twisted to face his opponent at the same time. He heard Kysen shouting, but he and

Tanefer were engaged in a battle for possession of the dagger.

Although he knew things were happening quickly, he saw them as if in a sea of chilled honey. The blade writhed in Tanefer's hands, then pointed at Meren. Without warning, Tanefer leapt on him.

Caught off guard, Meren felt his body overbalance, and he fell beneath Tanefer. He hit the ground, his head cracking against the packed earth. Desperate, he kept his grip on Tanefer's wrists. But as they struggled, he felt his strength wash from him, receding like a spent sea wave on a beach.

His hands were wet with blood, and they shook. His muscles screamed at the strain, while above him Tanefer pressed down on the dagger, aiming it at his heart. Knowing he had little time, Meren heaved upward with his whole body.

They writhed, tangling their legs and rolling. He sank beneath Tanefer's weight again. He was slammed against the ground, crying out as the impact jarred his wound. His hands slipped as they tried to deflect the dagger. He twisted the weapon at the last moment, just as the black shadow of Tanefer's body descended upon him. He felt the blade puncture flesh, glance off bone. Hot blood spilled over him. He couldn't breathe.

Tanefer gasped in his ear. "Forgive me, brother of my heart."

"No." He felt Tanefer's body relax and he swore.

Suddenly he was free of Tanefer's weight. Meren blinked up into torchlight. Kysen and Abu were lifting the body off him. Kysen dropped to his knees and began prodding.

"Are you hurt? Damnation, answer me!"

"I don't know."

He winced as he tried to sit. Kysen helped him, and by the time he was upright, he realized that he wasn't seriously wounded. He watched Kysen's hands tremble while they touched the flesh near the wound on his shoulder.

A charioteer appeared with cloth, which Kysen pressed against the wound. More charioteers arrived, bearing torches. A pool of light formed, revealing Tanefer. He was lying on his back, his chest covered with blood from a wound near the heart. Meren cursed, then shook his head as his vision blurred. He couldn't remember stabbing Tanefer, but he must have.

"Gods," Kysen said. "I saw that arrow and started running, but you fought so quickly. By the time we got here, I thought he'd killed you."

Meren's vision filled with the sight of Tanefer's ruined body. Crimson stained the sheer white of his robe and dappled the electrum at his wrists and neck. Death seemed such a violation in a body full of brightness, wit, and youth. Turning his face away, he allowed Kysen to bind his wound.

"This will do until Nebamun can treat you."

Abu held a cup of water to his lips, and as Meren drank a shadow fell between him and the torchlight. He pushed the cup away and raised his eyes. Ebana stood over him, holding a bow. Kysen helped Meren stand, and together they stared at his cousin. Ebana bent down and retrieved a bloodied arrow. At the appearance of Meren's cousin, Abu and the other charioteers retreated out of hearing distance.

"It was you!" Kysen said. "You fired that arrow at Tanefer."

"You piqued my curiosity with your worry about your father, so I followed you," Ebana said.

Meren leaned on Kysen and studied the scarred blankness of Ebana's expression. "Did you try to kill him to save me, or to stop him from using you against pharaoh?"

Ebana didn't answer.

"I don't understand," Kysen said.

"Tanefer has been planning a revolt all along," Meren said. "He was using Ahiram and Qenamun to devise the desecration of Akhenaten's tomb in order to provide funds for his mercenaries. The pure one, Unas, stumbled upon their plot, and Qenamun killed him."

Kysen was shaking his head. "Then Qenamun was the dung-eater who tried to kill me."

"Yes," Meren said. "But Qenamun's foolhardiness and our inquiries caused Ahiram to become overwrought, so he killed Qenamun, only to find he'd aroused Tanefer's fury by calling attention to the first murder. Tanefer tried to rid himself of Ahiram at the hippo hunt and failed, and Ahiram fled, thus exposing their intrigue. That was when I finally searched in the right direction." Meren gave his cousin a pained smile. "And that direction leads from Tanefer, through Ahiram, to the priests of Amun."

"We knew nothing of this foul plot against pharaoh," Ebana said at last.

"Why should I believe you?"

Ebana remained silent while he unstrung his bow. Then he began winding the bowstring. "I saved your life."

"Yes," Meren said. "Now tell me why."

Ebana came closer and glanced at Meren's wound. "Perhaps I didn't want you to die."

Meren lifted his brows and waited.

"Perhaps I thought you and pharaoh easier to deal with than Tanefer."

"You were right. Eventually Tanefer would have killed you as well as me."

"And of course, I'm telling the truth. The temple of Amun never plotted against the life of pharaoh."

"What do you want, Ebana?" Kysen asked.

"A bargain."

Meren exchanged glances with Kysen and nodded for Ebana to continue.

"Let us declare a truce between the temple and the court, cousin. We offer an end to all this hidden warfare in exchange for—how shall I phrase it—a cessation of these awkward inquiries of yours. Qenamun was the only priest among the evil ones who have so disturbed the peace of the living Horus."

"Why should I make this bargain?"

"For several reasons," Ebana said. "One is that you've no proof that anyone else from the temple has committed any transgression."

Ebana eyed him as he said this, but Meren wasn't about to agree or disagree.

"Another reason is that with the threat of the Hittites growing and the invasion of all these renegade soldiers and bandits, you can't afford to be at odds with Amun as well."

Meren began to scowl as he realized the truth of Ebana's reasoning. Then his cousin lowered his voice and stepped nearer so that he could almost touch Meren.

"And also, my suspicious, cynical, and jaded cousin, because I might have saved your life simply because it was yours."

Meren studied Ebana, his gaze traveling over that lean jaw, the thin white line of the scar. What real evidence did he have that the priests of Amun had been involved in the desecration of Akhenaten's tomb? Words spoken to him by Tanefer, who was now dead, and who had confided in no one left alive. Fragments from a bowl with mere traces of writing that could be explained away by anyone as clever as Ebana. The murder of Qenamun by Ahiram implied that they had participated in the crime together. Yet without the capture of the actual thieves who had dug into the royal tomb, he could hardly expect the powerful priesthood of Amun to admit guilt.

So far none of the search parties sent after the thieves had found them. Meren suspected that they'd fled by way of the Red Sea already. To accuse Ebana or Parenefer he needed more, and the priests seemed to have concealed their actions well, even Qenamun. Qenamun! The gold pen holder.

"Well, cousin?" Ebana said.

Leaning on Kysen, Meren turned to the house. "Come with me."

He led them back to Ahiram's bedchamber and to the shrine of Ishtar. Releasing his hold on Kysen, he plucked the pen holder from the niche. He swayed a bit, causing Kysen to slip his arm around his waist. Summoning his remaining strength, he opened the top of the case and tipped it. Nothing fell into his hand. Meren stared at the blood drying on the back of his knuckles, then gave his head a little shake. He slipped a finger into the tube and drew out a papyrus wound into a tight roll. He handed the pen holder to Ebana.

"No doubt you recognize this?"

"No," Ebana said.

"Come now. You must have seen it many times in the House of Life."

"Don't be irritating, Meren. I assume you mean this is Qenamun's."

Meren was unrolling the papyrus. He skimmed the flowing script that filled the sheet, studied the name written at the bottom, and lifted his gaze to Ebana's.

"I should have expected him to blame Ahiram and Tanefer and keep silent about—"

Ebana stopped him by reaching out and grabbing his forearm. "Don't say it. You've no evidence, so don't be foolish."

Meren yanked his arm free and handed the papyrus to Kysen, who read it aloud.

"I, Qenamun, lector priest of Amun, call upon the good god as my witness. Amun came to me in a dream and said unto me: Go forth and cause me to be avenged upon the great heretic for his sacrilege. I have done this, with the aid of Prince Ahiram." Kysen broke off. "There's more about Akhenaten's heresy, but no mention of anyone else at the temple."

Wincing, Meren leaned against the wall. "I think he meant this as a record of his greatness, possibly to be put on his tomb." He glanced at Ebana. "But such a text could only be inscribed if someone else besides pharaoh or his heir ruled Egypt."

"Or if pharaoh one day changes his opinion about his brother," Ebana said. "Qenamun might have had a dream about that also."

"By the gods, Ebana, you don't expect me to allow this evil to pass without consequence."

"I expect you to report to pharaoh that Prince Tanefer plotted a revolt against him, that he suborned Ahiram and Qenamun into helping him loot a royal tomb to pay for his war and his treason, and that there's no evidence against anyone else from the temple."

"The divine one will never believe that Qenamun acted alone, that he hired mercenaries and bandits on his own."

"What the golden one suspects concerns me not. Only his actions are of import at the moment. Do you want a truce or not, cousin? And take care that you answer as pharaoh's advisor."

Meren pressed a hand over his wound. The bleeding had stopped, but he needed to see his physician soon. His eyelids felt as heavy as ingots, and he was so weary. But he had to think. A truce between the temple of Amun and the court would allow Tutankhamun to grow to maturity without threat from the only power to rival pharaoh in Egypt. The boy needed time, time to gain strength and wisdom, to build alliances with other princes, other temples, the army.

A truce would make no difference. He would still watch the priests, still not trust them. But perhaps the danger would recede for a while. Certainly Parenefer would cause no more trouble, for fear of provoking pharaoh's wrath again and getting himself killed. Yes, Parenefer and Ebana would live in fear from now on, always wondering when Tutankhamun would decide to retaliate against them. Perhaps a truce would be a good thing.

"I shall consult pharaoh," Meren said. "The welfare of the Two Lands depends upon harmony and balance between the servants of Amun and the son of the god."

He shoved himself away from the wall and stumbled. Kysen was beside him instantly and pulled Meren's good arm around his shoulders. Meren cursed, his eyes closing as he tried to keep his legs from folding. Someone slipped an arm around his waist. He opened his eyes and found Ebana supporting him. His cousin began helping Kysen walk him out of the house.

"Don't look so astonished," Ebana said. "If you die of this small wound, who will speak to pharaoh on my behalf?"

20

$\triangledown$

On the third night after he'd killed Tanefer, Meren was in a palace chamber near the royal apartments with Ay and Horemheb. The general was striding about the room while Meren rested on a stool beside Ay. His wound was itching where Nebamun had cleaned and stitched it. Egypt was famed throughout the world for its medicine. Meren just wished the physician didn't insist upon using a needle fresh from a white-hot flame; he could have done without the magic of the fire. They were going over the precautions taken in rounding up Tanefer's nest of traitors, including the guards he'd placed near pharaoh. Rahotep had been given the task of finding the enclave of mercenaries lurking in the desert.

"A messenger came not an hour ago," Horemheb was saying. "Rahotep is chasing the renegades north. Those he doesn't kill will flee into Palestine."

Meren nodded wearily. He hadn't slept well since he'd discovered Tanefer's betrayal. He would never understand how his friend could have plotted to kill Tutankhamun, but deep in his ka, he had some understanding of how one so brilliant could lose control after years and years of enduring the damaging rule of an unfit king.

Meren himself failed to divine the purpose of the gods in inflicting Akhenaten upon Egypt and then allowing the middle brother to die untimely so that

Tutankhamun came to the throne too young. A plague of misfortunes had driven everyone to desperation until Akhenaten died, but Tanefer had suffered more than most. His mother's country had endured far more at the hands of the Hittites than Egypt had at the hands of its heretic pharaoh. And Tanefer had witnessed the destruction.

How much of his rebellion had been impelled by the desire to spare Egypt from a like fate, and how much had been simple greed for power? He would never know. And the pain of losing so close and beloved a friend remained with him, an interminable affliction.

Horemheb had finished his summary, and Ay rose and leaned on his walking stick as he talked. Meren listened without comment. He had already reported to pharaoh the night his friend died, giving him the entire story of the deaths of Unas, Qenamun, Ahiram, and Tanefer. He'd given the report without comment, his spirit so weighed down with grief that he had little attention to give to his estrangement from the king.

He'd been honest about his suspicion of the priests of Amun, for the king's view was the same. The offer of the truce was discussed. Then he'd left. Nothing was said by pharaoh regarding their personal difficulty. During the days that had passed since then, Tutankhamun had consulted Ay and Horemheb in his effort to reach some decision. He hadn't sent for Meren at all.

Ay's wrinkled hand descended to his shoulder. "You aren't listening, Meren."

"Forgive me," he said. "You were talking about moving the royal tombs from Horizon of Aten."

"I know Akhenaten decreed that his house of eternity never be moved, but we can no longer abide by his wishes."

"Yes, yes." Meren heard the impatience in his own voice, but sometimes Ay could be so circuitous.

"Now that the body has been restored," Ay said, "it's time to move all the family burials to a place of concealment."

Meren stared at the vizier. There had been little of Akhenaten left to restore. Whatever had been effected had been done to assuage Tutankhamun's troubled ka more than for any other purpose.

"We must choose a place, perhaps Abydos or Memphis," Ay said.

"Then get on with it," Meren snapped. "Put them in a simple, unmarked tomb in the Valley of the Kings. It's the most guarded place in Egypt, and it's the only place where they have a chance of remaining undisturbed. Here, where pharaoh's power can protect them."

"And right under the noses of the priests of Amun," Horemheb said with a chortle. He had been in riotous spirits since he'd been absolved of evil by Meren.

"Put no mortuary temple above to mark the site," Meren continued. "Move them and be done with it."

Ay's walking stick tapped the floor tiles as he strode toward Meren. "Your temper grows worse each day, boy. What makes you so hot-bellied?"

"Treasons and plots may be like meat to you, but I find them unpalatable."

His scar began to itch. It always did when he was thinking about Akhenaten's death. He'd stopped counting the times he'd cringed at the hypocrisy of his position. He had hunted and killed Tanefer when, not many years ago, he had ignored hints of a similar plot against Akhenaten that had led to the king's death. He had saved one king, but allowed another to die. Oh, he doubted he could have stopped Ay. Should he have tried, at the cost of more lives and the continued rule of a madman?

"I know you had great affection for Tanefer," Ay was saying. "We all did. You didn't want to kill him, young one, but he would have killed you if you'd hesitated."

A door swung open to reveal the overseer of the audience hall. Meren watched him without interest as he entered, stopped to arrange the complicated folds of his robes, and pounded the floor with his walking stick.

"The living Horus, Strong Bull arisen in Thebes, rich in splendor, the Golden Horus who conquers all lands by his might, the King of Upper and Lower Egypt, Nebkheprure Tutankhamun saith thus: 'The Lord Meren will attend my majesty. He is to come alone'."

Meren glanced at Ay. The vizier leaned on his walking stick, his back so bent by age that he resembled a lurking vulture.

"Go on, boy. It's time you two talked."

Sighing, Meren worked his sore shoulder. He was wearing an Eye of Horus amulet to guard his health. Nebamun had insisted upon it, and he couldn't have worn a broad collar over the wound anyway.

The overseer of the audience hall was leaving. Meren followed, gripping the amulet. It was suspended from a heavy gold chain. Long ago, the god Horus lost an eye in combat with the evil Set over the murder of his father Osiris. Toth, god of magic, retrieved the eye and healed it. Later Horus gave the eye to Osiris to eat in order to restore him to life. Meren wondered if the amulet could work its magic and restore to health his relationship with pharaoh.

Tutankhamun received him in the audience chamber reserved for formal events. Two Nubians of the royal bodyguard swung open golden doors, and the overseer paced slowly into the room between high columns. Meren followed him, his pace equally slow, and as he walked, he grew cold. Pharaoh was seated on his throne on a raised dais wearing the double crown of Upper and Lower Egypt, his body draped in gold, in his hands the crook and flail symbolizing his rule over the Two Lands. They would never reconcile if Tutankhamun continued to hide behind that aloof royal demeanor he'd learned to wear so well.

The overseer announced him and retreated. Meren sank to the floor before pharaoh and bent his head. If pharaoh wished formality, he would give it to him.

"Rise, Lord Meren."

As he stood, Meren heard the overseer return. He never liked noises at his back, but before he could glance over his shoulder, pharaoh beckoned to him. He mounted the dais and took up a stance slightly behind and to the right of the throne. Between the rows of columns the overseer preceded his cousin, who led a procession of priests bearing ornate boxes and caskets of gold, ebony, cedar, and ivory. Ebana was as ornate as his offerings in his court dress. A heavy necklace of malachite rested on his shoulders, while a long wig gleamed black against the shining green stones.

Meren watched priest after priest place his burden before the dais. He couldn't stop one corner of his mouth from curling as he realized how worried Parenefer must be to try to bribe pharaoh. Ebana caught his eye, and he pulled his mouth into a straight line. He shouldn't gloat. After all, Ebana had saved his life.

The overseer began to intone the phrases of formal address to pharaoh. Then Ebana spoke.

"The good god Amun has heard the prayers of his living son, the divine bull, the golden Horus. His care for his son knows no boundaries."

Ebana began to open the boxes. Inside lay stacks of ingots, gold ingots. The priests were still coming, and soon the floor was covered with boxes filled with gold, silver, and electrum. Meren stopped counting when he reached fifty. He cast a sideways glance at Tutankhamun, but the boy appeared to be taking this flood of riches with composure. Of course, much of Amun's wealth originally derived from royal generosity. No doubt pharaoh had seen greater riches on his visits to the royal treasury with Maya.

Two priests threaded their way through the fabulous litter, bearing a casket between them on carrying poles. They set it before Ebana, who removed the lid to reveal an interior filled with jewels, products of the workshops of Amun. Meren saw several necklaces fashioned of electrum, the links in the shape of beetles. There were diadems, fillets and headbands of gold, pectoral necklaces with inlay of carnelian, lapis, turquoise, and malachite.

Anklets of beaded amethyst rested on top of gold falcon collars and long, heavy earplugs of the same metal. There were several collars made entirely of thick lenticular gold beads in five rows each. The weight of just one of these made them a burden to wear. Ebana lifted a belt of electrum and deep green malachite. Bowing low, he placed the token at pharaoh's feet.

"Life, health, and strength to the living Horus, son of Amun, shining seed of the god, great of strength, smiter of Asiatics, he who—"

"Yes, yes," Tutankhamun said. "My majesty acknowledges this . . . small expression of the good will of the god my father."

Ebana straightened and waited. Tutankhamun stared at him wordlessly until Ebana resorted to glancing at Meren. Meren let him suffer a few moments longer before whispering to the king.

"Majesty, this humble cupbearer believes the Servant of the God begs privy speech."

A scepter waved in the air, causing overseer, priests, and guards to vanish. Once they were alone, Tutankhamun nodded to Ebana. Ebana gave Meren an uneasy look before speaking in a voice just above a whisper.

"The chief prophet of the god greets the divine one and asks if the matter discussed with Lord Meren has been agreed upon."

Still Tutankhamun didn't speak. A bead of sweat appeared from beneath Ebana's wig and snaked down his forehead to stop at his scar. The golden crowns remained motionless. Held in crossed hands, the crook and the flail seemed immobile. Ebana's gaze darted to Meren. Meren kept his expression as blank as the face of a desert cliff. When he thought Ebana's jaw would break from being clenched, pharaoh broke the silence.

"My majesty has listened to the speech of the Eyes and Ears of Pharaoh, the Lord Meren. Even now criminals are being sought for their transgressions against us." Tutankhamun shifted on his throne and rested his arms on those of the golden chair. "As we speak, my wrath seeks out those who would destroy the order of my kingdom. Justice and balance will be restored, according to the eternal and everlasting harmony between my majesty and the god, my father. There will be peace."

"Thy majesty's will is accomplished in its utterance," Ebana replied.

Tutankhamun waved a hand in dismissal. "My majesty's heart desires harmony and order above all things."

"As does thy father, the king of gods." Ebana bowed and retreated through the forest of boxes.

When the doors shut behind him, Tutankhamun let out a long breath. The scepters faltered as he slumped from his rigid posture. Meren found himself the subject of scrutiny from those great, dark eyes.

"Your wound doesn't trouble you?" the king asked.

"No, majesty."

Tutankhamun rose, and placed the scepters on the throne. Meren helped him lift the heavy headdress and set it beside the crook and flail. The king ran his fingers through his hair, then rubbed his temples.

"By the gods, those are heavy. They make my head ache."

"Shall I send for the royal physician?"

"No," Tutankhamun said. "No. I wanted to ask about Tanefer's men."

"Several of his officers tried to flee the city. I sent Kysen after them, and he's turned them over to Horemheb. They've been questioned about the location of Tanefer's mercenaries, and Rahotep is pursuing them. None of them seems to have been told about the desecration of the royal tombs."

"And the actual violators of the tomb?"

"No word, majesty. I begin to think they never left Egypt. The criminals are most likely living among us." He didn't mention Parenefer or Ebana. It was unnecessary. "No doubt they're busy dismantling the jewelry, melting down the gold into ingots, prying out stones, and so on."

They both glanced at the boxes full of ingots

"So that the source of the gold and stones can never be discovered," Tutankhamun said.

"Yes, majesty."

"You see that I've taken your advice. Both Ay and Horemheb said you were right, but I did so want to feed Parenefer to the crocodiles."

"Thy majesty needs time and peace in which to gain expérience."

"I'd rather have revenge."

Meren turned away from the brilliant piles of loot to face the king. "Revenge might cost you your throne."

"Ay said you would say that." Tutankhamun lowered his gaze to the floor. He cleared his throat.

"Um. I haven't had a chance to tell you that Maya

has remembered that it was from Tanefer that he first heard the rumors of Horemheb's treason."

"I thought it might be so, majesty."

Tutankhamun looked away. "And while you were gone chasing Ahiram, Tanefer kept reflecting upon the past, about how greatly you suffered at the hands of my brother, how Akhenaten had your father killed and tortured you." His voice faded and he gave Meren a look of appeal.

"I see, majesty."

"Do you?"

Meren heard the distress and pain in those two words. All at once he realized he'd just received for the second time something unheard-of in Egypt, a pharaoh's apology. Just as suddenly, his spirits lifted, and he smiled for the first time since Tanefer's death.

"Yes, majesty, I do."

He nearly jumped back when Tutankhamun gave a joyful whoop, dashed at him, and gripped his wrist. Although startled at the contact, Meren returned the gesture, gripping the boy's wrist, warrior to warrior.

"I've missed you," the king said.

"I have longed for thy majesty's presence as well."

Tutankhamun dropped his arm and peered into Meren's face. "You look weary."

"I'm well, divine one."

"I don't think so. Ay says you aren't sleeping."

Meren cursed Ay's inquisitive and interfering nature, which caused the king to laugh.

"Now that I see you, I agree with him," the king said. "Once we're certain we've purged ourselves of traitors at court, you will go to the country and rest."

"But, majesty, there is much to do."

"And Kysen will go with you to see that you abide by my orders."

"There's no need," Meren began.

"There is a need," Tutankhamun said. "Because my majesty declares it to be so. Now go home and rest. Ay says you've been working since before sunrise, and it's almost dusk. You must recover your full strength."

As Meren stepped down from the dais, a suspicion snaked into his thoughts, and he turned back to the king. "You want me to recover so that I'll take you on a raid."

"You did say I needed experience. Now that we have a truce with Parenefer, I have the time and freedom to get it. And those bandits are still plundering villages to the south."

"I knew it. Majesty, thou art shrewd and full of guile, like the cobra."

Tutankhamun walked over to him, folded his arms over his chest, and smiled. "I'm apprenticed to a master skilled in shrewdness and guile. How could I be otherwise?"

Meren shook his head as the king gave him a parting smile and left the audience chamber through a door behind the dais. Meren left the way he had come, and outside found Kysen coming toward him, flanked by Abu and Reia.

"Horemheb has just sent three of Tanefer's officers into the desert."

Nothing else had to be said. Criminals had been sent into the desert since before the time of the god-kings who built the pyramids. Meren wondered if Horemheb would be merciful and allow the men to kill themselves rather than be staked out in the sun and elements to die slowly. It was a matter in which he couldn't interfere. Meren fell into step beside his son.

"You're ready to go home?" Kysen asked.

"Yes."

Kysen gave him a worried glance. "You saw the king?"

"Yes. I'm to rest."

"Good."

Meren heard a relieved sigh and knew that Kysen had understood him. It wouldn't do to discuss the king's repentance in the palace.

"I'm to rest so that I'll be well enough to take the divine one on a raid as soon as I'm fit."

Kysen's steps faltered, and he gave Meren a chagrined look. "Oh, no."

Meren slapped Kysen on the back as they threaded their way through courtiers, servants, and government officials.

"It seems not even treason or murder at the god's gate will prevent pharaoh from becoming a true warrior."

Kysen snorted. "And what if the golden one is killed on this raid?"

"That's what you and I must guard against."

He listened to his son grumble, and he almost smiled. It wasn't but a few years ago that Kysen had been just as eager to test himself as pharaoh. The memory of youth was short. No doubt Kysen had forgotten his near-fatal initiation into warfare. Meren hadn't. He'd nearly lost his son to a dirty knife thrown by a thieving nomad.

What he needed was respite from restless youth and court intrigue. He would obey pharaoh and retire for a few weeks to the country. Surely he would find refuge there.

Coming in Spring 1997,
Lynda S. Robinson's next chapter
in the mystery series
featuring Prince Meren, the "eyes and ears of
Pharaoh Tutankhamun."

MURDER AT THE FEAST
OF REJOICING

Turn this page for more of Ancient Egypt's
intrigue and vivid atmosphere, which only
Lynda S. Robinson can render with such
accuracy. . . .

Look for MURDER AT THE FEAST OF REJOICING.
From Ballantine Books

1

▽

Year Five of the Reign of the Pharaoh Tutankhamun

Kysen hadn't wanted to come to the ghost-ridden and deserted city of heretics. But what son of Egypt would dare refuse the wish of the living god, the Son of the Sun, Tutankhamun? He walked to the railing of the barge that had brought him to Horizon of Aten, leaned over the water, and listened to the slap of waves against the side of the vessel. The scribe who was taking down his letter stopped writing and waited patiently, rush pen twirling in his fingers. When Kysen failed to return, he shifted uneasily.

"Is something wrong, lord?"

"No . . . no, I don't think so. Did you hear anything?"

"No, lord."

"I thought I heard . . . I'm sure it's nothing." Since coming here he'd been on edge, certain that renegades, outlaws, or some chance intruder would penetrate the isolation so vital to their task.

Before him along the east bank of the Nile stretched a city once filled with courtiers, government officials, servants, and royalty. Its carefully planned avenues, so different from the snarled and twisted streets of older cities, were now empty—empty and silent. Even the men on the five barges moored in a line beside them were quiet.

Kysen brushed his hand over his brow. "Is was nothing."

The scribe remained seated, awaiting orders. He was one of Meren's. He would wait all night if Kysen ordered it.

The sun was setting, but there was still enough light to see the tiny figures of infantrymen standing guard on the cliffs to the east. Kysen glanced over his shoulder, and movement caught his eye. A charioteer drove over the rocky surface of the western desert, the first of a long, widely spaced line of vehicles that patrolled the environs of the city.

Inhabitants of nearby villages had been evicted, as had the royal mortuary priests and necropolis guards. Akhenaten's capital city was truly abandoned now, except for pharaoh's soldiers and the fleet of barges, freighters, and service ships. The whole of it had been Meren's idea.

The ships' crews were in fact royal sailors, the passengers royal agents assigned by the king and his advisors. Traveling in a group designed to look like a flotilla on an expedition to the south, Kysen and his companions affected to be traders of the temple estates of Ra. Traders of the temples, royal institutions, and great households plied the waters of the Nile and markets of Egypt, dealing in commodities both rare and abundant; Kysen's cargo was rare indeed.

After criminals had desecrated the tomb of Tutankhamun's heretic brother, the Pharaoh Akhenaten, the king had asked him to witness the secret removal of the bodies of Akhenaten, and his queen, mother, and daughters from their houses of eternity. He was to aid in the execution of a plan to keep their bodies safe until new tombs could be provided, a task better suited to great generals and priests. Yet pharaoh had chosen him, and a few others whose faces weren't well known, for this sacred effort. It was almost finished.

Some of the grain and fine limestone on board had

been put ashore to make way for the intended cargo. Kysen watched a pair of sailors carry a load of grain suspended from a pole on their shoulders. Timing their steps, they crossed the gangplank and stepped onto the bank.

Others on deck rearranged bags on top of a long, tarp-covered mound. The outer layer of this mound consisted of grain, precious Tura limestone, and natron. Had this expedition been real, the ships would have returned from the south carrying gold, incense trees, leopard skins, and, sitting on the mast, baboons. Catching his lower lip between his teeth, Kysen tried not to think of what lay beneath the tarps and ropes.

He would never forget his first sight of the most precious of all their cargo, lying in the royal tomb, bereft of outer shrines and draperies. Urged on by the commander of the expedition, he had stepped into the wavering torchlight as master craftsmen strained and grunted to lift a heavy weight. Into his vision emerged a wall of gold. Then Kysen realized why the craftsmen were straining so hard. The heretic's innermost coffin wasn't of wood overlaid with gold foil like the outer ones—it was of solid gold. He hadn't slept through a night since.

He was only the son of an artisan, of such humble origin that he would never have dared look into the eyes of pharaoh. It didn't matter that Lord Meren, pharaoh's most trusted confidential inquiry agent, had adopted him. Deep in his bones, to the innermost recesses of his ka, his soul, he was still a carpenter's unwanted son. And to look upon the body of a pharaoh in a coffin of gold made him want to sink to the dirt and hide his face in fear. He hadn't, though, for that would have disgraced his adopted father and his new, noble lineage.

So now he awaited the arrival of that golden coffin in the form of a man. A special place had been reserved for it inside the hollow mounds lined with the dismantled outer coffins of the king and the Great Royal Wife, Nefertiti. The queen had already been gently shoved into place. Other family members would be concealed on the accompanying barges, to be hidden in out-of-the-way places assigned by the vizier Ay. There they would await the preparation of eternal houses in the royal burying grounds at Thebes. At the moment Kysen was waiting for Nentowaref, called Nento.

Nento posed as the chief overseer of the expedition, head of the so-called traders of Ra. His real titles were numerous, as Kysen had discovered to his regret. Nento was most proud of the simple appellation Royal Scribe, but he also loved to be called Scribe of the Royal Treasury, Overseer of the Seal, Overseer of the Magazines of the Temple of Amunhotep III, and Bearer of Floral Offerings to Ra. His most important duty on this expedition was to serve as a makeshift priestly guardian to their royal charges.

Kysen couldn't remember any more of the honors Nento kept repeating to him. When they'd first set out, Kysen had thought Nento officious and suspected him of condescending to a youth of common blood. Then he realized that Nento was trying to impress him—because of Meren. Nento had many titles, but none of them included that of Friend of the King.

Leaning on the railing of the barge, Kysen gazed down the road that led from the quay to the city. He heard a low rumbling sound before he saw them. Slowly, their paces matching the beat of a drum, a line of men and oxen rolled a sledge over logs toward the barge. The cargo was padded with linen to protect it and disguise its true shape. It was covered by tarps lashed with ropes. Ahead of the sledge, glancing back every third step, rode Nento in a chariot manned by a driver. Nento couldn't drive a chariot without tripping both horses. Charioteers rode on all sides of the group around the sledge.

His eyes darting to the cliffs that formed an arched backdrop around the city, Kysen checked once more for a soldier out of place, a suspicious movement. He swept his gaze over the rooftops of the city, then across the river and over fields and the encroaching desert. Nothing but charioteers and infantry. What was he doing? More experienced men than he manned strategic posts and scanned the horizon for just such clues. All at once it seemed as if a stone slab lifted from his chest. He sucked in a long, deep breath.

He could envision the scene in the eastern desert now taking place, the disguised priests of the royal Theban necropolis huddled around the restored blockage of the royal tomb shaft, the application of thick plaster, an arm moving in wide, swirling circles. Then at last, and forever, a seal pressed into white dampness, the seal of the heretic royal cemetery. It would never be used again.

Soon the mortuary priests and guards would return to Horizon of Aten. Sacred rituals would resume. Patrols would sweep the desert, watching ceaselessly for intruders. Kysen wondered how long they would keep vigil over empty tombs.

Sighing, he walked back to the scribe and lowered himself to a camp stool beside the man. "Very well, we can begin."

He'd already accomplished the frightening task of actually addressing a letter to pharaoh. Writing to Meren would be easy. That is, it would be easy if he didn't have to disguise the real contents of the message.

"The usual salutation," Kysen said.

He paused while the scribe wrote "Tjerkerma," the name Kysen had adopted for this journey, Meren's name and titles, then "year five" followed by the month and the day in the waning season of Drought.

He cleared his throat. "Tjerkerma greets his lord, Meren, in life, prosperity, and health, in the favor of Amun, King of the Gods, of Ptah, of Toth and all the gods and goddesses. May they bestow upon you love, cleverness, and favor." It had taken him years to master the formal letter-writing style.

"See! I am about to embark from the place, Refuge of Maat, upon the morn with good speed. All is in readiness. The cargo is disposed as you ordered. The traders sail to their appointed destinations."

In this prearranged phraseology, he let his father know that the royal family and their burial furniture would embark in the morning. With raised sails they would float south from Horizon of Aten in the direction of Thebes, and the journey would be a slow one. On this journey they would have to pass Thinis, ancient seat of his father's family, and Abydos, sacred city of the god Osiris. As he continued to dictate the letter, his guts began to twist like cobras in a basket.

He hated Meren's plan. Oh, not all of it. Only the part that risked his father's life, for that was what the effect of this design would be. Not three weeks earlier Meren had almost been killed. He wasn't fully recovered either from wounds received while thwarting the rebellion of one of his closest friends or grief at the friend's death. Yet in a few days he was going to do something that might place him in as great a danger as any he'd faced while tracking down that traitor.

His father was supposed to be resting in the country. Upon hearing of Meren's plan to go to the family seat, the estate of Baht, Kysen had tried to dissuade him. He knew Meren's family; visiting them wasn't the way to gain peace and solace, especially while dealing with this new, added burden. It exasperated Kysen that Meren still thought he would be able to rest when his plans came to fruition. No doubt he would continue to think so until the demons of chaos struck, as they were sure to do when he was dealing with the secrets of god kings.

Dawn had long given way to the furnace of early morning by the time Meren finished his correspondence. He left the cool shelter of the palace at the royal way station to brave the sun and the west wind that scoured its way across the valley. There were many such mooring places along the Nile, kept in readiness for times when pharaoh, his family, or favored friends might need to seek refuge during the long journey up- or downriver. This one was half a day's sail from his country home.

Followed by a pair of charioteers, Meren walked up the long ramp beside the palace. It led to a high brick platform on which his traveling household had set up their tents. A flight of stairs brought him to the walk on top of the defensive wall. Few sentries stood guard. He was going home to rest and wasn't on official duty. The walls had swarmed with guards a few days ago, when pharaoh passed on his way to Memphis.

As he gazed out at his ship, *Wings of Horus*, Meren furrowed his brow and rubbed the sun disk scar on his inner wrist. Pharaoh had promised to confine himself to military exercises in the practice grounds near the Sphinx. Meren could only pray to the gods that no bandits chose to raid any nearby villages while the king was in the capital. If only the golden one hadn't asked Kysen to be his unofficial witness to the arrangements at Horizon of Aten. Meren had counted on his son's presence among the king's war band to distract Tutankhamun from his obsession with acquiring real battle experience.

Shaking his head, he drew his gaze back to the long, sleek lines of his ship. Painted black, with lines of red and gold, it outsailed every other craft on the river.

Only a few ships in the king's fleet could match it. Not long ago, *Wings of Horus* had sped him on his way in pursuit of a traitor. Soon it would take him home. Already most of his household had removed there, including Nebamun, his physician, and Remi, Kysen's son. His aide, Abu, was in charge at his house in Thebes. As Meren indulged in a moment's admiration of his ship, another slid past it going north with the current, in the direction of Memphis.

Meren squinted at the vessel and motioned to the charioteers behind him. "Reia, Iry, isn't that Lord Paser's yacht?"

The two young charioteers joined him in peering at the slow-moving craft.

"Yellow with a green deck," Reia said.

Iry nodded. "Aye, lord, it's the same one we saw yesterday."

"And the day before," Meren said. He folded his arms over his chest. "Hmmm."

Paser was one of a faction at court that was growing around Prince Hunefer. Hunefer fancied himself better fit to advise pharaoh than the vizier Ay, who was the craftiest of statesmen. Although Hunefer's heart was far from clever, dissatisfied place-seekers had flocked to him in hopes of using the prince to topple Ay.

The question was, why would Paser follow Meren? He was only going home to rest and give the shoulder wounds Tanefer had given him a chance to heal. Everyone knew that. Everyone should know that.

Meren was considering the unlikely possibility that either Paser or Hunefer was more clever than he'd thought when Reia gave a startled exclamation and pointed to the canal that ran beside the royal mooring place.

"Look, lord!"

A skiff floated up to the bank and unloaded three fig-

ures, a man and two girls. The girls hopped ashore and
started running. They vanished inside the way-station
gates before their companion could tie off the skiff.

"What—why—?" Meren glanced at Reia, then at Iry.
Both men appeared expressionless, but he could see the
corners of Reia's eyes crinkle in amusement.

Pressing his lips together, Meren composed himself.
He would remain where he was and let his two youngest daughters find him. He wanted an explanation.
They were supposed to be at home, waiting for him, not
sailing on their own with but one servant to accompany
them. He hadn't long to wait before the two came racing toward him across the platform, long tresses flying
behind them.

The older girl, Bener, slowed as she approached, but
Isis flew past her and flung herself into his arms.

"Father, Father, I knew we'd find you! Aren't I
clever? I said you'd be delayed, and here you are. Bener
thinks she's the chosen one of Toth, with her writing
and her ciphering, but I'm the one who found you. It
was my idea, and she thinks she's so quick-witted."

Meren hugged his youngest child, and as her words
streamed over him, he forgot his resolution to be stern.
He'd spent months maneuvering through vicious intrigues, guarding his every word for fear of betraying
his king, keeping his senses alert for danger. Until now
he hadn't known how great the strain had been.

Kysen and Tutankhamun had both warned him of his
weariness. He hadn't listened. But as Isis babbled to
him in her golden voice, the muscles in his neck and
shoulders loosened. He'd lived with them twisted as
tight as the rope of a wine press. The demons that
jabbed spikes in his temples vanished.

Isis squeezed his neck. "I missed you, Father."

"And I you, my little goddess." He loosened his grip
on Isis and looked over the top of her head at Bener,

who had walked up to them sedately. She was standing with her arms at her sides, radiating composure. Was this his little girl, the one who climbed palms and stole pomegranates from the kitchen? She was almost as tall as Kysen.

He held out his arms. "Bener, my sweet."

To his consternation, she met his eyes, then glanced at Reia and Iry as if asking for their dismissal. Hoping his jaw hadn't fallen open, Meren waved the young men away. Once their backs were turned, Bener chuckled and floated into his arms.

Laying her head on his shoulder, she murmured, "I've missed you, Father, and I know you're angry at finding us here, but we had to warn you."

"It was my idea," Isis said as she tugged on his kilt.

Bener drifted out of his arms too soon, leaving him disturbed by her composure. She glanced down at her sister.

"I told you not to throw yourself at Father like a monkey. You're never dignified."

An argument erupted, but Meren was too busy studying his daughters to interfere. They had changed in the few months he'd left them in his sister's charge. Idut had warned him, but he hadn't taken her seriously. He should have. Bener was a woman now, tall and slender as a papyrus reed, but her arms and legs bore the elongated muscles of a leopard. Her face still held some of the plumpness of childhood, but she moved with the stateliness of a priestess and seemed to cultivate the demeanor of a woman three times her age. She reminded him of her great-grandmother.

And Isis. Isis frightened him, for she was beautiful, and he knew the dangers the world held for beautiful women. She had always been pretty, but she had matured into a double of her mother, who had always startled people by her resemblance to the fabulous

Nefertiti. Once she left behind the immaturity of childhood, Isis would make men step on their tongues when she passed.

What was he doing? He was imagining trouble before it arose. He'd drive himself mad.

"Enough quarreling," he said quietly. His daughters immediately broke off their exchange, which aroused his suspicions. "How did you get here, and why are you here? No, Isis, let Bener speak."

Bener exchanged a quick, apprehensive glance with her sister, wet her lips, and began. "It's not our fault."

"What isn't your fault?"

Again that quick glance.

"Remember your letter to Aunt announcing that you were coming home?" Bener asked. "Um, you see . . . That is, Aunt didn't pay attention to the part about how you wished your return to be private, just for us."

Isis burst in with an aggrieved tone. "I knew she'd ruin everything. We haven't seen you in months, and she's ruined everything."

"Father," Bener said. "Aunt has arranged a great feast of rejoicing in honor of your homecoming."

Meren leaned against the defensive wall at his back and scowled. "I made myself plain. I sent instructions."

"Aunt says she forgot," Bener said with a lift of her arched brows.

Isis kicked the wall with one sandaled foot. "My ass, she forgot."

"Isis!"

His youngest daughter lifted her delicate face to him, and he noted the way her fragile jaw set in place as if mortared there.

"She's ruined everything. How can we go sailing and fowling or even talk to you at all with all of *them* coming?"

Rubbing the back of his neck, Meren asked, "Who? Who has she invited?"

"Everyone," Isis said.

"Don't be a goose-wit," Bener replied. Isis ruined the elegance of her features by sticking out her tongue.

Meren fixed her with a stern glance. "Out with it."

Twirling a lock of hair around her fingers, Bener hesitated, then began a list that included Idut's son Imset, who was supposed to be studying in Memphis, Meren's cousin Sennefer and his wife Anhai, three of his uncles and their wives, and over a dozen of the local nobility. She didn't include the family retainers and supporters, tenants and servants who would flock to this grand celebration.

"Oh, and I almost forgot, Great-Aunt Nebetta and Great-Uncle Hepu."

He kept his expression blank as she spoke the two names he least wanted to hear. Surprise made him vulnerable to the burn of old, festering hate. How could Idut have invited Nebetta and Hepu? She knew he never wanted to meet them this side of the netherworld. She knew what they'd done to their own son. His beloved cousin Djet was dead, and they had killed him as surely as if they had stuck a dagger in his heart.

No, don't think about it. Your anger will grow until it swallows you. This isn't the time. Old grief compounded new—the loss of his companion in war and in celebration, the bright, merry, traitorous Tanefer. Djet and Tanefer, both gone. He might forget Tanefer one day. He would never stop grieving for Djet. He used to tease Djet that they were each other's twin soul. They had learned to shoot the bow together, to hunt, to fish, to sail. He and Djet had shared those early discoveries of the body that every boy experiences. They had even spent the night in the haunted temple near Baht on a dare. Together they had braved that isolated valley, slept within the crumbling walls of the temple, and screamed when, in the blackest part of the night, the desert fiends howled down the valley on the wind.

"Father, is something wrong?" Bener asked.

He shook his head and smiled. "Naught is wrong, my little geese. Now tell me how you got to the mooring place of pharaoh."

"That was my idea too," Isis said. "Uncle Ra was going home, and I begged him to take us this far."

"Ah," Meren said faintly.

He turned his back and gazed out over the river. Fishing boats, skiffs, barges, and pleasure craft sailed with and against the current. One of the yachts that floated past with its elongated rectangular sail unfurled to catch the north breeze had been his brother's. Ra hadn't even stopped. The reason was obvious to Meren, who knew his brother well, so well that from childhood he'd called the younger boy Ra after the powerful sun god. Ra didn't want to be there for Meren's grand return. He didn't want to see crowds rushing to the dock to greet Meren, didn't want to hear the cheers, hear Meren's name called, see countless backs bent in homage. And Ra knew how much his absence would hurt his older brother.

Meren's thoughts veered away from that idea. He had a more immediate problem. His private homecoming had been transformed into a grand celebration. Privacy was necessary, and not just for him and his daughters; quiet and calm, a sedate, unremarkable visit, these were conditions upon which he'd counted. If the feast interfered too much with his plans, he would have to leave his country house far sooner than he wished.

He hoped Isis wasn't right. He hoped his sister hadn't ruined everything. If she had, Meren was the one who was going to pay.

Lynda S. Robinson takes you back
to the cradle of civilization—
Ancient Egypt—where the River
Nile nourished a nation and where
mysteriously powerful rulers were
more than mere mortals....

MURDER
IN THE
PLACE OF
ANUBIS

In the shadows of one of Egypt's most sacred
buildings, a murderer lurks among the
embalmed bodies. And although there should
be safety under the watch of the gods, a
scribe has been found dead there. At the order
of the boy-king Tutankhamun, Prince Meren,
the kingdom's head spy, will explore every
facet of Egyptian society to find the killer.

MURDER IN THE
PLACE OF ANUBIS
by Lynda S. Robinson

**Published by Ballantine Books.
Available in your local bookstore.**